"A scene of summer beauty and morning splendour was this he overlooked; for the bosom of the calm deep gave back the richness of heaven, not in one broad roll of azure, but in dyes of blue, faint as the first glimpse of dawn and bright as the tint that ruled above it, and elsewhere of the violet's soft darkness; flecked in the far-reaching space, where sea and sky were one, by sails of ships; and in the south overhung with the silver fronts of clouds whose rear lay hidden in the morning mist."

It is with such magnetic, intense colour that W. Clark Russell consistently entertained his legions of readers and established a formidable reputation as a writer.

AULD LANG SYNE

AULD LANG SYNE

a novel by

W. CLARK RUSSELL

SANDNESS
MICHAEL WALMER
2022

Auld Lang Syne first published 1878
This edition published 2022

by

Michael Walmer
North House
Melby
Sandness
Shetland ZE2 9PL

ISBN 978-0-6452440-3-8 paperback

PUBLISHER'S NOTE

There are displayed in this book attitudes to, and nomenclature for, race that, though they were very common at the time of writing, are not acceptable now, and are not shared by the publisher.

This book is republished because of its significance in literary history and its excellence in many other respects.

*The publisher gratefully acknowledges the assistance of Robert Heatley
in the typesetting process for this volume*

CONTENTS

VOLUME ONE

VOLUME TWO

VOLUME ONE

CHAPTER I

GREYSTONE-ON-SEA

"And hark, my love! The sea-breeze moans
Through yon reft house! O'er rolling stones,
　In bold ambitious sweep,
The onward-surging tides supply
The silence of the cloudless sky
　With mimic thunders deep.
Dark reddening from the channelled Isle
(Where stands one solitary pile
　Unslated by the blast),
The watch-fire, like a sullen star,
Twinkles to many a dozing tar
　Rude cradled on the mast."—COLERIDGE.

IN the embrace of a curvature of this noble island of Britain, where the coast beheld by the passing mariner shines before his eyes with the pearly gloss and delicate shimmer of marble; where the land shoots out into the sea, scorning, with its iron heel stanchly planted, the thunderous shocks of the hurricane or the more deadly tooth of the lipping calm, and bearing on high at night its flaming beacon, like the fabled giant defying the stars with uplifted torch; stands a town whereon no man with a mind into which soft thoughts may enter readily can gaze without stopping to reflect.

In this little town, time and the handiwork of man have wrought lovingly together.

And generous Nature has backed them: glorifying the land around with calm enrichment of intermingling trees, and broad fields which pour their green or golden fruits down the hillsides and along the vigorous plains.

Upon so many of the houses, that all (save those that stand upon the skirts of the town) partake the tender characteristic, is the indefinable shadow which you shall observe the house-painter often deforms without obliterating, and which as surely creeps through all garish effacement as old age permeates the rouge and powder with which folly seduces the Dowager Threescore into a temporary pride of youth.

Beheld from a distance, this little town seems to dwell with something of the shadowiness of an ancient picture upon the English sea-shore.

Shadowiness one seeks as an element in pictures of a day which time has made dim. Greystone, in our own age, has this artistic condition in perfection. It is a ready-made vignette to adorn the little social legend which the gossips have handed down through the century.

Nor does the aspect of the houses, even when under close and familiar inspection—neither do the homely streets, with windy corners here and there to make the feeblest cough a piercing hint to the ancient lounger who lingers a minute in the blowing; nor the low, liberally windowed shops; nor the sign-boards that swing, with squeaks of rust and rot, over the uneven pavements; nor the worn lamp-posts, that shake in the soil on a windy night like the milk-tooth in a child's gum under the touch of the finger—belie the suggestion of drowsy, listless old age that is begotten by the soft shadowy confusion of the builded town when beheld afar.

Yet wanting in many a modern con-veniency, of which the omission hits hard the prejudice fostered by current sanitary laws, and that love of scientific despatch which is getting to exclude time as a condition of movement, here truly may we say is a town which a man being born in it he would dearly love, and make it his prayer to die in;—to form in the upright heart a memory as tender almost as anything human could inspire.

As this little town is now, I say, so, with scarcely a change of note to name—counting the laying of gas-pipes and the ejectment, in 1844, of Tobias Pipes the town-crier as nothing—was it in that year of grace, war, rapine, and high prices—to wit, anno 1806.

Yet with this difference.

It drowses now like an old man over a newspaper; like an old cat in the sunshine; like a hen upon sand with a July sky above it. It is a Borough. It has a Town Council; but what is their mission, save to read the minutes of the last meeting and confirm them, and then adjourn for a month? It has a police-sergeant and two constables; but what have they to apprehend, but the exceeding dulness of life, and the inadequacy of one and twenty shillings a week to the requirements of a wife and children?

But in 1806 the town of Greystone-on-Sea was wide awake.

Politics in it ran high and stormily.

The common fear of the Corsican kept its salt heart active and hating, and it was shouting with many nations over Trafalgar, and mourning with the deepest-hearted of them all over the setting of that glorious sun, "whose light," said the rector of Holy Trinity, in his memorable Sabbath sermon, alluding to the death of Nelson, "whose light unto mankind had been the peerless revelation of English courage, and who had gilded, with untarnishable lustre, the arms and valiance and heroic energies of our Island home. Yea! generations of weakly British sailors—could the imagination of his hearers bring their pride to apprehend the conceit of so dismal a posterity—should fail to weaken the terror which the spectacle of the British flag upon the sea should strike into the haughtiest foreign understanding, so prodigious, so unexampled, so surpassing all that may be found writ in the story of maritime conquest, ancient or modern, had been the influence of this most glorious victory upon the minds of the peoples of the Eastern and Western Continents!"

God save the king!

Therefore was there much to keep this little town awake:—

In scurvy dreams of flat-bottom flotillas.

In sinister shapes of crawling privateers, spreading their lips to show their teeth, as they sneaked, like beasts of prey, along the fields of the sea.

In dearness of meat and drink, which made poor Hodge's shilling scarcely worth a groat, though he wept and yelled over the recitals of the Gazette.

In such loss of national gods as Him of the Nile, and the lean, heaven-born Minister.

These are degenerate days. Fifty years hence they will be glorious times.

The clown out of the field and the fisherman out of the sea, and the gossips, whose haunts are in the midst of the houses, wander now in Greystone, with slow and indolent legs along their ways, in the dull trade and languid pursuits of the place finding no such demon of profit as elsewhere gives the whip to men's souls, and sets them running to and fro, as Scripture says.

But in yonder year of this story there was busy life in the thoroughfares:—

Much marvellous activity of tongue.

The sound of hammers in the boat-yards.

A lively beach of smacksmen.

Much traffic sea-wise.

Fish and smugglers' booty travelling inwards.

A fair river of imports of the fruits of the land from the lovely tracts without, and the produce of towns and villages behind the hills, chiefly for the calling cruisers and for the tall merchantmen that backed their topsail-yards off the shore.

There goes, now, and there went then, a narrow pass up to the westward of the town, out of the waste of silver sand which the water never covered, unless driven to it by a conspiracy of moon and gale.

By two walls of rock, spanned for the footpath along the cliff's edge by a rude bridge, looking, from below, to rule the sky with a slim and giddy filament; by great protuberances of stone and rugged hunches of chalk intermitting a sandy, rushy herbage, with yellow grass in places, and a moist, faint-coloured moss of the hue of the jelly-fish when it slowly oozes to the surface of green salt-water—you passed into a verdant lane, and the moan of the surf sounded hollow behind you through the echoing ravine.

Here, at the point where the hedges of the lane met and terminated in the deep fall of the pass, stood a coastguard's hut—a tarred, and, with its thatched roof, a feathery-looking thing, but of a most powerful scantling, and a fit stronghold for the grim Government gentry who, with gleaming hangers and heavy muskets, tramped round and about it day and night, for ever sniffing the salt air for any contraband relish it might carry, and straining keen ears, when the night fell, for the *cheep* of rowlocks and the rasp of stave and bilge on rock.

Along this lane, that broadened presently out of the shadow of trees and the interception of hedgerows into a fair open road, you wound your steps towards the town, in the ripe summer time always losing the track a hundred yards ahead of you behind the tall crops of the fields; and when the roofs and chimneys of the town were showing over harvest crops to the right, and the square turret of Holy Trinity, with its gilt cross standing like a flame of fire against the sky, levelled its grey top with the green swell of the adjacent cliff—until you came to a house.

It stands to this day; but not now, as then, alone. It was the out-reaching building of Greystone in 1806, with a grand command from its upper windows of the deep, whose plain runs up like the side of a hill into the sky; and useful to mariners as a landmark for the just procession of angles, being backed by such prominent objects of hill and windmill and spire as made its covering of these things most useful compass bearings, and a trusty day-beacon for the malignant Race-Sand.

CHAPTER II

DR. SHAW AND HIS SON

"Mean and vulgar spirits, whose souls soar no higher than their sense, love to hover ever about home; lying still, as it were, at dead anchor, moving no further than the length of the cable whereunto they are tied, not daring to launch out into the main, to see the wonders of the deep. Such a one was he of whom Claudian speaks to have had his birth, breeding, and burial, in one parish."—JAMES HOWELL

ON a certain Wednesday afternoon, the walled inclosure at the back of this house presented an agreeable scene of boys at play.

There were not less than forty of them, with just half an acre of ground for their feet to measure. Now, the whole circumference of the horizon might truly seem a narrow scope for the impetuosities of their leap-frog, their "horses," and other extremely animated pastimes.

All memory of the stinging breech of the morning was gone from the sulkiest sufferer. Freedom was here on a short visit: there was a divine sky overhead, and a soft south wind to stir the chestnuts near the house, and the beeches at the base of the ground, into a tender utterance of twinkling shadow.

Let people quote "my lord's" face, and refer you to "the duchess's" laugh, and argue: My lord's face might truly fit Tom Tiddler the groom, for the coarseness and expression of decorous slyness in it; and better bred laughter than the duchess's fills the mouths of sluts and trollops, as her ladyship's lady's-maid knows: but all the same, and holding these examples in our hand that it may be seen we heed them, nothing do we conceive truer than that good blood sets its refining mark on all the seven stages; that "quality" (as our grandfathers exquisitely defined the thing) shines as surely in the serene eyes of the baby as it informs with gentleness the bearing, and with intellectual beauty the aspect, of the man.

Watching these boys in their sport—though they swept past and about in every contortion of riotous play, giving and taking blows, harlequinading with inconvenient legs, shouting hoarsely, and making the air quiver

with their trebles of laughter and angry call—
you would have known them immediately as
a colony of little gentlemen.

Among the shadows under the chestnuts a
young man was seated on a bench.

He held a book in his hand, over which he
pored.

Never was attitude of rapt studiousness so
intently expressed. The pastoral poets would
have figured the birds ceasing their pipes, and
the tall trees neglecting to nod to the passing
gale, in sympathy with this musing or diligent
shape. In all the shouting and leaping of the
boys, there was nothing to provoke a single
impatient lifting of the head of this figure.

But he never turned a page.

He was of a slender build, yet with
shoulders broad enough to warrant him a
man. His feet were such compact curves as a
woman's eye would love to dwell on, for the
mere sake of the breeding and prettiness of
them. His bountiful auburn hair fell curling to
his shoulders, as the fashion then was among
men who were forswearing the wig, yet
sticking to the traditions of luxuriant head-
clothing.

This was all of him now visible.

Yet enough to make a picture of gentle masculine grace, and a shape of strong and nervous beauty.

He paid no more heed to the boys than they to him, though he was there to keep them in order; to overseer their tremendous spirits, to guard them against those recreations of blows and blood-letting into which—O fond British mothers!—the youth of this nation will diverge on any irrational excuse of grin or epithet.

Whilst he thus sat, there came briskly on to a platform (whence a flight of steps led to the playground) a short, plump old man, in black stockings and tail-coat, and frill spreading out like a fan from his bosom.

Catching hold of the rail, he ran his small, brilliant black eyes (taking a power of illumination from shaggy white eyebrows and a dusky skin) over the tumbling figures of the boys, and then looked steadfastly at the young man, whose back was towards him.

By degrees the boys grew aware of his presence.

Their shouts slackened, their mirth grew constrained, their antics got flatter.

They became objects for philosophical contemplation. Germs of future courtiers courted the monarch's eye by a decorous cessation of sport, by an attitude both timorous and wistful.

Germs of future parasites went apart from their mates on a sudden, and looked good lads, with eyes askew upon the platform, ready to laugh, to slaver, to sadden, to peach, as Frill might require.

Germs of sturdy Britons—two of a bunch that were fighting fell stupidly away, but kept their eyes upon each other in the corners of their sockets, and their neglected finger-nails punched little pink semicircles upon their palms.

The frolicsome spirit of others was not to be restrained on a sudden, but had vent in little spurts and pushings of play, like the breakers of an ebbing tide, until presently the ground was silent.

Still the befrilled figure stood staring on the young man, and the young man sat bending over his book, lost, in some deep kind of contemplation, to all external change.

"Cuthbert!" shouted the old man.

The young fellow looked around quickly, as though alarmed by the voice, or rather by the meditations which the voice had disturbed.

He arose and went towards the house.

"What book is that in your hand?" inquired the old gentleman, with his eyebrows knitted, and the hair of them glittering like frost in the beam of sunshine that fell straight on his face through the trees.

"Juvenal, sir."

And as the young man spoke he glanced upwards with a pair of true blue eyes, and disclosed a beautiful and winning countenance.

"Juvenal, indeed! Much of Juvenal have you read since I have stood here with my eyes upon you."

"Really—"

"No, no; that's not your task. And give me leave to see that, whilst you are wool-gathering, Bateman senior and Francis Tremaine have earned a flogging for using their fists. That was proceeding in a true line with your nose, and all the waggeries of the poet should not keep you from noting misconduct, if your mind was not elsewhere than in your head."

This was spoken in a low tone, not wanting in sharp distinctness.

The young fellow addressed as Cuthbert made no reply. He stood in passive posture, with no more than a little deepening of the expression of thoughtfulness on his face, and his eyes bent down upon the ground.

The old gentleman, having made an end of his rebuke, gazed at him fixedly for several moments, and then bidding him "step with him into his study," wheeled about and went into the house.

The boys, left to themselves, fell to their sports again with an uproar that took a new edge from its short suppression.

Dr. Shaw's study was a chamber well graced with books and portraits of men in ample wigs, with here and there a mezzotint, the festive rosy-bosomed nymphs of which, with loosened zones and dimpled smiles, could contribute nothing of their own gaiety to the sense of dulness prevailing—thanks, perhaps, to the dark curtains and the looming presences of sidereal and terrestrial globes, and such agglomerations of scholastic suggestions for the gratification of parents' eyes.

The doctor seated himself in a crimson velvet armchair, and motioned to the other to sit. Then, crossing his legs, and nursing his knee with plump hands, on the forefinger of one of which was a great signet-ring, he fixed his eyes on his companion with a gaze which, for severity and keenness, should have bored his mind through and through.

"Cuthbert," said he, speaking in a clear, firm voice, not perhaps destitute of a touch of suavity, "I have long had it on my mind to bring you to book with a plain question. Living under my eye as you do, do you conceive it possible, sir, that the remarkable change your character has undergone should have escaped me? Come, I will speak intelligibly. It strikes me that you grow weary of your apprenticeship. Understand me. You would rather not be a schoolmaster. Is that it? Look me full in the eyes, man, and remember that your father abhors a lie."

Cuthbert raised his eyes, but they fell instantly. Still he answered quickly—

"I don't grow weary of it. Why do you challenge me? Has a single murmur ever escaped me?"

"What! is discontent to be expressed by nothing but groans? Give me leave to tell you that a man can murmur with his face, sir, without opening his mouth. Pray understand that—murmur with his face, sir."

"Well," said Cuthbert, with a little drooping of the head and a reluctant manner, "I will say that if I did not know how near your wishes concerning me lay to your heart, I—I——"

Here he shrugged his shoulders, smiled faintly, and fell silent, beating the ground softly with his foot.

"Pray finish your sentence. You would correct a pupil, I hope, for stammering," broke in the irritable doctor.

With an expression in his eyes which made it very difficult to tell whether be was quite as much in earnest as his speech represented him, Cuthbert exclaimed, with a certain fastidious emphasis—

"I think no young Englishman who reads the papers but must sometimes feel a generous ambition to share in the glories and perils of the deeds which British soldiers and sailors are enacting in all parts of the world."

The doctor stared; his face hung between a scowl and a grin; then he burst out sharply—

"The world is before you! It is only your own legs hinder your *generous ambition*. What else stays you?"

"Your wishes."

The doctor sneered.

"Or I had better say my duty," said the young fellow, in a soft voice, looking for a moment eagerly at his father, and then turning his eyes aside and biting his lip.

"Duty!" cried the doctor, sarcastically. "Are you stopped by the duty you owe me, or the duty you owe yourself? If you want to illustrate fine thoughts, give me something better than brave words for proof. If your father's calling is too low a pursuit——"

"Low, sir!"

"I said low."

"Indeed, then——"

"Hold your prate! How dare you interrupt me, sir! I say that if your father's calling is too low a pursuit to satisfy your vaulting mind, why, shake off the mean burden, loosen your wings, and leave your duty behind you. Tut! tut!" he cried, motioning with his hand; "if those are your fancies, I'll not balk your gratification of them, trust me! It is nothing, of course," he continued, with a bitterness he could not conceal, though he would imagine his satirical smile a good mask, "that for twenty years I should have been sturdily plodding on in hope of leaving you an established man of sound report and name, narrowly holding my earnings, with the blessed help of your dead and sacred mother, that I might give you an Oxford training;

nothing my vigorous toil, my slow and painful reaches to competency, of which what should you know beyond what you have gleaned from your poor mother's tales of our early struggles? Pshaw! get you gone, my dear! There is glory abroad, indeed!—murder, lust, and fire! Now go and add your mite to the general destruction, by the demolition of your father's hopes!"

This was high-tragedy rant. Something to make a modern laugh. But old gentlemen used to spout somewhat in this way in those days; and sons who called papas "sir" listened respectfully to stronger stuff than this, as you may see in the comedies of the age and learn from the tales of your grandfather.

"Father," cried Cuthbert—and there shot into his face a sudden expression of deep appeal that made its beauty as touching and as soft as a woman's—"you are not just to me. I do not wish to leave you. I glanced very lightly at my fancies. Fancies they are—most trifling; without influence, indeed. If there is anything in my manner that causes you uneasiness, I will reform it."

But once more his glance went downwards, and the keen gaze of his father's black eyes assuredly belied their owner's sagacity if he did not detect that something stood between him and his son's honesty.

Yet, divining no other reason that his son should not be honest with him than that he was smarting under youthful impatience of dull routine, he stuck like a man to the skirts of Cuthbert's own suggestions.

"I don't say," he remarked, in a softened manner, "that the business of educating boys is not tedious. But, after all, name me the calling that has not something objectionable. The lawyer's trade dry-rots the understanding. The heart of the painter sickens over depreciative custom. The cultured priest starves on a footman's wages. If you have a mind for fighting and the glory that is got out of massacre, think of the personal pains, the wounds, and hollow applause—scarcely substantial enough to replace a missing leg or extract a festering bullet; and the settlement of a good home, the charm of books, the noble servitude of directing young passions and filling the growing mind with virtues and the useful wares of learning, shall not seem such disgraceful compensations as you hold them."

"I have said that I am content to remain as I am."

"Is that really so?"

"Truly so."

"Yet you are not yourself," said the doctor, gazing doubtfully at his son: "something is amiss. Just now Juvenal was under your nose and—let me see the book."

Cuthbert handed him the volume.

"Well, it is Juvenal; but that is mere luck, for you never looked at it. What distracts you? Absence of mind is intelligible in old men; but *you* are moon-struck in the midst of your classes. Yesterday I heard Worthington give you a foolish answer which you did not notice; and no exercise comes before you that you do not bend over it with a more puzzled look than the boy had who made it."

The young fellow folded his arms and remained silent, slowly swaying his foot.

"I date this change in you from the day of your return from London," continued Dr. Shaw, drawing from his pocket a small gilt snuff-box, and taking a pinch ready to apply when anger should set him sniffing. "I put money into your hand for the holiday, and trusted to your discretion to make it a cheap purchase of enlarged views. What did you do in London? I need not ask you. You have told me—you went sight-seeing—and I believe you."

Cuthbert bit his lip.

"That is enough, sir—I believe you," continued the doctor, answering with emphasis the brief glance that Cuthbert threw at him. "Now, am I to suppose that this holiday upset you? Come, come, you are not a yokel, that you cannot walk London streets without your ambition taking fire from every printshop."

He paused, his hand with the pinch of snuff in it suspended, and a light of angry triumph in his eyes, as though he should say, "The secret cannot elude me, but I hate the discovery."

Cuthbert rose and walked to the window, and looked out upon the green swell of cliff and the blue faint space of sea beyond.

That there was a secret in his mind might be known by the pain in his eyes, and a contraction of brow which told of a sudden inward wrestle.

But these signs faded, leaving him not paler than he was before, and with a tranquil smile, sweet with the melancholy and docility in it, he turned to his father and said—

"Nothing is amiss with me in the way you suppose. Give me a day or two for reflection. I shall then have something to tell you, and God knows what indulgence you shall show me."

The doctor arched his eyebrows, and, with a stiffening of his back, made his frill project fiercely.

"I don't like your strong expressions, sir. And pray, what have you done, that you should hesitate to avow it?"

And he stuck his head back until the hollow in his throat showed above his white neckerchief.

But if Dr. Shaw could be angry, so, too, could Cuthbert his son be obstinate; and the touch of the mule that is in the composition of most men shows nowhere more transparently than in a handsome face.

"Give me your permission to leave you, sir," said Cuthbert.

The doctor waved his hand, and Cuthbert walked out.

Isaac Shaw was doctor of laws and this much could be said of him—that better blood than his did not flow in any man's veins in all that town of Greystone, and that more of the learning which is not so much wisdom as scholarship thickened no man's wits within the municipal area.

But Isaac Shaw's learning was more to his profit than honour, as it brought him pupils but gave him no social advance beyond fellow-townsmen, inasmuch as not the rector even had weight of erudition enough to sink to the depths of his knowledge.

On the other hand, his blood was more to his honour than profit, as it made him haughty and exclusive, with a rattle of insolence sometimes, so that he was an unpopular man at Greystone, which supplied him with one only of the forty pupils who studied and struggled on his premises.

This Dr. Isaac Shaw loved his son Cuthbert with that kind of love which makes a man unkindly critical, vicious in perception of small weaknesses, and a very strait-jacket unto the object of its affections, that it may walk with moral erectness all the days of its life.

For many a year the current of the boy's existence had flowed gently down the channel of academic routine, with never a break of froth in it, nor sudden hasting, nor sharp divergence.

Tractably imbibing all notions that the doctor in his wisdom decanted, and with grave docility discharging such offices as should qualify him for the inheritance of his father's shoes, no possible uneasiness nor question of the regulation of his aims could this young man excite in the doctor.

Until suddenly—but the heavens know not without cause—there fell upon his moods a shadow so like melancholy that the doctor took counsel with himself and reasoned thus:—

"He is mewed up here, and we take few holidays. Every man requires now and again a change of scene. Ergo, Cuthbert requires a change of scene. He has asked for such a change of scene, and he shall have it. I will furnish him with twenty guineas, and he shall go to London and see life for a fortnight."

But lo! concession, instead of casting out the one devil from his son's mind, merely liberated the imp to return with seven worse imps than itself.

"What is on his mind I cannot conjecture," the doctor mused, looking at the door which Cuthbert had closed. "He says he is *not* weary of this life."

With a gloomy brow and a puzzled wrinkle of the nose, he snuffed up the pinch he had held throughout the interview, and muttered—

"But then he may lie."

Now, Dr. Isaac Shaw hated strong expressions.

CHAPTER III

CUTHBERT'S SECRET

"Of all actions of a man's life, his marriage does least concern other people; yet, of all actions of our life, 'tis most meddled with by other people."—SELDEN

UTTER silence falls never on a boys' school. Not even on the dormitories, wherein the snoring of dull stomachs and mutterings of young slumber, and the restless sprawling of limbs that makes the bedsteads creak and the bedclothes slide, are sounds audible throughout the night.

But there should be peace at prayer-time.

That hour is arrived; and now we certainly find a tolerable stillness on the benches, young knees and fitful tendency towards laughter notwithstanding.

One likes to think with reverence on young souls lifted up in prayer; but bright eyes squinting through open fingers, and breeched convexities topping legs of irregular lengths, are unfortunately circumstances of commonplace that detract from solemnity.

Yet all goes well; not a single half-suppressed cackle to make Dr. Shaw dart his eyes from the Bible. Hear the childish trebles—all virile voices long ago, and silent in the grave how many!— chasing the doctor's recitation of the Lord's Prayer in a subdued chorus that sounds like the singing of a summer wind.

The resident ushers at the corner of each form, their fingers to their eyes, stand erect. Cuthbert kneels near his father. A breeze from the sea keeps the chestnut leaves at the windows shivering, and through the twinkling of them the faint gold shine in the west comes and goes, with the large stars in the nearer sky, and the growing whiteness of moonlight on the fields.

Then to bed decorously, as becomes the recipients of the benediction.

As the boys file out through one door, Cuthbert walks out behind his father through another door.

Though watched on the whole by his father more closely than he merited, seeing that he had long ago abandoned petticoats, Cuthbert enjoyed every evening an hour and a half of liberty what time the doctor, having dismissed his scholars to bed, withdrew to his study to relax his mind in all ways that pleased him after the tension of the day.

His little spell of evening holiday was come, and as the tails of his father's coat fluttered through the study door, Cuthbert swung down his hat and left the house.

In the young moonlight, and the glimmering memories of crimson over the dark line of the cliff, the ocean breeze, snatching land-fragrance from the nestling crops, was sweet as honey.

No tenderer and more peaceful scene ever bared its dark breast to the mild scrutinies of the moon, than the rapt broadlands which ran their dreamy spaces from the edge of the sheer cliff to the shadowy phantoms of the horizon. Soft were the voices of the breakers upon the hidden beach, joining their feathery cadence to the chant of the night-wind moaning along the land.

And yonder, a blazing globe amid the pale-eyed constellations, was the beacon of the giant foreland-rock that hung its immemorial shadow in the deep.

Down the broad white road, whereof the dust powdered his shoes as neatly as meal a miller's face, his lean shadow growing into sharper outline as he walked, Cuthbert went swiftly, pausing once to pull a watch from his fob. The sound of the sea followed him like the murmur of a shell to his ear—a hollow reverberation fit to quicken a pallid fancy (in the eye of the delicate moonshine frosting stirless shapes) into uneasy perceptions.

The road led straight to the town.

Coming presently to the brow of the western slope, the town lay in a fog of moonlight at his feet, the lamps threading it in veins of fire-sparks, and the sea creaming a wash of white foam on the semicircle of beach.

And so forwards and downwards, his shadow growing smaller in his wake, and the dusky crops on either hand rippling their ears on a level with his shoulders, until a row of noble wayside elms bury him in their heavy gloom.

Here he halts.

It is a weak-hearted love that is not punctual in its promises; and what should excuse delay, when the lover waits and the summer moon shines out her sweet invitation, and the soft wind sets the trees bending stately heads to behold the coming of the tardy one?

But lo! a figure steals around the bend of the road from behind the plumage of the fields, and in a moment lips are meeting.

The embrace is a warm one, wanting in coyness, and the richer in tenderness for the want. Something to stiffen Dr. Shaw's frill into ferocity, and to rob the finest Scotch of all flavour in his nose.

"It is barely the quarter," the girl said in a low voice; and she clasped her hands upon his arm, and strained her eyes at his face. "We are both before our time."

"Both impatient, Jenny."

"Ay; but I will take most credit, for the way is all uphill for me, dear."

"How long can you give me, pretty?"

"Not above five minutes."

"Indeed; then those minutes shall be long ones."

"Not above five minutes, I say, Cuthbert; and I feel the pity of it this lovely night, when the moon is so pretty, that I shall cry to go to bed."

He kissed her hand.

"Mother thinks I am gone to see Kate Oliver," she went on. "so I must not stay, for fear she should ask father to fetch me. There are troops of fishermen in the market-place, and the streets are full of people, and mother does not like me to walk alone."

"Would she think you safe with your husband?"

"Ah, would not she! If father had her heart——!"

"Put away your hat, that you may lay your soft hair on my shoulder. Here is a dry cushion of grass, with a streak of moonlight on it for me to see you in. Have a little patience while I talk to you. Mother will not be wondering yet."

So they seated themselves on the verdure, where the moonlight fell in a lance of tremulous silver; and she, dutifully removing her hat, bent her cheek to his shoulder.

Thus they sat, with no other sound to disturb them than the moaning of the sea, and the rustling of the leaves over their heads.

In the moonlight a lovely woman's face takes a sad and moving beauty.

No blush glows through the pearl of the light upon it.

Lips which are red as the rose in the sun, are pale in this light, which denies passion to them.

All expression of thought is chastened into pensiveness.

Richness and sensualities of lid and lip are refined into a subtle fragility.

It is the true virginal lustre, wherein beauty grows a vision, and passion dies on eyes and mouth.

Not a sweeter face ever smiled in the love of man's eyes than Jenny's, though marred by the moonlight as a mirror for the emotions, which, in the glory of the day, gave it colour and archness, and a hundred turns of grace.

Cuthbert's hand toyed with her cheek, and his lips often pressed her forehead before he spoke again. Time was precious to him and her; yet the sweetness of silence was a drug to heedfulness just then, and powerful care was powerless to break the deep spell upon them, and disengage their amorous being from the mystery of passion and moonlight and stillness.

"My little wife," said he in his gentle voice, "I have been closely pressed to-day by my father. I put him on a scent that puzzled him; and really he went down to it greedily, for his anxiety to find out the meaning of what he chooses to call my altered behaviour is perfectly wonderful. I hinted—merely hinted—that the news of our sea-fights, and our battles ashore, had set my heart beating for higher feats than cramming boys with learning. Well, it was time that lie noticed some change in me."

Jenny counted with her fingers upon his shoulder, softly smiling and listening to him the while.

"He said to me," Cuthbert went on, "'I date the alteration in you from the day of your return from London.' He draws near, you see, dear. He is dreadfully close at my heels. Still, his notion is odd, seeing that I have not moped since as I moped before I went that trip."

"How like our adventures at home are! Only to-day mother came up to me, and. took my ear in her hand and said, 'Jenny, Jenny, I will squeeze *hard* if thou art not honest. I hear you sighing in your sleep just like my old school-mate Sally Mattocks did when the silly wench brought trouble upon herself by listening to a gipsy woman's lies. Father watches you closely, and I know him very well as a man who never troubles himself to stare, unless there be something to see. What is it, silly?' I pulled my ear away and made it burn to run from her, and I laughed that she might think her talk nonsense. But oh, my dear, I could not help crying just two or three tears. I do not fear mother—indeed, she would be very proud of my own, and love him for his own sweet sake, and make him her boast, as I know she would; for often father tells her that she has made her godmothers sad fibbers, though what he means by that you shall tell me, as I have not one little bit of thy cleverness in my head, sweet—but father's eyes, when he is angry, make me shiver. What bold things a girl will do for love! And yet it does not make her brave."

She put her hand over her eyes, and peeped at him through her fingers; not for the coquetry of it, but that she might not lose sight of him a moment.

"Jenny, I will tell you what it is—there is no help for it but honesty. And that we need not be afraid of."

"Oh no, indeed! The Lord forbid. We are both truly honest, I thank God."

"Honest and reticent," he exclaimed, with a subdued laugh. "But where are we to begin?"

"Ah, that is for you to tell me."

"Well, good sense tells us to begin at the worst end first. But I should prefer to hold over my father till I have done with yours."

"Both ends are the worst," said Jenny with a sigh.

"I will begin with your father, Jenny. That is my resolve; and one's own wishes are the easiest way, love. To-morrow evening I will see Mr. Strangfield and tell him we are married."

"To-morrow evening!"

It was a long way off for their next meeting, but *very* close for bitter business.

"It is not too soon?" he said, soothingly.

"No, it is not too soon," she answered, with a little shudder. "But I wish it were over—I wish he knew."

"Every moment of delay," he continued, "is a new wrong to you, my pet; and surely I am no loving husband, Jenny, if I wrong you. What excuse have I for delay? So far it has been cowardice. But I can end it if I choose, and to-morrow night it is done. Will your father be at home?"

"I dread to say yes. I shall not dare to face him."

"Jenny, you must not be so timid. You are not alone."

"But I can hear him crying, 'Jenny, Jenny, come down from your room!' with his face like wood, and the angry stoop of his head, which he will lift in flames, as I saw him once when he charged his niece Martha, who is dead, with an evil deed."

"This is no evil deed, my pretty?"

"Did not I just now say we were honest? In my heart I feel we are; yet what should my conscience answer if father calls me deceitful?"

"But, you see, there are so many kinds of deceit. There is one kind that injures people, and another kind that injures no one. Whom have we injured? Dearest, there is nothing to fear?"

"Father will call this an evil deed—he will say it is an acted lie."

"Jenny, we have chosen our own road, and if we have walked upon it secretly, your father shall know our reasons. Have we done wrong in loving and marrying? Our duty now is to confess, and that is all that remains. We shall know no peace until the secret is out of us, and we are spoken of as man and wife."

"My own husband, I pray God you may not suffer because you love me."

He shook his head and kissed her.

"I know that your father will think you have degraded yourself," she went on, "by marrying Michael Strangfield's girl; and did I not tell you, Bertie, that I was not your equal, and that you had no right to love me? But you have given me your heart," she cried with a sob, "and never comes a night that I do not kneel down and bless God for thy love, and pray that I may be thy true sweet treasure."

"As you are, as you are, Jenny! God judges me as I speak."

"I cannot help fearing my father," she continued, in a trembling voice, "for though he is very stern he loves me; and I dread the thoughts his love will fill him with when he hears that I have deceived him and mother."

"The worst is not so bad as the dread of it, dear."

"He is so terribly religious."

"Ay, a Baptist; and my papa is a Tory Churchman! And we are to be impaled on their prejudices! Thank the Lord, old men are scant of breath, and when their lungs are empty, young men may——"

"Hark! here are the coastguards."

The tramp of men, deadened by the smothering dust of the road, fell upon their ears; and soon a little company of dark figures, with the moonshine kindling silver stars in the polished points of their weapons, turned the corner and strode sturdily, in silence, up the hill. There were twelve of them, for the reliefs along the cliff: they went up the white road with wreaths of dust hanging to the heels of the hindmost, and were presently a black line upon the hill-top.

"It should be half-past eight," said Jenny. "I must be going, Bertie."

"We have not been together five minutes, Jenny. Your mother will not be thinking of you yet. Stop, my pretty, till we have settled to-morrow's business."

"Oh, Cuthbert, how sweet it would be could you take me to a home to live with you! The tiniest house would do. I should love to wait on thee; and mother will tell you I can cook better than she, who was fifty-one last March."

"First let us subdue your Puritan father," replied Cuthbert, tickling her face with a spear of long grass and smiling as she smiled. "He shall find me his match in texts."

"My dear, you are a thousand times more clever than father. He will not reason with you; he knows better. He may show thee to the door and bid me follow you, and so I shall be turned away and bring no blessing with me."

He loved her too tenderly, and was too gentle in all moods to feel impatience at her words, though they were a tweak to the nose of his pride, that, being a gentleman of honourable descent, a shipwright should act to him as Jenny suggested.

"I am not so greatly afraid of him," said he, smiling still, and leaning his head on his hand, which posture made him a figure of grace like a carving; "the harder nut to crack is at the school-house yonder. They say astonishment petrifies; and if my father's heart is as strong as I sometimes think it is, what impenetrable stuff will surprise at my confession make it! Cast-iron will be as putty to it, love. But he cannot divorce us; and so, either he must receive us both, or lose me wholly. Which, now, will he do?"

"Heigh-ho!" she answered.

"It is the spin of a coin, Jenny, that has but two sides; not a cube, not a die, that multiplies risks. Is it the king's head? then our fathers are our friends. Is it the king's tail? then God be with us. We can make our fight like others.

It is something that we start honestly: and, for my part, like faithful Kent, I can keep counsel, ride, run, and deliver a plain message bluntly; so that, dear, we are stocked to begin life on."

"Your face is so serious that I do not understand your words," said she, straining her sweet gaze at him. "Hush! there is the quarter striking! Oh, I must be going, indeed. Good night; say good night to me, Bertie."

They both rose, their hands clasped.

"To-morrow night, at half-past eight, watch for me at your window, Jenny. My mind is resolved. I will speak to your father first, and then tell mine the story. We shall sleep the sweeter for it. A clear conscience before all things, and that will come by honouring ourselves."

"Yes, it is right," she whispered with a little shiver. "Kiss me, and say good night."

He strained her in his arms, and she went away, but slackened her pace and fled back to him out of the moonlight. Then, slipping from his lips, she ran across the road and was gone.

CHAPTER IV

BREAKFAST-TIME

"*Prince Prettyman*. But prithee, Tom Thimble, why wilt thou needs marry?"—*The Rehearsal*

"I think a man must be of a very quiet and happy nature who can long endure the country, and, moreover, very well contented with his own insignificant person—very self-complacent."—LONGFELLOW

THERE is a little reconciling fiction handed down by father to son, and never disputed by the schoolmaster.

This fiction declares that the happiest time of life is schoolboy time.

Now, a man need not be in a bad temper to deny this, recalling the kicks and tasks, the surly ushers, the tooth-splitting Greek, the brain-twisters of Euclid, and that tingling commentary on most things—

"UNBUTTON, SIR!"

But in this matter let every man speak for himself: for some, in after life, suffer in so many parts, not corporeal merely, that it may prove to them a pleasant memory to recall the days when they ached in top and bottom only for the sins of their understanding.

But passing from them who are taught to them who teach, be it declared that under the heavens there is no worse drudgery than the life of an usher.

There is the permanent trial of the spirits.

There is the tempered mind buckled up in scholastic routine, like good steel in a bent scabbard.

There is the prim repacing of first principles.

There is the weary twisting of the gimlet of intelligence into heads of wood.

These things make the usher's knee-bagged breeches and shiny coat the raiment, in just eyes, of a martyr.

"Whereas," groans poor George Herbert,

> "Whereas my birth and spirit rather took
> The way that takes the town,
> Thou didst betray me to a lingering book,
> And wrap me in a gown.
> I was entangled in a world of strife

Before I had the power to change my life."

The Lord help him!

Out of his bed rose Cuthbert, to the tune of the school-bell, swung by the man who cleaned the boots, and thrived on pocket-money errands, to the destruction of youthful digestions.

His own mild hint yesterday, by which he had hoped to put his father off from grappling questions, had stirred him into perception of new sympathies in his nature. With thoughts of his wife, and the secret to be divulged before another night should come, had mingled impulses of freedom, a yearning for the shows and struggles of an outer world, and a placid weariness of spirit, when the schoolroom rose in his eyes, with the tasks to be set, and the ignorance to be corrected.

His resolution to proclaim his secret was a quickening spirit in the soil of his mind, germinating seeds there which he himself knew not of.

"Why need I fear my father's anger?" he thought, as he threw open his bedroom window, and stood in a stream of sweet warm wind, fresh from the blue water; "I have served him dutifully, and will yet justify all his fine thoughts of his calling by sticking to it, if he will love Jenny, and bear with me for marrying her. If not, the world is big enough to find me work, surely! What I am fitted for shall not trouble me; but what I can get to do, I'll do."

This honest soliloquy done, he betook himself to dressing.

Never a looking-glass gave back a handsomer face than that into which he glanced. Such a picture of dark auburn hair, white brow and blue eyes, bright with mind, as would set a heartless beauty dreaming like a faithful sweetheart.

Neglectful of the mirror's blandishments, which, so Heaven has willed it, are often condolences for the beautiful and flatteries for the ugly, Cuthbert beheld a vessel under full sail come sweeping round the foreland point.

The water boiled with the brilliance of snow under her bows, and the brass on her decks gleamed in a hundred stars of fire.

Of all man's handiwork, the most stirring and noble detail furnished by him to nature, is a ship in full sail leaning down to a wind and sweeping softly, amid a hum of froth and the melody of breezes upon tautened shrouds, across a lustrous breast of sea.

Here now was this proud show, and the meteor-flag at the gaff-end made it a sight, in those crimson times of British history, to quicken the dullest eye into light.

For the Frenchman's flotilla was still at Boulogne; and the shipwrights of Brest were pushing briskly to avenge Trafalgar.

Collingwood was off Cadiz.

Russell was off the Texel.

Those glorious spirits, Cochrane and Hood, were sharpening their swords for red work in the Garonne.

Consequently pig-tailed Jack was a lovely presence to the British gaze, and his ship a brillianter beauty than a toast.

As this vessel came round the point, the nautical eye fixed her for a ten-gun brig, just now a Channel cruiser, with teeth sharp set for the clamorous fare of Gallic privateers, or the harder pills of Yankee Doodle's navy.

But what doing so close inshore could not be guessed; until, behold! halliards and braces were let go, tacks and sheets raised, leechlines and buntlines manned, staysail, jib, and peak halliards released; her light canvas fluttered and melted into thin lines; round came her wheel, the spokes flying through the beating hands of the men; then made her bowsprit a handsome sweep, her large canvas vanished, and every yard was dotted with rows of heads.

In a few minutes she had dropped to the length of her hempen cable out of Cuthbert's sight under the tall cliff.

And now for the day's dry work, the first stage of which was the meeting of the boys in the schoolroom, to await, amid crackling of yawns and restless shuffling of feet, the arrival of Dr. Shaw in that academic gown of his, which he donned only to read the morning prayers in or to birch a boy.

He was a schoolmaster all of the olden time. He never omitted to pray for Church and King.

If his orisons betrayed special solicitudes, the preservation of these two divinities of his high-heeled toryism were the things concerned.

His prayers just here were a kind of accentual damning of Dissent; and the boys knew well, and the masters better, when to put in the loudest and deepest amen.

There was a poignancy in his tone this morning that made Cuthbert wince a trifle. Not a roll of the eye but that prejudice pulled the strings of it.

And such keen ears will conscience prick, that Cuthbert was ready to swear his father's manner of praying exhibited distinct perception of irremediable relationship with the Baptist deacon Strangfield.

Between prayer-time and breakfast-time there was a half-hour, to employ which profitably to his spirits, that stood sorely in need of regenerating influences, and also to escape his father's eyes, the twist of which, when they all got off their knees, he did not relish, Cuthbert went into the fields before the house; and so, through the glorifying sunshine and the narrow footway in the barley, down to the short grass of the cliff edge, on the swell of which he stood within a fathom of the sheer fall.

A scene of summer beauty and morning splendour was this he overlooked; for the bosom of the calm deep gave back the richness of heaven, not in one broad roll of azure, but in dyes of blue, faint as the first glimpse of dawn and bright as the tint that ruled above it, and elsewhere of the violet's soft darkness; flecked in the far-reaching space, where sea and sky were one, by sails of ships; and in the south overhung with the silver fronts of clouds whose rear lay hidden in the morning mist. In the clear, sweet-flavoured wind, the semicircle of shore, with the bare black fishing-boats upon it, sipped at and soothingly fingered by the lapping yellow foam; the houses close upon the beach, with windows shining out of the grey of the walls; and the ship-of-war at anchor, with her boats leaping in the flash of waters like fat infants straining at their mother's gown, made a picture of pure and homely beauty, such as few eyes could behold without dimming.

But Cuthbert was toiling with a giant in his mind, and nature was only blue and green to him; for there is nothing dainty to a troubled mind but ease, and this our young friend could not get, neither by sitting nor by standing.

Whilst marriage remains merely a fulfilled love-dream it is a sweet commerce; another passage, and a deep one of the trance. So Cuthbert had found it. A soft diversion, catching a relish from subtlety, and the unpressing need of disclosure easily postponed. But, now that confession was to be made—and his honour could contemplate no hindrance of this—the true meaning of marriage was to be compassed; signifying heavy obligation, and the discharge of it in such wise that the bloom in Jenny's cheek should not fade.

Now, God knows, a girl's bloom is a colour that young men and poor find difficult to fix.

But no use standing moodily conjecturing trouble. So back again to the school-house through the crops, which went whispering to the passage of the wind, as though they had snatched a secret from it.

To the ushers—this old-fashioned term is very meaning—was conceded the privilege of breakfasting with the boys. But Cuthbert would have been glad to exchange places with any one of them that morning, so little fancy had he for a *tête-à-tête* with his father.

It was his duty, however, to be in the room when the boys assembled, and observe that grace was duly said by one of the masters, and deliver the order for the boys to fall to.

Under the clock he stood, punctual to the hour, and in a hungry swarm the boys tumbled in, crowding to their places with a swoop as of crows upon a field of pickings, making ready, with furtive looks one at another, to snatch at the crusts which crowned the pyramids of bread and butter.

Grace having been said by a bachelor of arts, and the order to begin given, out sprang forty hands from under the tables, and the pyramids lost their form and substance.

Then Master Cuthbert, with a pleasant smile around him, left the room.

Old Dr. Shaw, with his legs crossed, and showing no prodigy of calf, bent an eye upon his son as he entered the room that seemed to twist round and round into him.

Cuthbert took a chair and waited, with his father, for the servant to bring in the ham and teapot.

Until these things were forthcoming the doctor held his tongue with a napkin laid cautiously over his frill, and so tucked under his chin that the lower part of his face upon it was like a cameo, he fell to the repast with the zeal of a man who suffers nothing to interfere with the first duty of the day.

Then wheeling round, cup in hand, and the saucer poised on thumb and forefinger, after an old-fashioned habit of drinking tea, he looked hard at Cuthbert.

"I have no right yet, I suppose," said he, in a level voice, "to ask you to explain your mysterious hints of yesterday?"

"It was understood, sir, that I should have a day or two for reflection."

"For reflection on what?" demanded the doctor sharply.

"In asking that, you ask all, father."

"All!"

The doctor uttered the exclamation with a most embracing emphasis. Cuthbert made no answer.

"I should be glad to have my doubts set at rest," continued the doctor, with a gloomy nod of the head, intended to serve as a challenge.

Still no reply from Cuthbert.

"Indeed," exclaimed Dr. Shaw, with a great deal of the schoolmaster in his face and a flourish of the saucer, "I have a right to *demand* an answer from you."

So you have, sir, unquestionably."

"Then give me in a few words the meaning of this change in your behaviour."

"A few words will convey nothing."

"Then," shouted the doctor, "be elaborate. Give me prolixity if you will, so that you explain!"

"Pray, sir, moderate your impatience. I pledge myself to be open with you shortly."

Dr. Shaw grew red in the face, and deposited his cup and saucer, that he might gesticulate unconstrainedly.

"*What*," said he, subduing the passion in his voice, "*what* I desire to know, is this matter—in your mind, that is—not yet ripe for confession?"

Cuthbert swung his foot.

"You do not, perhaps, perceive that these empty hints of yours may convey false impressions, and disturb one with a sense of some LARGE wrong-doing!"

The implication produced nothing.

"When—when—why are you silent, sir? It is your business to contradict me eagerly!"

He stopped, with his ear inclined.

The expression in Cuthbert's face grew more mulish.

"I say that your hints put wild notions into my head!" And with a little shout, as he darted his head at his son, the doctor cried — "WHAT HAVE YOU BEEN DOING?"

"It comes to that, sir," responded Cuthbert, gently.

"Pray continue."

"I have promised to tell you."

"When, sir?"

"Possibly to-morrow."

"So, sir, it *is* a secret?" said the doctor, with his eyes full of exasperation.

"So you will have it," replied Cuthbert, scarcely smothering a smile.

This was stubbornness dreadfully mortifying to the doctor.

Yet there was a gleam of comfort in it too; Bœotian comfort the doctor would have called it, implying muddled complacency.

Depravity is not apt to show in this guise, and possibly there might prove a littleness in the confession—some boyish caprice to be morally whipped most easily into the old discreet paths of thinking—which would make the doctor's curiosity a ridiculous thing to remember.

But, in any case, the best compromise to justify present anxiety and preserve his dignity in the future, was a dark brow and a chilly demeanour.

These were not hard to come at, and under their shadow breakfast ended.

CHAPTER V

IMPRESSED

CUTHBERT might well be thankful that there would be no need for him to meet his father again that day in privacy unless summoned.

It was not quite clear to himself why he should choose to make his and Jenny's secret known to old Strangfield before he spoke to his father; but men in mental straits yield often to inclination without much inquiry; and that his father, to his way of thinking, was, of the two doses to be swallowed, the more ill-flavoured for his honesty to gulp at, was the only reason he could have given you for carrying his bit of news to Strangfield first.

Into the schoolroom he went, with his nervous brooding and face of unpeaceful thought, and mounted his stool, loathing the pantomime of his actions. New discoveries he made with every cast of his eye: that the yellow maps appareling the wall sickened the sunlight; that low human nature was in the ushers who made machines of their sensibilities for lucre and a bed; that the hands of the clock were painted to mock his longing for the hour of solitude; and the hum of the boys, making their lips whisper their tasks to their memories, more vexing to his ear than the bagpipes to a sleepy man.

Yet, predominating over all the pulsating anxieties, were his native gentleness and sweetness of voice and manner. The little gentlemen around his desk had frank eyes for his, and a pretty willingness to learn that they might spare him; and no better flattery could he wish to receive, nor truer tribute to his own clear instincts. He spared the stick, but did not spoil the little rogues by that economy; they loved him, and when before him were brave in their harmless ignorance and quick to profit. And that he should have been constrained to his high stool that morning, advantaged him after all; for solitude, with her specious allurements, could have profited him nothing (if the devouring of one's own heart be held profitless); whereas there was better light than the sunshine in the generous young faces attentive to his words, and a mild distraction to his trouble in the thought that he was making a pleasant memory for himself in their small hearts.

At ten o'clock, with the punctuality that invites awe, entered Dr. Shaw; up rose the forms and the desks to salute this head, as wigs in the law courts spring into a flourish of vegetation when "my lord" comes rustling to the judgment-seat. With a short bow—for pomp is difficult to five foot six of stocking and tail, though swelling with frill—the doctor took his seat, and with a smart rap on his desk, summoned the Grecians to their labours. But the rich rotundity of the dead vocables (the only corpses that keep their souls) could not hold the doctor from many an askew glance at his son's pale and beautiful face, drooping under his thoughtful hand in sham attention to his duties. A beautiful face indeed, full of most noble sculptural harmonies, and even, to the doctor's searching eyes, the more winning for the pensive shadow that overlay it.

Alas! what was drawing the boy from his old zeal?

To no Homeric measure went the doctor's thoughts. If the youngster's mother were alive, she would get at his heart.

But the passage was too narrow for a large frill.

Noon was the hour for a frisk in the playground.

To escape his father, Cuthbert joined the boys, but had no heart to mingle in their sports, though invited by some of the elder lads.

The English master, a cautious, reddish-haired son of the Borderland, but of speech untainted by Erse, unhaunted by Runic germs, came to him with a trim politeness of air and extolled the sky.

Well, it was a sky to applaud, with a meeting of archness and benignity in its blue and of its gracious tenderness making most delicate relievos of the trees.

"Sir," said the English master, clapping some book under his arm, "this is weather to make boys fat with pleasure."

Cuthbert smiled.

"When I was a lad I ran most nimbly when the sun was hottest. It must please your father's son, Mr. Cuthbert, to see these boys so hearty and spirited."

"No doubt he is pleased," rejoined Cuthbert, listlessly.

"You will observe, sir, that health is a larger condition in the eyes of parents than education."

"It should be so."

"One should be a boy to lead boys, Mr. Cuthbert."

"Sometimes one gets tired of boys, though."

The English master took what you may call a Lowlander's peep at the young fellow's face, and with a little sigh as of a man disburdening himself of something more than a trifle, said—

"That is very true, Mr. Shaw."

"Unless," continued Cuthbert, thoughtfully, "one is a father; but, even then, one would occasionally wish one's boys girls."

"I have my doubts about girls," replied the English master.

"At the worst they are gentler than boys, if not more docile."

"Ay, sir, but they have more morals to be looked after than boys. I knew a schoolmistress who went mad, and all her friends owned it was morals."

"How very odd! Few ladies die of their morals."

"Meaning discipline, I should have observed, Mr. Shaw."

"Do schoolmasters ever go mad? asked Cuthbert.

This was a joke to be slyly relished.

The master laughed under his breath.

"I sometimes think," said he, snatching courage from the other's suggestive manner, "that this is no calling for a man of spirit."

"It is a duty that some one must discharge."

"But for a man of spirit, sir!"

"Why, it can never be a question for spirit to decide; for the spirit is gone, when the decision is wanted."

The English master shook his head.

"If I had my time over again!" said he, in a voice like a groan.

"You would do what?"

"I would break stones, sir."

The old alternative, which is always preferred when too late to adopt.

Cuthbert looked at this man with a little thrill of pity.

The sounding of human minds was a new art to him; and to him, as to all beginners, the first ground-touch of the plummet was a shock.

"How they must talk together, these masters!" he thought.

But it was a sympathy he had a mind to borrow from.

"A man must be content to get his living somehow, I suppose," said he.

"Maybe, sir," rejoined Mr. Saunderson, doubtfully.

"Times are always hard to the poor."

"True, sir; and hardest upon the educated poor."

"Simply because gentility is a restriction instead of a privilege."

"One reason, Mr. Shaw. Culture, you see, is a rich man's boast, but it is a needy man's despair. For what," he suddenly cried, with an expression of intolerance in voice and face, "did my father spend his savings in giving me a university education? To make me a gentleman! Lord, help me! Better had he sunk the learning to teach me skill in tools, or the business of the counter. At forty, one can excuse one's want of manners and knowledge, if one has a home and children to love."

He dropped his warmth and smiled by way of apology, a sudden gush of self-interest making him anxious that Cuthbert should not accept him too narrowly. The smile was more depressing than the outcry. Cuthbert returned no answer, and the other, not fully perceiving what might come of this babble of his, sought safety in proving Cuthbert his seducer.

"It is plain, Mr. Shaw, that you find this business of teaching boys irksome."

"I need not deny it," replied Cuthbert, candidly, with a glance round the playground.

"But—pray pardon my freedom—you are a younger man than I, of bright promise, Mr. Shaw—forgive me—and ardent, as I may fairly presume from your abilities. If I rebel now and again, my kicks are jaded—idle dreams stir me; but they are soon resolved by necessity, and I go to work again with a thankful spirit. But you—how can I doubt it?—find these walls narrow. They obstruct the horizon, and that is always a pity in vigorous eyes. I sometimes respectfully wonder that your father does not give scope to your ambitions, and deliver you, with such opportunities as his position warrants, to the world you could not fail to grace."

"Ah, Mr. Saunderson, there is much to wonder at," replied Cuthbert, gently, not liking this servility which had fallen over the man's candour. "Time squares everything, if we have patience for the routine of phases. There is the little baronet crying—who has been bullying him?" with which excuse he left the English master.

So the day wore away and the evening came, and when the boys had trooped to the dormitories, Cuthbert went to his room to prepare his mind and person for the beginning of a difficulty. He had no acquaintance with Mr. Strangfield, but knew him well by sight, of course, as Jenny's father, and by hearsay as a mule of a man in prejudice, rancorous as a Moslem in his manner of belief, and with those disdains of blood-precedence and factitious rights which filled the pot-houses of the time with eloquence, and gave a strut to the low man's stride. So, as a tactitian should who knows that big ends are often compassed by small provisions, Cuthbert dressed himself in his soberest apparel—a well-worn monkey-jacket and dark small-clothes—resolved, at least, with true world-cunning, that the hard-eyed Baptist should find nothing foppish in his dress to smell rankly to prepared prejudice.

Then, with his lips twitching to the strength of his silent arguments, our hero went lightly down the staircase, and softly passed his father's study, and out by the house door.

He had hoped to get away unseen; but lo! in front of the garden gate stood Mr. Saunderson, smoking a pipe and contemplatively enjoying the strong evening breeze. The twilight was small, and the moon reddening behind the glowing foreland lamp. Had Cuthbert chosen to walk on, Mr. Saunderson would not have recognized him; but in his embarrassment he must needs stop and speak, whereat the master whipped his pipe out of his mouth and stared ceremoniously.

"A fresh evening, Mr. Saunderson. Pray continue to smoke."

"It is, I may truly say, my only indulgence," replied Mr. Saunderson, giving his pipe a loving shake. "There is less chance of my being observed here by the boys, than were I to light my pipe at the back of the house. You are going for a stroll, sir."

"Ay; one cannot do without exercise." And with a nod Cuthbert went on his way.

Mr. Saunderson looked after him earnestly, and when the young fellow had vanished in the folding shadows, shook his head and betook himself to his pipe again, sucking strongly.

Now, after a day of brilliant stillness, a shrill evening had come, a gloom clamorous with wind, with but fitful promise of moonshine amid the straining shadows of clouds. The air rang with the clash of trees, and the boiling of surf under the cliffs, and the silken sweep of the corn-billows rushing through yellow fields. Along the road pursued by Cuthbert, the dust rose in shapes of corkscrews, and whirled away in volleys; and the lights which spotted the landscape twinkled like winter stars.

Mr. Strangfield's house was a long twenty minutes' walk from Greystone school, stepping it briskly; but even if the dust, when the curve was compassed, that drove full in his face had proved no hindrance to Cuthbert, the obnoxiousness of his mission, and the thoughts that it bred tweaking savagely at his nerves, would account for the frequent drag of his pace. He could have come to a standstill at times, when he considered how he should open his business and what state of mind he should find himself in if Strangfield, after hearing his story, should turn him out of his house. Such treatment was to be apprehended on the evidence of Jenny's own fears. Then, after a loitering caused by such thoughts, his mind would betake itself to Jenny, watching with lovely timid eyes at her window, brightening with love and alarm to every figure that passed; and on he would push again, until he was half-way down the hill, where the dust was more quiet and the wind less sturdy, being no longer the rushing army that poured its invisible hosts along the upper plains, but mere flying scouts and subtle sharp-shooters, making swift leaps at his cap, or plunging, with a glitter of dust into his face, out of the lanes in the corn-fields, or swooping straight down upon him from the open sky.

By this time the moon had changed her copper into silver, and was kindling growing and waning phantoms all about; sometimes brightening the road into a clear-shaped way, then leaving it a short passage into shadow.

He had passed his trysting-place, and had turned the elbow of the road which laid the town broad under his eye, when the sounds of men's voices came up with the wind; and, in a few moments, he perceived a crowd of persons approaching him. The moon, stooping clear of a pillow-shaped cloud, threw out a full radiance, by the which he saw that the crowd was a company of sailors—some ten of them at least—and that they walked in two gangs, one on either side three men, who strode abreast with heads dejectedly hung and their hands pinioned behind them.

"Deserters," thought Cuthbert, stepping aside.

"Stand!" shouted a youthful voice, "in the king's name! Thompson, here is a toe-and-heeler for us. He'll make the complement, and no more sweethearts to break our heads with frying-pans."

The word "Stand!" though very forcibly delivered, produced no effect on Cuthbert, who could scarcely credit, indeed, that it was meant for him; and he was passing on, when a young man in a cloak stepped in front of him.

"Now, my bantam, turn about! You're wanted."

"Do you address me?" exclaimed Cuthbert, so much amazed that he looked behind him, half persuaded that there must be some one there for whom the accost was intended.

"You or the man in the moon, my hearty; whoever is nearest."

"Suffer me to pass you, sir."

"Now, this is too bad," cried the young fellow, in a mock voice of consolation. "Oaths we are used to, but politeness in a son of a quid is fit for nothing but to get lush on tick with. Stand, I tell you! Damn it, don't you understand king's English?" for Cuthbert was pushing past.

"Make way for me. You are over-stepping your duty, or labouring under an error."

"Ay, ay, we always do that. Thompson, give him a sheer to port. We'll argue as we walk."

A bushy-whiskered fellow approached Cuthbert, who sprang back a yard before the outstretched arm.

"Touch me at your peril!" he shouted.

"Come, come, take it coolly, man. All the arguefication in the world'll do no good. The Sarvice wants ye, so give us your hand upon it!" With a bound the bushy-whiskered man grasped Cuthbert's arm.

The three pinioned men looked on with a dull interest; the sailors turned their tobacco-junks unconcernedly, glancing back at the town or up at the moon, and muttering over the wet pull before them.

Cuthbert had one of those nervous systems which, in a fury, make steel of the hand and steam-engines of the muscles. His white fist sped, like a snow-flake on a rush of wind, right into the bend of the man Thompson's brow, and a pigtail wriggled in the dust, and a pair of boots tried to hit the moon.

Now, having done this, had he used his heels, he would have saved himself, for he was of the build for swift running whereas sailors are bad runners, though decent dancers. But his chivalrous courage, not disdaining flight, for the honourable reason that it never thought of flight, held him rooted, with nostrils quivering and gleaming eyes.

In the moonlight, shining steadily for a space, the scene of men made stationary by brief amazement at so much pluck was a picture to impress the mind. What! one to ten, with a front upon him as if he were ten to one! Here was stuff wanted for mounseer! The three captives chewed their lips as they wriggled their wrists. Lord! an their hands had been free! And the dust before the wind twisted away in spurts of gossamer powder among the men who would not lift an arm until commanded.

Thompson, of the bushy whiskers, gathered himself off the road, and rubbing the bridge of his nose, looked with a cast in his eye at the young gentleman in the cloak.

"We want no bloodshed," exclaimed that worthy. "Thompson, Jenkins, here, three of you make his hands fast and bring him along!"

This was an order not to be disobeyed under pain of a whipping: willing backs must not be bloodily ploughed for boyish obstinacy. So they went with a rush: the dust soared in a cloud as from under the heels of a flying horse. It was a wild fight, a mad resistance, with the hard-hitting which the age of Mendoza and the slogster Crabbe made free with. But a sudden blow must end the unfair contest. Down went Cuthbert like a snuff-seller's Scotchman under the lurch of a drunken man. In a moment his hands were bound; but his legs declining to exert themselves, he was hoisted on to the shoulders of a couple of stout seamen, and the party proceeded smartly up the hill towards the gorge that led to the sea.

CHAPTER VI

THE STRANGFIELDS

" 'We ought to be very careful how we entrust this affair to him,' interrupted the wicked duenna: 'you do not know Don Lewis; he is too nice in punctilios of honour to be assisting secret amours; the very proposal of a private marriage will offend him.' "—*The Devil on Two Sticks*

HARD by an open space of yard, rudely railed, stood a house of wood; a fair-sized house, and strong as an oak-built hull.

Scarcely would you have known it for wood, so artfully were the scantlings matched, so cunningly had time wrought upon the walls the hue of stone, so dexterously had the trainers laced themselves, to show among their summer leaves or winter tendrils no more of what they embraced than would suffice to deceive you.

The roar of the sea was always in the ear of this house, for only the length of this yard was between it and the breakers on the beach; so that on angry nights, when the wind blew fiercely from the south and east, the torn spray would come flashing upon the back windows of the building in slaps and slobs and bubbles of yellow froth, until the whole house rang hollowly with echo.

The town lay upon either shoulder of it.

Up the High Street looked this house; not fully, but askance, in proper keeping with its modest retirement behind the little tract of flowers and grass and reposeful evergreens, and the veil of the bounteous parasites which trimmed its walls.

So that the heart of the town ever beat in its eye, for from its windows the market-place was a clear picture; under the pillared shadows the faces of the wenches and the men showing, and their eager utterances coming duly down to the house in plain syllables.

The yard that adjoined this house was a shipwright's yard; and often as the tar-cauldron belched its smoky stench in the midst of it, the fumes could never kill the sweet-flavoured smells that filled the air around from the white deals and shavings of the pine, and the blocks of red-hearted oak and teak from India.

With sheds for the storage of tools and the costlier woods, with masts and booms, quaint figure-heads and pieces of ship-work, with blocks and capstans, bulkheads to be fitted and timbers snarling with huge red nails, deep-sea leads, dock-fenders and strands of hawser, in one corner an old kedge, yonder a heap of ring-bolts—the yard wore a well-furnished look.

And now even at this stagnant season, when the Frenchman's and the Yankee's love of small sweet pickings was so voracious, that the art of the British coasting trade was a plucky coquetting with wind and haven, even now in this yard were the skeletons of two vessels—a lugger and a schooner—to be finished, equipped, and afloat by August, under the signed contract of Michael Strangfield, who wanted neither pen nor witness to make his word binding.

On this evening of Cuthbert's impressment, the master shipwright sat in the parlour of his wooden home, filling the room with the mist of navy tobacco. In this matter of the pipe his flesh was weak.

A lamp in the centre of the table sent forth a strong light, which disclosed one of those quaint interiors a man must search England inquisitively to become acquainted with in these days.

The low-pitched, heavily joisted ceiling, with a slight set towards the sea, as though the wooden foundation had sunk somewhat in that part of the house which looked upon the water; the patiently carved panelling; the flowery mantel-piece (high as a man's chin), with a framing of dappled china tiles; the windows, filled with narrow panes of bottle-glass (or something exceedingly like it, and more especially that part of it which appears to be manufactured for the sole purpose of falsifying the measure), which allowed no man to look in and no man to look out; the high-backed chairs; the mirror, reflecting dimly, like an old man's memory; the faded paintings, representing the *Queen Charlotte* off the Galloper, the armed lugger *Fan-fan* chased by a Dutch frigate, a hog in a gale of wind, and the smack *Wanderer* (built by Mr. Strangfield's father), with her trawling gear overboard, and the yellow sands of the Goodwins on her starboard beam.

These details Hogarth himself might have designed, for the sportive mixture of the queerness and the picturesqueness of it all; for the challenge to the eye from the meanest detail, and for the garnishing by the chisel of the woodwork wherever it gave license for a flourish of taste, sometimes thinly disguising grossness by clumsy choice of classic subject.

Mr. Strangfield sat in a high-backed armchair near the table, and opposite to him was his wife.

Both of them were busy; the one with his pipe and a design on paper of the hull of the schooner—a skeleton yet in the yard—and the other with knitting-needles.

On the table, at Mr. Strangfield's elbow, was a big horn Bible.

"I believe," said he, in a slow, hard voice, withdrawing his pipe and speaking slightly through his nose to retain the flavour of the tobacco, "that the lines here laid down be those that'll give Mr. Wainwright the speed he looks for." He eyed the paper earnestly. "Here be the small bow-displacement that makes the *Rattler* on a bowline a match for the *Imperoose*. And here's as pretty a swell of the sides as ever I saw, with a sweep to the stern-post that'll keep those hanging quarter waves so flat that they shan't reckon an ounce in pull. And I don't deny that there's something about this bow that makes it look first class: a proper lean, and that sort of look which the stem wants to cut a clean strip out of the water, like a shaving under a plane—and that's how speed's got. Vessels had need to walk in these days, with the French Papists our enemies, and Satan teaching them how to build ships."

And as he said this he laid down the drawing, and looked at his wife through a pair of thick-rimmed spectacles.

The spectacles of those days were disfigurements, as all persons know who are familiar with old prints and paintings.

But neither the irresistible enlargement of Mr. Strangfield's eyes, nor the goblin circles through which they surveyed Mrs. Strangfield, could deform the stern and worn beauty of his countenance.

Fifty-five his age was, and ten years added would still have left his days behind his face— due to a half weary expression of asceticism, and the puckering of an overhanging brow, and an acidulated droop of the under lip. His dark hair, well laced with white, hung in decent profusion over the white collar of his coat, and his attire was grey coarse stockings, stout broadcloth, furnished. with dingy metal buttons, and square-toed boots, with soles thick enough to warrant him no skulker.

"If the moon wasn't so clean, I should allow there was a gale of wind in the sound of the sea."

He yawned loudly.

"Wife, I've smoked enough, and enough is contentment to a thankful heart."

He rose to place his pipe on the mantel-shelf, and reared a figure that brought his head close to the low ceiling.

"Jenny is in her bedroom, and there she sits and sits. What ails the girl? Hast thee noticed her, Michael?" said Mrs. Strangfield, who, though she put her questions with a touch of fretfulness in her voice, went on knitting very placidly.

This was a woman to be admired for her pretty hands, soft eyes, and rich brown hair, neatly smoothed beneath a full cap.

Otherwise, her face disarmed criticism by its vacant good-nature and cheerful insipidity.

Strangfield turned to look at her, and resumed his chair.

"You have seen me watch her," said he. "Why, therefore, do you say, *hast Thee noticed her, Michael?* You are apt to speak without care, wife. Your lips go one way and your mind another."

"Well, well, I have my faults."

"Truly you have, my dear."

"As Gospel says, Who is without sin? Unless it's thee, Michael; and that one should know, by your readiness to cast stones."

Mr. Strangfield frowned, but was wise enough to hold his peace.

"What ails Jenny, then?" continued the mother. "You should know. You be a man of long sight. *I* never could hide a secret from thee."

Mr. Strangfield sat for a space behind his spectacles pondering, while his wife lay down her needles to pass her hand over her hair.

"What should be the matter with her?" demanded Mr. Strangfield, presently. "Her health is sound?"

"I hope so!" cried Mrs. Strangfield, nervously.

"No one has been meddling with her heart, to my knowledge."

"Meddle! Certainly not. Should I not know?"

"Unless," continued Mr. Strangfield, "she be fallen into that state against which the Apostle warned the Corinthian damsels, putting it in this way — that the unmarried woman careth for the things of the Lord;

81

which was, doubtless, a true thing to say of those ancient people, but will not hold now."

Mrs. Strangfield shook her head softly.

"If she had a sweetheart she would tell me," said she, looking rather vaguely, however, at her husband, as a woman might whose conscience does not place her perfectly at ease.

"I could not imagine that she would not," said the husband, sternly.

"As to Mrs. Mead's gossip, it's idler than the wind. Nay, that says nothing for the wind will cool thee when thou'rt hot, and so it doth good. 'Tis idler than her old body, which fusses everywhere, and is like a needle for the sharpness of its pricks, and the eye it carries with it. Jenny has a sweet face, and is as true a lady to speak with as Squire Flashman's wife."

Mr. Strangfield waved his hand. He could not endure this sort of praise.

"Being known to her somehow," continued Mrs. Strangfield, who was not very easily repressed, and who, when she had a point to get at, always travelled to it along the most roundabout paths—"for the chit will not explain how their acquaintance began—is it not proper that Mr. Shaw, who is a born gentleman and knows manners, should take off his hat to her and pass a pleasant word when they meet? Now, through some block-head neighbour, Mother Mead hears of their talking on the beach, whither Jenny had gone for shells for a pin-cushion. And to me she comes with a wise tossing of the nose. But, says I, 'Ma'am, I am my daughter's mother, and what concerns me shall be my proper trouble, under Providence, that our neighbours may have full time for their own affairs.' That was well said, Michael, dost thee not think?"

"Let Mrs. Mead beware how she meddle with Jenny's name! But there should be no cause, neither for her nor any other gossip, to talk."

"Cause!" cried Mrs. Strangfield, opening her mild eyes, with a little toss of the knitting-needles. "A pretty pass, truly, if Mr. Shaw cannot pull off his hat to Jenny, and praise the weather, without his politeness being called a cause. A cause to set Mrs. Mead's tongue going? You need not stand on your head to do that."

"I'll not have Mr. Shaw's name chimed with my wench's," exclaimed Strangfield. "Beelzebub himself is not harder on us than the doctor up at the school-house. 'If he's not a Papist,' said Mr. Baldwin to me t'other day, 'it's because he has too much lust to deny himself meat in the week.' Do you remember his lecture against us last year? Dissenters and Baptists especially are enemies of the Gospel, and traitors to the Throne, he says, and I keep those words in my mind. 'Tis an old saying, that 'honest fowls never take serpents' eggs to hatch.' Let Mr. Shaw keep out of my nest. It's bad enough that Judith Mead should talk."

"Dear heart alive, I know naught of Mr. Shaw," exclaimed Mrs. Strangfield, with a corner glance at her husband. "If Jenny has set him gaping, his mouth is not the only one her beauty has opened. I like to look at his handsome face in the street when I meet him, and his eyes never were matched for the blue of them. These are the Lord's doings, and a woman may admire the works of creation, I hope. But Jenny would not make a sweetheart of him without opening her heart to me, I promise thee. Leastways, I should hope not. Every wench has her fancies, and if you would have them give you no trouble, you must let them be. You knew that others had my thoughts before thee, Michael; and you were quick to excuse me, my man, when I said thee ought'st not to love me for having loved others."

Mr. Strangfield gloomily put these little vanities of memory aside, by the easy method of not listening to them. To be candid, he was a trifle suspicious of the soft smirk (that looked so much like mild triumph) which sometimes rose to the surface of this topic of their courting days.

"What does Jenny do in her bedroom all these hours?" said he. "These mopings have come upon her since her return from Sydenham. Did she leave her heart behind her there?"

"Now, how you talk! Were that so, would not Rachel have written?"

"Jane, Jane, I do not like thy habit of fleering. It is an old taint of sauciness."

"I'll go and call Jenny, and she shall argue with thee herself," said Mrs. Strangfield, quite unruffled by her husband's reprimand.

She put down her knitting, and leisurely rising, with a pretty waddle left the room. Up the staircase, wide enough for a big house, she went, and with a smart turn of the door-handle, entered a bedroom. Here all was dark; until a few moments' gazing exposed Jenny's figure seated at the window, with the windy moonlight streaming upon her, and the summer gale tossing her hair.

"Jenny, Jenny!" exclaimed Mrs. Strangfield, advancing quickly, "what sickness art thou courting at that open window, foolish child?— letting the cold wind fill your bones! Come away from the draught, and shut the window. Father wants thee downstairs."

"It is past nine, mother. What does father want? I like this cool wind, and the stars are pretty to watch, running among the clouds."

"Father does not understand your moping. Here have you been sitting for above an hour. We have been talking about thee, and he has some questions to ask."

"What questions?" exclaimed the girl, quickly. "Let me stay here, mother. It will be time for bed soon. What questions has father to ask?"

"Why, you speak as if you were scared! Jenny, if you would fly in the face of the Lord, the way to do it is to flout thy mother. What ails you? A dozen times I have asked, and you say nothing ails you. Are you not well? is there some secret to trouble you? are you weary of home? Come down, come down, and open your heart to your parents." And saying this she took Jenny's hand, but finding it cold as stone, cried out, "See, now, if this wind will not put thee in a sick bed!" And in a little passion of anxiety and annoyance she closed the window sharply.

The sweet and faithful heart, bidden to watch for her husband's coming, felt the closing of the window to be the true ending of her hopes and fears for that night. It was a reprieve that left deep yearning and faint-heartedness and sorrowful wonder. Never had he failed her before. It could not be fear that made him shirk the interview he had himself planned; neither fear of her father, nor want of passionate love for her. With ears straining to catch at every sound, she gazed through the closed window at the vision of dancing lights without, and the flare of the moon sweeping beyond the clouds and silvering the tossing tops of the bay trees.

"What questions has father to ask, mother?"

"Why, what these mopes signify. He doubts if you brought your heart back with you from Sydenham. But *I* say it was your spirits you left there."

"Mother, let me be here. I am low in spirits to-night. Father would easily make me cry, and what would he think to see me in tears?"

"Jenny, just tell me this, then, that I may answer him when I go downstairs —hath Mr. Shaw talked soft things to thee? Come, come, speak up, my child. Surely I need not be angry, if your beauty has pleased him, and he hath saddened you with foolish fancies. Is that it? We will make you smile again, when we know what troubles you, sweet-heart!"

Jenny's head drooped, but she made no answer. Not to a lie could she stoop. Yet to confess but a part was to confess nothing; and to confess all was not in her courage, nor in the policy which her husband had concerted, and now sadly delayed. The mother, waiting for her to speak, wistfully eyed her, as she stood in the dim mist of moonshine that lay upon the window.

"Why do you say I mope and am low-hearted, mother? Is not my laugh merry? Am I not a cheerful help to you in the house? One cannot always be glad. The noise of the sea, and the cry of the wind to-night, and the struggling of the sweet moon with the clouds, have—have——" She faltered, and continued, in a voice as soft as a flute's—"Sometimes one has pleasant sorrows which one likes to nurse. There is no reason that I should mope. I can feel very happy—— Ah, dear Lord! would that he had come and saved me from another day of fear!" And breaking out thus, she threw her head upon her mother's breast and cried.

For some girls to cry is very little matter for mothers and others to behold.

As the blue heaven weeps its dews when all is calm and clear, so there are girls who break into tears when there is little of sorrow or shadow to find them a reason.

But Jenny wept rarely—at least, in her mother's sight; therefore the honest bosom on which her face was hidden was rent by the unaccustomed sobs, and anxious, plaintive sympathy spoke in the poor woman's voice, as she exclaimed, with her pretty fingers tenderly kneading the girl's rich hair—

"Oh, my child, my dearie! you will break my heart with your misery! What is your fear? Has any one wronged you? Kind Lord, what trouble is this that hath come upon you? Jenny, Jenny, raise up your eyes—see how bright the moon shines in the room; it makes thy hair like yellow silk. Oh, my pretty lamb, who is he that hath not come? and what is thy fear, Jenny?"

Now, the door of the bedroom and the door of the parlour both standing open, and the staircase measuring but a small space betwixt the low floor and the passage, it was scarcely possible that Mr. Strangfield, sitting in expectation of his daughter's arrival, should fail to catch his wife's words. When, therefore, in her clear, pained voice, she cried, "Who is he that hath not come?" and "What is thy fear, Jenny?" up rose the master shipwright, and the staircase groaned under his boots.

Jenny, hearing him coming, drew away from her mother with a quick movement of terror, and backed through the glare of moonlight into the shadow near the bedstead.

"Wife," exclaimed Strangfield, in his strong voice, "how is it that Jenny does not come to me?"

To which no reply was vouchsafed. He advanced by a stride and said, "What has the girl been saying? and what is her fear? Jenny, come forth. I can see you standing there. Give me thy hand, foolish wench, and now downstairs with us all. If there be aught to fear, pray that the Lord may deliver us from evil."

So speaking, he held forth his hand, and the shrinking girl, not daring to disobey, came to him fearfully, and dropped fingers of ice into his palm.

As they went down the stairs there was a lifetime of suffering in Jenny's thoughts. For what now was she to do? Must she confess, under the crushing gaze of her father's eyes? Beyond her strength of voice, beyond control of passionate weeping, would the confession take her. Cuthbert would be here anon—to-morrow, surely—and shift the heavy load of her secret upon himself. And with him at hand those stern eyes would not be terrifying, nor the anger unbearable.

In the lamplight, how pale and sweet she looked!—lustrous with emotion, her large eyes, and the glorious disorder of her wind-swept hair, making of her head and heaving bosom, and the womanly droop of her full and tender figure, a touching, lovely picture of frightened sorrow. Sit she would not, lest by sitting she should prolong the bitter task; so she stood at the table, and her mother near her, in half-protective, half-wondering posture, whilst the father returned to his high-backed chair.

"Now, my girl," said he, his voice insensibly softening under the beauty of his only child, "speak boldly, and acknowledge the trouble that has come to you. I will tell you," laying a forefinger on his thumb, "when this habit of moping first became visible to me: that was a full month before we sent you to your aunt Rachel. That visit did not improve thee, but, on the contrary, has made thee worse. Now you have your date, and so you shall not be at a loss for the reason."

The girl tried to meet her father's eyes, whereof the severity appeared intensified by the spectacle-rings that concentrated their forces of fire and feeling; but to stand to them hardily was an impossible feat; her gaze went downwards, and in a scarcely audible tone she replied, "I do not mope, father; sometimes I like to be alone."

"Be honest, wench, be honest!" exclaimed Strangfield, harshly. "What was the meaning of those words your mother was repeating just now?"

"Jenny, they were, *'Would that he had come and saved me from another day of fear!'*" whispered Mrs. Strangfield. "Have no fear, my pretty. Thy father is stern, but he loves thee."

The girl refused to speak. Then Mr. Strangfield repeated his question, and her lips turned pale, as under the pressure and torment of a thousand words which they would not part to deliver, and one most tearful, wildered, pleading look she cast around. Her father watched her steadily, and with an ever-deepening shadow on his face.

Her want of speech was want of honesty, he thought; and his mouth took a sullen curve.

"Jane, speak to her. She may answer thee."

"I have questioned her, Michael. Jenny, Jenny, answer thy father, dear heart. Tell him thy trouble!" and she snatched at her breast with both hands, crying, "Oh, Michael, what has come to our child?"

"Jenny, will you answer me or not?"

"Father, you shall be answered, but not by me."

"Who is he that should have come and saved you from another day of fear?"

"Oh, father," cried the poor girl, clasping her hands, "have pity on me—do not question me now."

"Not question you!" returned Strangfield, in an inexorable tone. "Not question you! What has happened to you, that you are not to be questioned by your father?"

She shook her head and sighed, with a low moan in her sigh. Ah, that she had the courage to speak the truth now, and intrepidly make herself known! But it was her husband that should speak for her, and he would be here to-morrow, surely! Oh, she might be sure.

Now, in her sweet innocence, having no knowledge of other moral wrongdoing in her than sly procuration of her darling's name and heart for life, she would not conceive that her frightened obstinacy and evasive answers were filling her father's mind with a fear that touched her sacred honour. Yet that such fear was in him she might know by his cheek's pallor, and by that expression of eye a man has who, being wounded, bleeds inwardly. The wife had tolerable sight for change in him, and watched him under a wrinkled forehead.

"Child," he cried, in a grating voice, "I have asked you for the truth. Have it I will, if it cost thee and me our lives!"

To say which, and in his bitter energy, he jerked his body forwards, whereat the girl shrieked and became hysterical. "O mother! O mother! what would he do to me! O mother! save me from him!" and with wild alternate sobbing and laughter, she backed away from the table, until she felt her mother's arms about her, when she fainted, as a person dies, with horrid suddenness.

CHAPTER VII

AN ANXIOUS PARENT

"*Edgar.* My tears begin to take his part so much,
They'll mar my counterfeiting."

Lear

NOW, at that self-same hour, at Greystone School, Dr. Shaw sat alone in his study, in that ease of posture which he loved: his starched neck-cloth replaced by a silk handkerchief, a soft cushion cherishing his form, slippers on his feet, and his waistcoat band liberally eased off. The boys were long since gone to bed; the ushers were congregated in a living-room set apart for them. No risk, therefore, of sudden intrusion surprising his relaxed dignity; and with spirits and wine and biscuits on the table, and the soft lamplight toning down all scholastic angularities of furniture, the study had somewhat of a hospitable air.

The booming of the wind in the chimney, and among the trees outside, where it swept the leaves into a sound like the boiling of breakers on a beach, was a chant or chorus for the ear, snugly lifted from the down of cushions, to relish. So, with the diversion of a triple distraction—in the tumbler to be sipped, the book to be glanced at, and the wind to hearken to—the doctor might find solitude not unpleasant. Yet wholly pleasant it was not; for neither his book, nor his glass, nor the voice of the wind, could subdue in his face an expression of thought which could have no reference either to what he did or what he heard.

Closing his book, he drew out his watch—a fat dial that popped like a cork from his fob—and sat erect to inspect it. Half-past nine exactly; observing which, he pulled the bell.

A maid-servant opened the door.

"Has Mr. Cuthbert come in?"

"No, sir."

Now, the proper hour for Mr. Cuthbert to return from his evening spell of an hour and a half, was nine o'clock. Punctual to the moment latterly he never was; but before this night never had he delayed his return by half an hour.

This was a liberty. This was a bad example. The doctor's soul rose in resentment.

How could he reprimand unpunctuality in another, if his son, the school's exemplar, as his father had striven to make him in all things, flagrantly omitted the first of virtues to the disciplinarian?

Anger, being excited, must find vent somehow; and Dr. Shaw fell to pacing the room actively, meditating thoughts harsher than reproof, to be delivered when Cuthbert should appear.

For a quarter of an hour this idle activity endured, with now and again a pause between, that his ear might strain at the blowing wind.

Then he pulled the bell-rope again sharply.

"No, sir, Mr. Cuthbert ain't come in yet."

"How do you know?"

"His slippers ain't in the rack, sir."

Now passed another short time.

The doctor looked at his watch, opened the study door, and listened.

The house was full of soft moaning, delicate echoes of the strong voices without. And nothing else was audible, unless it were the muffled tones of one of the masters reading aloud in the ushers' room.

The doctor walked to the house door and hesitated, with his finger on the latch; then slipped the iron tongue, and the door flew open, letting fly a shock of wind that set the loose coats on the pegs whipping the wall with the tails of them, and whirled a handful of dry brown leaves along the floor-cloth.

The land was flying in the summer gale.

Great shadows were speeding over the white ground of moonlight.

The tree-tops were stooping like the heads of runners; all things seemingly pursuing the route of the torn clouds, which swept like volumes of steam across the moon and down the slope of stars.

Bare-headed the doctor stood, leaning against the wind from the doorstep, directing his glance into the far reach of the road, along the whole length of which the dust in columns was sailing steadily.

Then stepped the old man back again into the hall, and with a sturdy push drove the door against the wind to its fastenings.

"What keeps him! what keeps him!" he cried to himself.

Presently he must step into the hall again to listen.

Anger was melting into alarm. A tremulous busy-ness of memory kept him breathing quickly. And, above all things, his heart yearned for his son.

As he stood, with head inclined to bring his ear to full reception of all sound without the house, Mr. Saunderson came from the ushers' room, humming a snatch of song.

But down fell the honest man's indolent jauntiness like a garment when he beheld the doctor, and stiffening his figure into a decorous mien, he approached with a bow, not unmingled with the surprise he felt at the old man's listening posture and negligent dress.

The doctor turned to look at him.

"Oh, Mr. Saunderson," he exclaimed, "will you be pleased to tell me if you have seen my son since he left the house this evening?"

"No, sir, not since he left the house."

"That is very strange, Mr. Saunderson."

"Is not he returned yet, sir?"

"He is not. It is past ten o'clock, and his usual, I should say his prescribed, hour is nine, as is known to you, Mr. Saunderson."

Mr. Saunderson of course looked at his watch.

"I am mortified by this unaccountable behaviour," continued the doctor. "There is nothing that should detain him. Does it not strike you as very singular, Mr. Saunderson?"

"Why sir, it is somewhat odd, perhaps," rejoined Mr. Saunderson, a little too diplomatic to pledge himself to an emphatic opinion before he had acquired a larger knowledge of the doctor's views of the subject.

"I repeat," exclaimed Dr. Shaw, "that there is nothing that should detain him. He knows the rules, and this defiance of discipline, this—defiance, I say, Mr. Saunderson, is—is——"

Well might he stammer and stop in such a strain of lip-reasoning. He looked eagerly at the door, and drew out his watch for the twentieth time.

"Sir, this procrastination cannot be mere unpunctuality—there *must* be a substantial, a reasonable cause for his delay," observed Mr. Saunderson, rattling his *r*'s.

"I think so, sir—I think so."

"If agreeable to you, I should be happy to walk to the town and make inquiries."

"No, I am obliged to you; not at this hour. I'll not suffer myself to feel anxious. My son has shown himself restless lately. There have been signs of impatience in his behaviour, as though our discipline fretted him. This conduct to-night must mean a resolution to— to free himself from the traces—he must think it manly to defy us, sir. But," cried the fiery old man, "my house shall be locked up at the usual hour; the last person in the world to merit my forbearance in a matter of this sort is my son."

"Surely, sir," cried Mr. Saunderson, with a rich roll of the "r" in sir, "you do not consider that he has left you?"

"Left me! What has put such a thought into your mind?" said the doctor, in a sharp, febrile whisper, and his eyes shone under his white eyebrows.

"Why, sir," stammered Mr. Saunderson, who wanted time to recollect himself and apprehend his own meaning, "it seems to me a strange thing, sir, that you should bolt your door upon your son, Dr. Shaw, unless you believe that he does not mean to come home, sir."

"I do not understand you, Mr. Saunderson. Pray step this way and oblige me with your meaning," exclaimed the doctor, with excitement half suppressed in his manner; and, closing the study door, he said in a sharp voice, "Mr. Saunderson, if you can throw any light upon my son's absence, I desire—I have to beg you will do so."

"I really can throw no light upon it, sir—none whatever," replied Mr. Saunderson. "By your threat to lock up the house, I judged you to be aware that your son would not return to-night."

"I am aware of nothing," cried the doctor, loosening the handkerchief around his neck, "beyond what I have told you—touching his behaviour for some time past—— Hark, Mr. Saunderson! is not that a footstep?"

"I hear nothing, sir."

The doctor seemed to lose himself in thought; and Mr. Saunderson stood with his eyes fixed on the carpet, that the doctor should not think he took notice of the wine and spirits.

"You may be pretty sure that he will return home presently, sir. That he should be uneasy under the discipline of this school is a good reason to account for his present loitering. And there is no doubt, Dr. Shaw, that he is uneasy, sir," said Mr. Saunderson, with a nod at the doctor, who, at the first words, had looked up and stood listening with his head on one side.

"You are right, Mr. Saunderson; he is uneasy," replied the doctor; "and I do not doubt that lie disguises his impatience less to others than to me, who yet have heard enough from his lips to judge him."

The twist of his voice put a note of interrogation to this observation, and made it a question for the other to answer.

"I believe, sir, your son covets a larger sphere of action, Dr. Shaw."

"He has admitted this to you, Mr. Saunderson?"

"Well, sir, he has."

"And when, pray?"

"Why, sir, if the truth must be told, this afternoon."

"But if I understand you rightly," said the old man, with a pale smile which proclaimed many other things than the ease of mind it was intended to depict, "nothing escaped him to warrant you to suppose that he does not mean to return—to-night?"

"No, sir; I can recall nothing to that effect—nothing, Dr. Shaw."

"Thank you, Mr. Saunderson. I need keep you no longer. I am obliged to you for your company. Good night to you, sir."

Mr. Saunderson bowed and retired. The doctor looked at his watch. Twenty minutes to eleven. He rang the bell angrily.

"Is the house locked up?"

"Not yet, sir. Were a-waitin' for Mr. Cuthbert."

"Lock up and get to bed, all of you!" cried the doctor fiercely. And the bristling of his eyebrows, and the fire in his eyes, despatched the girl from the room in a bound.

He seated himself at the table, with his elbows upon it, and his face in his hands. He heard them bolt and chain the house door, and the slippered tread of the masters as they went whispering upstairs. Now through the silence moaned the wind, with rattle of dry leaves eddying, and the threshing of the chestnut boughs.

Presently rose the old man and drew the curtains from the window, whereby the shine of the lamp would be visible to the furthest bend of the glimmering road; returned to his chair, and with his watch on the table under his eye began a vigil.

This was an only son that had gone forth, and not yet returned.

CHAPTER VIII

THE "CLEOPATRA"

"With sloping masts and dipping prow,
As who, pursued with yell and blow,
Still treads the shadow of his foe
And forward bends his head,
The ship drove fast, loud roared the blast,
And southward aye we fled."

Ancient Mariner

A GREAT sight is the boiling of froth in the moonlight; the streaks and dissections of its cream upon a dark beach, the swift and hissing rush of breakers thundering in their struggles, the quivering gloom of a windy sea beyond.

But great sights to the eyes are sometimes scurvy knowledges to the body, and the yeasty splash and combing coil of the southerly tumblers on the Greystone sands were beauties to be quit of as fast as good ash oars could strike fire out of water.

So, with a British will that made the rowlocks creak like an iron door swinging on harsh hinges, the oarsmen in the *Cleopatra's* boat flung their backs at the lacing spray, and drove the wedge of their boat's bow into the blast of the wind and the ebon hills in their path.

Right under the moon, and in the broken shimmer of it on the water, lay the man-of-war brig, bowing to the land like some restless colt flinging furious heels at the wind.

The yellow lamp at her yard-arm swung athwart the stars in sweeps and jerks, and seemed to dodge them. Beyond where the boat was dragging and vanishing, the land was a vast black shadow, and its burning eye upon the foreland to the left marked the junction of the heavens.

But in the hollow, the haze of the wind and the moonlight was as luminous as the clouds when they swept the zenith in folds resembling steam; with protrusion of dis-jointed outlines that made the scene fantastic, and a foreground of winking lights and a semi-ring of stationary foam.

Urged by six heavy blades, the boat ate her way stubbornly; dishing the surging spray in sheets and souses until she was awash, and the backs of the men lustrous for the drenching.

Meanwhile Cuthbert had recovered the uses of his brain, thanks to copious splashing, soon after the boat had shoved off.

Beholding the stars and the flying clouds, and feeling the jump and wobble of the sea in the strain and ache of his own timbers, he immediately comprehended the dreadful character of the misfortune that had befallen him, and raising his voice, attempted to address himself to the young gentleman in the cloak who was steering the boat, but was instantly silenced by a kick and a promise of a flogging if he opened his lips.

"You cannot be aware——" began Cuthbert.

"Hold your jaw, you lubber!"—here came the kick.

"Sir, you're——"

"By the Lord, you shall be flogged until your back is as green as your brains, you villain, if you move your tongue again!"

So there was no help for Cuthbert but to resign himself to broken-hearted contemplation of this bitter divorce from the woman of his love; and with his hands bound he reclined, gnawing his lips with misery, and watching with distracted eyes the land they were leaving, while the foam flew in his face, and the gale in his ear howled down every movement of hope.

In this condition of mind was he when the boat went rolling alongside the brig.

It was something to see the big and bristling hull stoop to the upward leap of the boat. It was as though a mother leaned down to embrace her little one.

Briskly the crew handed up the prisoners; then sounded the keen pipe of the boatswain; and while the boat soared to the davits the pawls of the capstan jerked out a music on the gale like the hammering on an anvil while the furnace roars. With quick leaps and runs, and the disciplined rush, and the steady pulls of men-of-war's men, the anchor was cat-headed, the yards dropped their dim spaces of canvas; round swept the shore-lights, and down lay the cruiser to the wind. And then you heard the squattering of ploughed froth humming at the bows, and the shrieking of big sails in the high gloom.

The four impressed men were left standing near the foot of the mainmast under the eye of a marine. The business of getting under weigh was achieved with the swiftness that war-time teaches, and all to the windy whistling of a pipe, the brig being snug in less time than a woman takes to brush her hair. While the shore-lights were veering into a faint line upon the quarter, and the great foreland lamp was thrusting its red flame among the cloudy stars well to the right, a brawny fellow came to the prisoners with a battle-lantern swinging in hisgrasp, and made them a visible group.

Then approached two men from the opposite quarter of the deck, and the lantern flashed in the bullion and buttons of uniforms. Behind them stood others, and forward was a crowd of seamen staring at the four men; and this was the picture of the deck, adding to it the detail of a savage row of carronades, black as ink in the watery moonshine.

"Are these your men, Mr. Towplank?" said one of the uniform wearers, the tone of whose voice was as good a warrant of his office as his epaulets.

"Yes, Sir Peter—four of them, sir," replied the young gentleman who had done Cuthbert the honour to impress him.

"Well, you look likely men, my lads; and I suppose you don't require me to tell you that you are wanted to serve the king, and fight his

Majesty's enemies? There is glory and prize-money to be got if you do your duty; and, as British seamen, you'll never want me to tell you what your duty is, I hope."

With which flourish Captain Sir Peter Grahame, Bart., in command of H. M. S. *Cleopatra*, was about to slue himself round on his heel to go aft, when one of the men spoke up.

"If you plaze, sor, me name is Matthew Murphy, and I'm an Imirikin. Your honour therefore persaves that it's not me duty to fight for the king, God bliss him!"

"Ah, I see—an American born in Kilkenny."

"Indade, then, your honour, I was born in Galway," responded Murphy, at which murderous admission there went a smothering of laughter among the men forward.

Hereupon Cuthbert spoke.

"I have to represent to you that I am not a sailor, sir. My father is Dr. Shaw, of Greystone School. Your officer has committed an error in impressing me."

This had in it the matter of a rebuke, and was a trifle downright for quarter-deck hearing; but then it was delivered in a soft and cultured voice, and he who spoke it, with figure lighted up by the flare of the battle-lantern, and handsome face showing, looked a gentleman.

Sir Peter gazed at him inquisitively.

"Mr. Towplank," said he, "where did you meet this gentleman?"

At the word *gentleman* applied to the man he had kicked, and which same word was a definition he was the last midshipman in the service capable of making with true application, not because his father was a retired undertaker, but because his father's son was a cad, Mr. Towplank's eyes began to roll and the wind to feel chill upon his small-clothes.

"Meet him, Sir Peter? Why, sir, coming down a hill. He gave us a deal of trouble, sir. He knocked the bo'sun down. I never took him to be better than the mate of a coaster, sir."

"I can vouch, Sir Peter, that there is a Dr. Shaw living at Greystone, and that he keeps a school there," exclaimed the first lieutenant, who stood near the captain. "I know this to be so, because my friend Lord Cosgrave told me that he has a son with Dr. Shaw."

"Yes, sir, young Middleton is a pupil of my father," said Cuthbert.

"Quite right; Middleton is the name," returned the lieutenant.

A large name helps out a case grandly in a Briton's ear. Mr. Towplank drew his squat figure out of the glare of the lantern.

"Your impressment is a mistake, Mr. Shaw, and I much regret it," said Sir Peter Grahame in a kind voice. He then held a whispered consultation with the lieutenant and walked aft.

There is poor satisfaction in the apology or regret that does not right a man to his own wishes. With clasped hands and downbent eyes stood Cuthbert, a bitter mourner; for every burst of foam struck out of the hurrying waves by the vessel's bow was a mark of increasing distance from all he loved in this world; and he was like to go mad when his mind went to Jenny waiting for him to come and speak to father—waiting and marvelling, and then sickening for the strangeness of his absence, and the cruelty of his silence.

His three companions in misfortune were led forward to be converted into trim men-of-war's men.

"We shall have to treat you as a passenger," said the lieutenant, addressing Cuthbert, "until we can land you. We will swing you a hammock in a spare cabin, and you will mess at our table."

"Can you hold out any hope that I shall be landed shortly?"

"Why, you see, we are bound to the chops of the Channel. Gantheaume is at Brest, and there Cornwallis means to keep him. There is talk of the *Guerriére* being about, and it is Sir Peter's dream to fall in with her, when there'll be tough work for all hands, for she's pierced for thirty-six guns, and carries three hundred men. Should a slant of wind serve, Sir Peter might put you ashore off the Start; or he'll turn you adrift, no doubt, if we fall in with a homeward-bounder. But you had better make up your mind for a cruise. It will be a new experience to you, Mr. Shaw, and something to tell the boys about—not to speak of the chance of your seeing a blazing sea-fight."

"You speak very kindly, and I can see that I am to be well treated. But my absence may break my wife's heart." He covered his face with his bands.

"Phew! A wife! Lord help you! Is there not always a petticoat in every man's trouble, either causing it, or making it worse? But come below, Mr. Shaw, and try the flavour of our rum. Nothing like honest Jamaica to steady a man's eye for trouble."

CHAPTER IX

A SAIL RIGHT AHEAD

" 'Hillo! who have we here?' said I, as the black sails and lofty spars of a large vessel, diminished by distance into a child's toy, were hove up out of the darkness into the clear sky, in strong relief against the increasing light of the lovely background, rolling slowly on the bosom of the dark, tumbling swell . . . . Presently the object appeared again, and this time, by the aid of my glass, I made out a stately vessel."—*Cruise of the Midge.*

THE Turk is a wise man who, when misfortune comes upon him, praises the name of Allah and smokes his pipe. Surely the most unprofitable altercation you can hold is a wrangle with fate. Prometheus in bonds, defying the Omnipotent, makes no such great moral figure as the poets profess. There is far better relish, if less tragic majesty, in the behaviour of Addison's honest Dutchman, who, when he fell from the top of a mast and broke his leg, thanked God very heartily that it was not his neck.

Much, undeniably, there was in Cuthbert's position to make him miserable. Could Lieutenant Transom have promised to put him ashore next day, the young fellow would have plucked up heart and swung his glass like a man; but there was bitter prospect of his detention lasting, with risks of death between, and never a chance (it might be) to send his story to Jenny. Scarce could he hold up his head pleasantly as Transom tried to rally him. Indeed, he was no philosopher, or rather, he was a very bad one. Having broken his leg, he regretted that it was not his neck. In other words, he felt miserable enough to regret that the blow that had knocked him down had not killed him; in which unwise state of mind he was conducted to a cabin.

To come to a tumbling sea, fresh from the steadiness of shore, is a privilege no landsman covets. A hammock by swinging, tolerably mitigates the effect produced on unaccustomed organs by the rollings and leanings of a ship. But a very little movement is sometimes worse than heavy motion; and when the nose is attacked as well as the stomach tossed, then no help for you but utter proneness and an intolerable servitude to the giddy pillow.

Such a night as Cuthbert passed a man had need to commit murder to merit. All through the hours the thunder of water sweeping past was in his ears, with the creak of timbers and the small yelp of the straining bulkheads; heavy footsteps beat a rhythmical tramp through the deck into his brain; sometimes sounded the pealing of canvas, the cheep of blocks, the smart fall of rigging, the shriek of the boatswain's pipe. The bull's-eye over his head had changed from ebony to silver before his pained and heavy eyes closed, and then for a while the poor fellow forgot his sorrows in sleep.

The bell on deck was striking when he awoke, and for some moments he could scarcely persuade himself that he was not in his coffin; such being the impression produced by the pinioning of his elbows by the canvas sides of the hammock, and the close-pressing ceiling of deck just above his nose.

With a scramble he got out of the hammock, somewhat refreshed by his spell of sleep, and less sea-sick. But he had nearly broken his head; for the deck was all aslope, and no other perpendicular for him to come at but such as his hands, on letting go the hammock-sides, gave him, so that, if he had struck a window-glass, he would have shot through it.

While he was dressing, a marine presented himself.

"The first lieutenant's compliments, sir, and, when you are dressed, will you breakfast with him?" said the man, as erect as a sentry in his box on the deck that kept Cuthbert staggering.

This invitation was of course promptly accepted, and in a few minutes Cuthbert followed the marine into a large cabin with a ceiling garnished with small-arms, stout lockers around hair seats, charts on the walls, and a table laid for breakfast. Here he found the first and second lieutenants. Both men were fine specimens of the naval officers of those days—the days of Cochrane and Strachan; Transom in middle age, and the other young, but both with hard, stern lines of resolution carved in their embrowned faces, both with the hearty, open look of brave spirits, dressed in uniforms that smelt of gunpowder, and one of them with a cutlass scar behind his ear, and the other of them with two stumps for fingers on his right hand.

They saluted Cuthbert with blunt politeness, and, breakfast being served, invited him "to fall to at once, for we are rising the royals of a big ship right ahead," says Transom; "and whenever there's anything visible on the horizon we always accept it as a hint to bear a hand in stowing ballast."

"How the deuce came young Towplank to take you for a seaman?" exclaimed the second lieutenant, scrutinizing Cuthbert admiringly. "If there was moon enough to see your hands by they should have satisfied him that you were not his man, supposing him sober."

"He was sober enough. I explained to your captain that this midshipman gave me no chance of representing myself," replied Cuthbert. "I can only trust that Sir Peter Grahame will put me ashore soon—anywhere on the coast will do."

Transom looked grave, but said, "Well, well, there's no telling what will turn up. Strange things happen at sea, Mr. Shaw; and it's odd enough that I should meet you, seeing that it was only the other day I dined with Lord Cosgrave, and heard him praising Dr. Shaw's school at Greystone as one of the best in England."

It might have been the conversation of these two kindly gallant men, the sight of their scars, and honest, hearty faces; or the snatch of sleep that had brought him fortitude; or the sense of the idleness of mourning and of the healthy wisdom of hoping; or these things united, it might have been, with his own youth and stirrings of a courageous though gentle spirit, that subdued in Cuthbert the bitter emotion of desolation and hopeless anxiety that had nearly driven him crazy with thought in the night, and that wrought a finer temper in his heart and nerves for the encounter to which adverse fate had summoned him.

And then again: "My dear man," Transom had said to him gaily, "when your people find you missing, be sure they'll start on such a hunt after you as will bring them to the true cause of your disappearance. It will be known throughout Greystone that our press-gang took three men last night, and do you suppose your wife and father will not hit upon the *Cleopatra* as the reason of your sudden vanishing?" A question that brightened up the poor fellow wonderfully.

And better than a cordial to a half-drowned man was the glory and freshness of the morning on deck; holding a sweeter delight, in the fulness and splendour of it, for the gloom and the smells he had quitted. The sea in the early light ran in curls and tumblers of quicksilver, under a steel-blue sky that was melting into richness in the east; while away in the south the flooring of the heavens was delicately garnished with oyster-shell-shaped clouds, compact as link-armour, and lovely with tints of mother-of-pearl.

Down to the flying wind was the *Cleopatra*, stooping with a leaning bow, ripping up the breast of the water as a dog slants his head to make a better lever of his jaw. The mighty press of sail filled the blue sky overhead with thunder, and the base of the sweeping tower of canvas was an acre of foam.

Sir Peter Grahame paced the deck aft with a telescope, which from time to time he levelled at some object ahead; he bowed to Cuthbert, but seemed too preoccupied to speak. A crowd of men were on the forecastle, pointing forward and conversing in low voices, some of them looking aloft, or at the water rippling past, with grins of satisfaction.

The first lieutenant came to Cuthbert, after exchanging a few words with the captain.

"There is a sail yonder," he said, "which we have reason to believe is the *Guerrière*. If she shows French colours we shall fight her. We are rising her fast, for nothing can stand against the *Cleopatra* on a bowline, and Sir Peter has instructed me to request that you will go below and remain there on the order being given to clear for action."

"Mr. Transom, I hope Sir Peter will not insist on my going below. I may be of use on deck, and am willing to fight with the men."

"Well spoken, Mr. Shaw, and, a generous offer," replied Transom, glancing with a smile at Cuthbert's hands. "But, my dear fellow, you must think of your wife. However, we'll leave the matter for the present. The ship may prove a non-combatant—perhaps an East Indiaman. One can't detect nationalities twenty miles off."

With which he returned to the captain, and they walked the deck together.

There is a stirring pleasure in pursuit at sea, the like of which cannot be tasted on shore; and though Cuthbert's heart thumped with a leaden pang when Transom told him what to think upon, yet his pulse rose again when he looked at the water foaming past, and discerned the star-coloured sail of the ship ahead, steady on the delicate line of the horizon. It was not in his English blood to stay the fire that coursed through it.

No man on board but was too busy in watching the ship to notice him or offer him company. All hands knew that the *Guerrière* was a heavy vessel, and a desperate match (even manned with Frenchmen) for a ten-gun brig. Likewise, they knew that if Sir Peter fell in with her he would fight her. Therefore for their lives did they watch the distant sail and speculate, and feel the itching palm that nothing assuages but the scratching of a cutlass hilt. Why, as they talked they spat on their fingers, and whistled to windward for more of the strong breeze that was driving the bows of the brig into a hill of foam.

An hour went by with nothing outside the chase to put life into it but a stretching of bowlines, a swing at the topsail halliards, and a flattening in of the jib-sheets; such little nursing did the *Cleopatra* want to point her bowsprit to windward of the stranger, whose lower yards were now above the horizon.

Suddenly the men forward heard the first lieutenant, who worked his telescope in the main rigging, sing out—

"She has clewed up her royals and top-gallant sails, sir, and her mizzen topsail yard is down on the cap. Now she hoists her colours! They are—oh, confound this jogging!—they are—they are——"

"French!" shouted Sir Peter, and down sprang the first lieutenant, and in a trice there was shrill whistling and quick movement among the men, and a coming and a going, and then a steady stand.

CHAPTER X

THE ACTION

"Vain was their brav'ry!
The fallen oak lies where it lay,
    Across the wintry river:
But brave hearts once swept away,
    Are gone, alas! for ever.
        Vain was their brav'ry!"

MOORE

AT ten of the forenoon the Frenchman lay plain on the sea, with colours flying, musketeers in her tops, and her bulwarks black with the heads of her men. A big frigate she was, of the graceful shape which the British were all too slow to copy in their dockyards; and the Gallic cocks in her hencoops might well have swelled their throats with derisive screams when they beheld the English sparrow sailing down to grapple with the hawk.

The first shot fired came from the frigate when she was still out of reach of the *Cleopatra's* guns. Cuthbert saw the glance of yellow flame and the smother of white smoke; the ball whirled up a little pillar of froth out of the sea close alongside, and then came the report, dulling its sting against the wind's teeth.

"My lads," exclaimed Sir Peter Grahame, standing at the quarter-deck capstan with his hat in his hand, "yonder ship is the *Guerrière*. None of the enemy's ships has done more damage to our peaceful merchantmen than she. She is a big nut to crack, but our heels are shod with British iron, and we'll grind the kernel out of her yet. Hold on all till you get your orders, then make one man of yourselves. Now God be with us!"

A cheer like a broadside was given; the helm put over, the loftier sails furled, and the *Cleopatra* drove bow on towards her enemy.

In those brave days, British naval tactics were no written discipline, but a man's own judgment; and though it was the boarding-pike and the cutlass that won most prizes, yet many a Frenchman was beaten by manoeuvring that kept him cutting capers in vain pursuit of his enemy's intentions, whilst the foe waltzed around him to a tune of thunder, slapping one ear while the other was rubbing, and piling carcases around the guns which exploded anyhow.

The captain of the frigate, beholding the *Cleopatra* making as though to run him down, might well believe that this was not her intention; but to say what a man will *not* do is not to know what he *will* do; therefore Captain Toufflet, not choosing to broadside the object which only two guns could cover, waited to see what would happen.

The *Cleopatra's* flying jib-boom pointed due amidships of the *Guerrière*; then by the length of a spoke was the wheel put over: round swept the *Guerrière's* helm, that she might rake the *Cleopatra* as she passed under her stern. But lo! the brig, twisting on her keel like a yacht, put her nose at the revolving Frenchman, and blaze! blaze! went her two bow-chasers, and down came the flag of the Republic, along with the gaff and a sputter of canvas shreds. A minute later the vessels lay broadside on to one another, as close as two houses on opposite sides of a street; and simultaneously from both of them leapt out a line of flame, with a roar as of a mountain rent in twain by an earthquake, and the smashing and splintering of woodwork, while all between was smoke.

Now had the action begun in earnest, and a sight for Cuthbert to remember was the deck of the English brig. Calm as a statue and as steady, Sir Peter Grahame stood some fathoms forward of the wheel, with powerful voice and slight gesture of the arm giving his orders. You would have said that he had eyes all over his body,—eyes for the helmsman at the back of him, and the yards and sails above him; for the grimy seamen sweating at the guns, and for every toss of the arm of the gold-laced French commander shrieking, after the manner of his nation, from the raised after-deck of his ship. What apprenticeship to the bloody business of a sea-fight shall teach a man to keep his wits in his eyes and heart? An inheritance this tranquillity in hellish uproar is; the Englishwoman's gift to her sailor-child, and carried with him through the shambles which, in those heroic days, littered the long road from the midshipman's hammock to the admiral's state-cabin.

Now being to leeward, the decks and rigging of the brig were smothered in the smoke of the guns; now being to windward, they saw the Frenchman clothed in fog, out of which red tongues of fire darted and the winking sparks of small-arms. With nimble feet and blackened faces the Englishmen danced round their guns, ramming home sea-blessings with every charge, raising hoarse cheers with every explosion, their disciplined audacity never shying; and the wounded, with their teeth upon their lips, working on until they fainted or dropped dead. The sun shone crimson on the splashed decks, and. the crowds around the guns began to thin; and the cockpit-ladder was never free of a burden of men helping helpless comrades to the surgeons. The musketeers in the Frenchman's tops were doing the mischief, and the swarms upon the frigate's decks seemed undiminished, though the yells and groans among them proved murderous duty done by British powder.

Now the English captain began to see that he should be overmatched if he did not lay the Frenchman on board; for his eighteen-pounders could make no fight with the enemy's heavy artillery, and there was small chance of prize-money and the glory of a gazetting unless the boarding-pike and cutlass came into play. But as he gave the order to man the weather-braces to sheer the brig alongside, his fore-topmast carried away, and all his head-sail with it. As a running man, shot in the leg, falls a cripple, and slues around in helpless state, so the *Cleopatra*, deprived of her forward canvas, rounded up into the wind's eye, whereupon the Frenchman sailed clean round her, drenching her with both broadsides in rotation. The second discharge was a murderous volley; for a ball smashed the wheel and killed the men at it, and a bullet hit Sir Peter Grahame under the arm, and he fell, mortally wounded.

At the beginning of the fight Cuthbert had stood at the foot of the mainmast, unnoticed by officers and crew—in the furious excitement and splendid horrors of the scene forgetting self—eager to help, but in his ignorance not knowing what to be at, when a cannon-ball struck a seaman in the back and threw him forward with a heavy smash, where he lay dead as dust, with his face a mask of blood.

This was the first man killed; but scarcely was he down, when a gunner leapt from the breech he was patting and tumbled backwards, moaning shockingly.

"Help me to carry him below!" sang out a voice; and, with a sick heart and damp forehead, Cuthbert buckled to the worst bit of work a sea-fight gives.

So to help in this way was his share in the action, and a stronger stomach than his might have found it difficult. Below, where the surgeons were at work, with bare red arms and gleaming knives, and wet handkerchiefs tied around their heads for the nerve the moisture gave them, the heat was overpowering, the thunder of the guns a dreadful sound; and the prostrate wounded, their anguish bleating through their stubborn lips, and their faces ghastly with grime and the whiteness of pain, a spectacle that wrenched the soul to behold.

He had returned on deck for the twentieth time, and was at his former post, ready to do what should be wanted, when the fore-topmast fell, with its heap of sail and rigging, and the brig shot round; and in a few minutes the *Guerrière* poured in the first of her two deadly broadsides. He heard the grape screech past him, and beheld the carnage of it; and then he saw Transom, with his hand to his ear, rush forward and call upon the men to clear away the wreck and "bear a hand, or the brig would be taken." Then it was a rush with the unwounded, many who were bleeding following madly, too; the guns were deserted, and the ear was deaf in the silence, whilst the seamen hacked and hewed; and with desperate hands rove halliards under the foretop, and bent them to the staysail, that they might get the brig's head to pay off.

And all the while the Frenchman was sneaking round to bring her port broadside to bear, and her small-arms men and topmen were discharging volleys of musketry at the small band of Englishmen on the brig's forecastle. Then, before the staysail could be hoisted, the *Guerrière* poured her second tremendous storm of flame and thunder and iron into the devoted brig.

Cuthbert saw the captain fall, and sprang aft. He placed his arm under the dying man's head to raise him.

"Too late—I am bleeding inwardly!" he gasped. "Tell Lieutenant Transom to strike . . . drag my body abaft the skylight . . . they are too many for us . . . my poor men!"

Then came Transom rushing aft with despair in his face, for he had seen that the wheel was gone and their case hope less. Beholding the dead body of Sir Peter, he started back, gazed despairingly around him, and buried his face in his hands.

"The captain's last words to me were that I should tell you to strike," exclaimed Cuthbert.

"Yes, yes," groaned Transom, "it must be done. God help us! Half our men are killed— the wheel is gone—I must stop this carnage."

And he went aft with a tottering step, and, grasping the signal halliards, hauled down the colours.

The *Guerrière* to leeward was working up to rake the brig again, but when her men saw the English flag hauled down, they sent up such a shriek as nothing less than the capture of a line of battle ship could have justified. What! all this clamorous exultation over the defeat of a little ten-gun cruiser of one hundred and twenty men by a great thirty-six-gun frigate of three hundred men! But a shout rarely provoked may well be a loud one.

And what was Monsieur's plight? It is known that the *Guerrière* had eighty men killed and one hundred and eight wounded in this action. The sun shone through her sails like a lamp through a sieve; her mizzen-mast, fore top-gallant mast, and jib-boom were gone; her figure-head smashed, and part of her bulwarks in splinters. She looked to the full as much a wreck as the *Cleopatra*. And if there is anything certain in naval history, it is that, could Sir Peter Grahame have put his brig on board the Frenchman, disorganized by havoc, he would have carried her. So let us fling the Union-jack over the valiant dead, and with reverent gratitude thank God that they were our countrymen.

CHAPTER XI

JENNY CONFESSES

"The winter it is past, and the summer comes at last,
　　And the small birds sing on every tree;
Now everything is glad while I am very sad,
　　Since my true love is parted from me,
The rose upon the brier by the waters running clear,
　　May have charms for the linnet or the bee;
Their little loves are blest, and their little hearts at rest,
　　But my true love is parted from me."

BURNS

IN Mr. Strangfield's yard brisk business was doing. On stages round the skeleton hulls workmen were sending up a clang of saw and hammer, some of them breaking out into songs, others calling jests to their mates, while the air was nimble with smells of wood, and the sun made tools of iron hot to the fingers. The high tide of soft blue water gurgling among the piles of the launch-stages, the wooden house with its shelter of green creepers, the brown hens awkwardly hopping out of and into the yard, through the tarry palings—such colouring as these things lent, homely and quaint; such colouring as the softly windowed houses beyond furnished, and the green of trees, the dazzling whiteness of chalk, and auric tint of sand—should make a brave show in Mr. Strangfield's eyes of the busy scene of his yard.

But if anything lovely there was, and relishable to his senses in the sight of it, no man could have guessed his pleasure in his face. He walked sedately about, his hands clasped behind him, pausing often, and challenging the men's work with eyes which they had good reason to believe could see through an oak plank. He rebuked no jest, he was deaf to songs; but if ever a hint of scamping showed itself, in front of the sinner he stopped, and stared at him, immovable, with face of wood; which method of correction was as effectual as storming in immediate efficacy, and in the long run more prodigal in good results.

Indoors, in the same sitting-room in which we have sat with Mr. and Mrs. Strangfield,

Jenny was at work on a gown, which, you know, in that age had short sleeves, and a waist just under the bosom, and a brave breast-opening for the divulgence of sweet secrets. This was a gown that Jenny herself had made, and toiled at with love and smiles and many a soft whisper; for it was to be put aside to furnish, with other work of her pretty fingers, her wifely equipment when Cuthbert should take her home.

But as she sat over it now, she would leave her needle in the stuff, while her chin sank into the hollow of her hand, and her dreamy eyes looked out through the open window upon the people in the market-place.

There was trouble enough to sadden her.

First of all, her father had not spoken to her that morning; with a sullen aversion of head he had declined her kiss, and with an iron manner turned from her.

Then her mother was peevish and short, irritated by the alarmed curiosity which Jenny refused to gratify, and wagging her head at her for an obstinate wench.

Such marks of displeasure would have been unendurable to Jenny's soft and affectionate heart, had not belief that Cuthbert would come that evening and tell their story brought courage and tender fancies more sustaining.

Yet, what had caused him to break his word last night?

So was she for ever dropping into reveries and running long conjectures into melancholy, from which she would break when she thought of his smile and voice, and ply her needle again.

In pensive posture was she musing when her mother came actively into the room, with skirt tucked up for kitchen work, and face red with scolding and serious cooking.

To milder natures than Mrs. Strangfield's—and truly mild was hers—has the "general servant," or maid of all work, as that age termed the Thing, proved a steady vexation; and there was a no more obliging, idle, willing, neglectful, tearful, and ignorant slut in Greystone than the Polly Baggs who "did" (in several senses) for the Strangfields.

"There's no trusting the creature a moment!" cried Mrs. Strangfield, leaving the door open that her voice might carry to the kitchen, and making Jenny a mere excuse for a parenthetical attack on Polly. "Will you believe it?—the knives are not yet cleaned; the slattern hath left your father's new boots all night in the scullery; and not a bedroom touched. This very afternoon," she exclaimed, raising her voice, "I will see her aged mother, who is bedridden and dependent on her daughter's work for her rent, and bid her take her away. I have preached and prayed; but her pleasure is a crimson riband, and soap she never touches; and since she will be a lady, then humble folks' bread is not fit for her, and so she shall pack!"

With which she slammed the door as a powerful full stop to her objurgation, and sat down, fanning herself with her hand.

"Still a-dreaming?" she presently exclaimed to Jenny, who, on her mother's entrance, had started from her musing and used her needle quickly. "Jenny, 'tis most provoking you will not open your mouth. A dozen silly blunders have you made me fall into this morning with thinking of your strange behaviour last night. What with Polly's sinful idleness, and thy moping face and dreadful swooning, I scarce know which end of me is upright. Tell me now, Jenny, if—well, well, say yes if I am right, then. Was it not Mr. Shaw whom you cried out about in the bedroom?"

The girl turned her pretty eyes upon her mother, and answered under her breath, "Why should it be Mr. Shaw, mother?"

"Nay, nay, it was—I see it in your face!" called Mrs. Strangfield, with a little burst of triumph. Jenny was silent. "Tell me it was—tell me it was. I shall not be angry, Jenny."

"It was," replied Jenny.

"Now, Jenny," continued Mrs. Strangfield, leaning forward in her eagerness, "tell me, in two little words, what is there between thee and him?"

"Mother, I told father last night that you and he shall be answered, but not by me."

"By whom, then, Jenny?" said Mrs. Strangfield, coaxingly. "See, my dear, I am not angry; I do but want the truth. Your father is in a bad way because of your stubbornness. Mr. Shaw is a pleasing young gentleman, and the Lord forbid that I should quarrel with a man of his quality for—for——" Here was a long pause, and then insinuatingly, "Now wilt thou not help me, Jenny?"

"Mother, mother, is it fair to press me in this way?" responded Jenny with a bewildered look, yet with something like spirit quivering in her mouth. "Neither you nor father will bide. He has not heard me, and yet he judges. How cold and hard was he to me this morning! Oh, mother, I have a secret—it will make him angry, and I fear him! I have not courage to tell it myself, but it shall be told you. Oh, be sure, mother, you shall know it."

And now, speaking thus, more fully than mere thinking could realize for her, did she feel the secret shiver and bitter fear that made her crave for Cuthbert's presence and support when the moment of disclosure or discovery should arrive.

Somehow it had become a habit with her to believe that when the secret was told to her father, he, in his deep wrath, would turn her from the house; a notion built by her terror on the fierce severity of his judgments on human weaknesses.

And of this conviction, intolerable to her when seized with sense of loneliness, the pain and shame and misery were only to be mitigated to her imagination by her resolve to hold her tongue until Cuthbert was beside her; that, should her father drive her from his roof, her husband's hand would be in hers.

Mrs. Strangfield stared at her as a stranger might.

Of this lovable child of hers—this sweet and placid girl, whose pure soul-workings had been heretofore as plainly figured in her lovely face as clock-work shows in a crystal box—she on a sudden could make neither head nor tail; for a virtuous and holy reason, indeed! that no question of her child's honour could arise.

The fall of the moon or the drying up of the sea sooner than such a thing.

And not hitting upon a secret marriage, what, then, could remain but love? which, to be hugged as a mystery, to hold the tongue obstinate, to set a body swooning, altogether passed her simple understanding.

No wonder, therefore, was she puzzled, and stared in perplexity.

With her honest wits at work, she tried her hand at a solution.

"If you are in love with Mr. Shaw, and letting him court you slyly, your father will certainly be angry when he hears of it; because he does not like under-dealing in man or woman, and would think it unpardonable in thee, who should'st know better. But this I may say, child, that though I should agree with your father in thinking ill, of a *secret* love, I would not allow him to say too much to you, nor set his face against the young man. You are fit to be a gentleman's wife, as I have told him over and over; and if you will just own *all* to me, Jenny, break it to him as his wife should know how, and the rest will be easy, my dear. *I* am not averse to Mr. Shaw—quite the contrary; though what *his* father will say is another matter. But, then, 'tis no business of ours. Young Mr. Shaw is a handsome youth, and not accountable for his father. Indeed, if he truly loves you, he will attend chapel, which would win thy father's heart. You needn't smile! I have heard of a man turning Hebrew Jew to marry; and if a man can deny the Lord for love of a wench, surely Mr. Shaw may easily become a Baptist."

Jenny's smile quickly faded. It seemed easy to say the few words, and if their effect could begin and end in the kind-eyed mother who watched her, long ago would they have been said. But when she thought of her father, her throat grew dry.

In the midst of the silence between them, both actively thinking in wide-parted ways, there fell a substantial knocking on the house door; whereat up jumped Mrs. Strangfield, to see to her cap and gown, and square up all dishevelment, whilst Jenny's heart thumped wildly, and the work fell from her lap to the ground unheeded.

"Now, surely," exclaimed Mrs. Strangfield, "this cannot be Mr. Shaw who should have come last night!" and she looked at Jenny's white face with an air of comical fright, for, loudly as she talked, she was sincerely afraid of Michael.

Presently in floundered dirty Polly Baggs, with the bustling importance a bad servant assumes when she thinks she has something of consequence to deliver.

"Please, missus, you're wanted."

"Who wants me? Did you answer the door with that smut on your nose? Oh, for shame, you baggage! Who is it? Be quick—be quick! Don't you see you're keeping them waiting?"

"It's a gentleman," said Polly, surlily passing the whole length of her arm over her face in pursuit of the smut, which she succeeded in lodging under her eye.

"Well, show him in."

"He axed for master fust."

"Show him in, I say."

Who should appear, bowing gravely, his soft hat under his arm, and his light hair oiled and brushed into a cone, but Dr. Shaw's English master, Mr. Saunderson. Mrs. Strangfield favoured him with a swift curtsey, and Jenny also prettily bent her knees, though fear made that an easier job than stiffening them again.

"Pray, sir, take that chair," said Mrs. Strangfield, with fussy politeness. "Do you wish to see Mr. Strangfield? He is in his yard, and shall be called at once, if you please. He hath much business on hand just now—two vessels building, and an order received for one yesterday, and likewise a galley for Mr. Jackson, of Mount Zion."

With much deliberation, undisturbed by Jenny's beauty, at which he flung several respectful, ardent glances, Mr. Saunderson put his hat on the table, divided his coat-tails, and sat himself down. That he was in no hurry was easily seen, which very considerably, in Mrs. Strangfield's eyes, heightened the mystery of his visit.

"I am truly glad, madam," said he, "to hear of the flourishing condition of your husband's business, and would on no account have him summoned from his duties. You and your charming daughter will, I am sure, be as fully competent as he to answer the question which has occasioned my intrusion upon you."

"Indeed, sir, we shall be glad to oblige you in any way in our power."

"You are most considerate. I must tell you that Dr. Shaw, of Greystone School, with which academy I am at present associated, is much troubled about his son Mr. Cuthbert, who, I believe, is known to you?"

This he said interrogatively, looking first at one and then at the other of them. Mrs. Strangfield gave her daughter a quick glance, and replied—

"Mr. Shaw is known to me by sight, sir, but I have not the honour of a speaking acquaintance with him."

Mr. Saunderson elevated his eyebrows.

"Why, then," said he, "I have been very greatly misinformed. I was told that Mr. Shaw visited here, and was on the most friendly footing with your family;" and he looked at Jenny with a smirk that gave a large meaning to his words.

"Whoever said that spoke what is entirely false!" cried Mrs. Strangfield, indignantly. "It would make my husband mad to hear that such dreadful stories were told of us. To my knowledge, Mr. Shaw hath never set foot in this house since we occupied it, and that would be quite ten years before he was born. My daughter there will vouch for that. Pray, sir, who gave you this piece of news?"

"An old woman named Mead, ma'am, who lives behind the market yonder. I was directed to her as a gossip who has all facts concerning this town at her finger ends. Says she, 'If you are hunting after Mr. Shaw, go to Michael Strangfield's house—the wooden house by the boatyard. If they choose to speak, they can tell all you want to know.' Which, with other observations," continued Mr. Saunderson, with his eyes on Jenny, "to which I paid no attention, brought me here forthwith. If you can enlighten me, therefore, ladies, you will greatly oblige."

"But upon what would you be enlightened, sir?" exclaimed Mrs. Strangfield, warmly. "Mrs. Mead is a shocking false speaker, and is most unbearably impertinent to use our name in answering you. There is no truth in what she hath said. If you seek Mr. Shaw, he is not here."

"Still, ma'am, I trusted that you—or you, miss—might know of his whereabouts. Last evening he left his father's house, and has not returned. If he has run away, he has gone foolishly to work—slyly and foolishly, ladies— for no man has seen him, and he has left with no more clothes to carry than what are on his back. It is idle to suppose he is dead, for the cliff has been searched, and the sands under the cliff, and all about the country we have sent our big boys and some men, and no sign of him visible."

Jenny sat motionless, staring at the speaker with unwinking eyes.

"However," continued he, slowly taking his hat from the table and rising, "it is plain that he is not here, and that you know nothing about him. His loss will be a heavy blow to his father, who had great hopes of him; though, for my part, I cannot help thinking that he kept him too much under, and so *forced* him, after a manner, to leave his home."

"But what is thought, sir? What doth his father think?" exclaimed Mrs. Strangfield, too much interested to notice the growing strangeness in Jenny's eyes and the singular blanching of her lips.

"Why, Dr. Shaw cannot conceive what has become of him; he is in a bad way, and there is no school kept this morning. Quite a sadness has fallen upon the boys, who talk together in subdued voices; for Cuthbert Shaw was a kind young gentleman, much loved by us all. As to what has become of him, I have my own opinion. Last night, a little before nine, I saw him leave the house, dressed more queerly than ever I had taken notice of in him. Shall I say shabbily dressed? That was it, ma'am. He was undoubtedly annoyed to find me posted at the gate, and addressed me very hurriedly, and was glad to make off. Now, I can put two and two together, as well as another: yesterday afternoon it was that he spoke to me of being weary of his life under his father—not precisely those words, Mrs. Strangfield, but his meaning. Now, what should his disappearance represent but the true significance of his language to me? That make up your minds to believe, ladies. He has fled in search of livelier work than tutoring; perhaps will enlist, for a sailor he never would make, with such little hands. And the doctor will have to need him for a time, if ever he recovers the truant."

Having delivered himself of which, Mr. Saunderson bowed low to Jenny, saluted Mrs. Strangfield, and went away, expostulating with the elder lady for coming to the door with him—though politeness was not so much her reason as a resolve to favour him with further views of her own respecting Mrs. Mead before she let him out.

Now, scarce had she re-entered the little sitting-room, when she uttered a shriek and ran forward to her daughter, whose aspect was one that might well excite a mother's terror. She stood rocking herself at the window, with both hands upon her heart, and her face of the dreadful whiteness of the dead.

Mortally wounded she looked, with her languishing eyes.

"Oh, my God! what is this, Jenny!" cried her mother, flinging her arms around her. "Was he so dear to thee, then?"

No answer came from the pale lips for some moments, only hard struggles for breath, with now and again a little moan.

"Oh, Jenny, rest thy poor head on my shoulder! Oh, little hands, how bitterly cold! My lamb, my pretty one—hath he betrayed thee? Why were you not brave to speak out your heart's secret to me? Whisper now, whisper now, that I may comfort thee."

"Mother, I am his wife!" the girl answered, and with a mighty effort overcame the nausea and the darkness of swooning, and drew away from her mother and stood erect.

CHAPTER XII

MR. STRANGFIELD'S CONSTRUCTION

"I do not like thee, Dr. Fell,

The reason why I cannot tell;

But—I do not like thee, Dr. Fell."

ANON

MRS. STRANGFIELD started and fell back with inimitable wildness of amazement. Her face was puffed out with the force of her surprise, and she drew no breath until a feeling of suffocation made her cry out.

"His wife!—his *wife*, Jenny, do you say!" she exclaimed, in a tone almost as deep as a man's, searching meanwhile her daughter's countenance for any hint to make her doubt the truth of what she heard.

The girl fell upon her knees, with her hands clasped above her head.

"We were married when I went to Sydenham," she said, in a voice that had lost nearly all its sweetness. "My fear of father kept me silent. But Cuthbert should have come last night to claim me before thee and him, and Oh, my heart!—where is he now, and why has he left me!"

With which, and with her tearless face in her hands, she fell to moaning—in her humble, heedless posture of woe, a piteous sight. Then must her mother begin to weep.

"Oh, Jenny, what hast thou been and done! Oh, my child, what shameful courting has made you stoop to this deceit! Alas! what a strange wild thing to do!" And with streaming eyes she poured forth her interjections.

Now it befell that the servant Polly, having cast herself down upon a kitchen-chair to indulge in one of those aggravating fits of whimpering, which seized her after every collision with her mistress, overheard some of Mrs. Strangfield's startling ejaculations, to which she listened, with her mouth gradually opening, and her head slowly lifting out of the greatness of her arm-sleeve; and being a blockhead as well as a slut (for dirt and ignorance love each other's company), and eager to show how forgiving she was, and how smart was the watch she kept over the interests of the family, the draggle-tail sped softly out of the kitchen into the shipwright's yard, and, deaf to various personal remarks on her figure called slyly to her by the workmen, ran up to Mr. Strangfield, and cried out, "Master, if ye want a to-do ye shall see it in th' parlour! There's bin a man, and missus is callin' Miss Jenny bad words; and sich blubberin' as is goin' on might fill a copper!"

Mr. Strangfield looked down with a scowl of surprise into the seamy face of the handmaid, and not choosing to risk any questions in the hearing of the men—for Poll's excitement was something to balance a stout voice upon—he sensibly concluded certain directions he was giving to one of the hands, and walked to his house.

On entering the parlour he found Jenny standing at the table, and her mother sobbing in her handkerchief. He was a man with a keen eye, but no sharpness of vision did he need to know that he stood in the presence of a sorrow the like of which had never before darkened his home. In the girl's short recoil as he entered, the sudden mutinous flash of the eye that changed the whole character of the face, the swelling nostril and passionate resolution of misery informing the whole figure of her, he read it. For, in truth, in the blight and shock that had come to her with the news Mr. Saunderson had brought, fear of her father was lost; her recoil was an involuntary effort of instinct; firm in her misery she stood now, and her eyes were steady on her father's face.

Though his wife heard him enter the room, she would not lift her head from the handkerchief. In her dread to tell him what Jenny had done, she gave the mischief a more sinister aspect than it need have worn, by preserving her weeping posture and silence. He knitted his brows and clasped his hands strongly to preserve an evenness of voice, and subdue the dull pain in his breast. But, do what he would, he looked a man striving with might and main, to prepare himself for a shocking disclosure.

"Jane," said he, in a low hard voice, "did you not hear my footsteps? Why are you crying, and what makes Jenny so white and wild-looking?"

He had turned his shoulder on his daughter, and gazed at his wife only.

"Oh, Michael!" quavered Mrs. Strangfield, talking in her handkerchief, "Jenny hath done a mad thing. She has just now owned it, and surprise makes a fool of me. But thou must bear with her, Michael. Deceit only is she guilty of—of nothing worse, husband. You will show her mercy, Michael; for is not she our only child? And the Lord's truth is in the saying, that 'stolen waters are sweet, and bread eaten in secret is pleasant.'"

"'But he knoweth not that the dead are there, and that her guests are in the depths of hell,'" quoted Mr. Strangfleld, in his deep tones. "What has our child been doing?"

There was a short pause, and then Mrs. Strangfield, removing her handkerchief from her eyes, and piteously looking at Jenny, feebly answered, "She has secretly married the son of Dr. Shaw."

Now most certain it was that Mr. Strangfield had expected to hear a worse confession than this; for it is a truth not flattering to the saintly severity of such natures as his, that their conjectures are apt to sink to the very lowest deep of wrongdoing, and stay there until drawn up again by discovery into pertinent bearings. For a moment, therefore, he was visited by a sense of relief; for not instantly could his mind get quit of the foul idea so as to apprehend strictly the meaning of his wife's words. But when once mastered, it brought with it a flood of amazement; and as though he discredited his hearing, as though his daughter had undergone some physical transformation that bewildered him utterly, he stared at her; then, in a terrible voice, cried, "Let me hear this from your own lips, woman!"

"Father, it is true. I am Cuthbert Shaw's wife."

He walked round the table to his chair as though intending to sit, but still stood.

"When did you marry him?"

"When I was at my aunt Rachel's."

"When you were at your aunt Rachel's! That is three weeks since. Give me the day."

"It was on a Wednesday, father—I do not know the date. I forget," replied the girl, trembling like one in an ague, yet never shifting her feverishly lustrous eyes from her father's face.

But both mother and daughter could see that he had no pity. Had his child fallen dying at his feet, his was the inexorable abhorrence of wrongdoing that would have wrung the truth from her failing breath, as in the old legend the man smashed the gem to remove the flaw in it.

"You will have to remember the date—name me the church."

"It was in London—I cannot tell the name. I will think presently;" and she pressed her cold hands to her forehead.

He looked at her with a kind of dread in his eyes, as though she were some unsightly thing. Yet, God knows, never did she appear more lovely, so exquisitely fair in her fear and misery, so tenderly womanly and helpless in her white sweetness of face, and bruised and broken mien, the more pitiful for her cruel struggles to seem brave.

"You remember nothing—neither the date of your marriage, nor the church wherein you were married?" he said; and, looking around him with a pathetic manner of uncertainty, he moved towards the door.

"Michael!" exclaimed Mrs. Strangfield in a whisper, laying her hand on his arm, "where art thou going?"

"To fetch the woman's husband, and examine him before thee. Let me go!" he answered fiercely, shaking her hand off.

"Oh, Michael, you will not find him—he hath left Greystone! Just now came a gentleman to inquire for him here. It was the news that overcame her. Poor Jenny!—my little one!" and she sobbed bitterly.

He turned upon her as a man would on an enemy. "Gone!" he shouted; then, subduing his voice, "*Gone*, do you say, wife?"

"Yes, Michael, indeed, indeed. Not ten minutes ago a gentleman was here to tell us. Mr. Shaw has not been home all night; and whether he is dead, or why he hath gone—Oh, Jenny! Look, Michael; she is dying! Oh, help her! help her!"

The girl was sinking on the floor, when the mother with a bound was at her side, and caught her as she fell. Bestowing a single glance upon the group, Mr. Strangfield strode into the passage, seized his hat, and left the house.

With long, resolute steps he swung his arms up the High Street, to the corner of the road that led to Greystone School. It was past noon, and the sun at its hottest, and a still day after the strong wind of the night; so that the sea, heaving softly like a woman's breast after a struggle, was, to the uttermost distances of it, as silk for the sheen, and glass for the pureness.

As he turned the corner, he had nearly upset an old woman who was coming round in a rapid hobble; and before he could pass her, she hooked his sleeve with her forefinger.

"Good marning to you, deacon; hurry you're in indeed to tumble a well-dressed lady like me! Now, don't I see that you're after young Cuthbert Shaw, and that there's hell-fire burning in your heart this very day? Well, well for the luck of old eyes! But you'll not catch the pretty man, deacon!"

And the old woman, who was veritably a hag, with nose and chin meeting, and a bloodshot eye, dropped her hand under her grey cloak, and grinned through her yellow fangs into his face.

"You have everybody's business in your head but your own, Mrs. Mead," exclaimed Strangfield, just stopping to say this to her; and was about to hurry on, but halted with a swing. "How come you to know that Mr. Shaw is not to be found?"

"It's all over the town that he's missing, my dear. Some say he's gone drownded, and t'others that he wur taken by the press-gang, as drew poor Billy Basings out of his wife's arms last night—the Lord curse 'em for the job! for his wife's my niece. But save ye, deacon, the Sarvice hath no want for soft little men. He hath done some mischief, and has run, like Georgie Moon, d'ye remember, as set poor Johnny Grouse cryin' for his Susie. Now do you know what it is, master? Ah, dear Lard, how terrible he looks!"

And, with a creak of stifling laughter, she hobbled around the corner.

With a bitter frown shadowing the expression of indignant shame in his face, Strangfield went rapidly up the hill, rehearsing with twitching lips the things he should say to Dr. Shaw. Often he pulled off his hat to wipe the sweat from his brow, and breathed distressfully with the haste of his walking. Indeed, his gestures and strides, and pale, beaded face, were those of one beside himself. A man coming down the hill, who knew him well, saluted him; but he passed without recognition, kicking up the dust as he went, and swinging his arms with his hand clenched.

The boys were at their games in the playground as he skirted the wall; for though true it was that no school was kept that morning, it was only partially true that the boys were downcast by Cuthbert's disappearance. A little awed they were in the early morning, when the whisper went round that he was missing, and surmises of his death bandied, and statements of the doctor's grief. But there had come pleasant consolation with the cake-woman and her tray of pudding-buns and brandy-balls; and obstinate indeed is the grief of that boy whom candy cannot cheer and a holiday make merry.

Mr. Strangfield walked to the house door with a resolved step, and pulled the bell. The servant examined his face curiously, as if she would read tidings of Dr. Shaw's son there, but hesitated when questioned if the doctor could be seen.

"Tell him that I have come to talk to him about the young master," said Strangfield; whereupon the girl admitted him, but left him in the hall while she went into the study. Then returning: "If you please, what name?" But Strangfield was in no temper for formality, even if he were one to admit its uses; he put the servant aside and entered the study, closing the door behind him.

The room was darkened by the curtains; yet there was light enough to disclose the figure of Dr. Shaw, seated near the table, his head lifted out of his hand, staring at the unceremonious intruder. In an instant he rose, and drawing himself erect, exclaimed—

"I have not the pleasure to know you, sir. I desired the servant to obtain your name."

"My name is Michael Strangfield, and my trade be ship-building. I'm a deacon of the Baptist chapel, in George Street, which is better than saying that only a bitter errand could have brought me into Dr. Shaw's house."

"Be pleased to sit," said the doctor, coldly, and stepped to the window and drew apart the curtains.

Now were the features of both fathers visible, and never was offered a greater contrast of faces. The doctor, who had not been in bed all night, had a haggard look, which showed strongly on his plumpness; his eyes were languid with anxiety and fatigue. Yet the dignity of good breeding was in the repose of his face, and in his manners especially marked. On the other hand was the worn and handsome face of the shipwright, scorn and shame gleaming with a half-smothered light in his eyes, and the iron will of his nature hardening the curve and set of his mouth, and inclining his head to a backward fall of half-derisive haughtiness. With both hands he held his hat to his breast, taking no notice of the other's invitation to sit.

"Sir," he said slowly, "there is a report below that your son is missing. But I am not a man to heed the town's gossip. Let me know from you that this is so."

"It is so," replied the doctor, eyeing him keenly.

"Is this sudden leaving of you unexpected?"

"Totally unexpected. Mr. Strangfield, if you have news to give me concerning him, I beg you, in the name of humanity, not to withhold it."

"Answer me this, Dr. Shaw. Do you know that he is married?" said Strangfield, breathing deeply, and speaking with difficulty.

"Married!" cried the doctor, with unmistakable astonishment. "Certainly not, sir—most assuredly not, indeed!"

"I pray you reflect before you speak, sir. As you answer me now, so shall you be judged by Almighty God, who will hold you accountable for this action of your offspring. By word or look has your son Cuthbert ever given you reason to suspect he hath a wife?"

"Mr. Strangfield," replied the doctor, shocked by the energy of this adjuration, "I have given you a plain answer, and still my reply to you is, No. What has put this extraordinary notion into your head?"

"Then your son is a villain and a robber! the plunderer of my child's innocence, and my name and honour! He hath enticed her into vile wrong, he hath taught her a deceit that hell itself would rebuke, and now hath left her to dwell alone in the disgrace and ruin he hath overwhelmed her with!" He let fall his hat, and buried his face in his hands.

The doctor stood petrified.

"In God's name, man," he cried, "speak out, and give some meaning to your charges. Dead or living, my son is outraged by your language, and before you leave this room you shall name me his offence, that I may establish his innocence."

With a shake of the head, as if he would clear his brain, Strangfield looked up.

"My daughter Jenny has this day told me that she is secretly married to your son. Do you heed me? That she is his wife, sir, which you would now make out a lie! Clear him of that!"

The doctor put up his hand. He was a man of decisive theories, and as bigoted at one pole of thought as Strangfield was at the other. So calmly confident was he his son was not married, that he would not even condescend to reason the matter to himself.

"Your daughter," said he, in a cold voice, "is either wilfully deceiving you, or labours under some astonishing delusion. I am intimately acquainted with my son's nature and disposition, and do most positively assure you that he is the last man in the world to contract marriage clandestinely."

He spoke with a little curl of the lip, for he was very confident on this point.

"But—" he was continuing; then stopped and frowned, with his eyes bent on the floor.

"You were about to say it!" shrieked the unhappy father. "Speak out and clear him, in the name of God! I have called him villain and robber—clear him!"

"I must beg you to restrain your impetuosity," returned the doctor haughtily. "If my son has acted the part of a villain, you will not mend matters by clamouring at me. Statements have been made to you by your daughter, and their verification is a simple matter. But, mark me, she is deceiving you!" he exclaimed, with scornful emphasis; for though the grief and consternation of Strangfield seemed genuine enough, yet the doctor's profound dislike of the sect to which the man belonged, and the absolute unlikelihood of Cuthbert connecting himself by marriage with this rugged, humbly bred

Dissenter, made the visit wear the habit of a conspiracy, against which it behoved the learned little man to be on his guard.

With a heavy effort Strangfield calmed himself; and, with a struggling face and twitching fingers, essayed to speak reasonably.

"You say my girl hath deceived me. This truly has she done, be she speaking Gospel or a devil's lie, in what she hath told her mother. Yet you must know, sir, that up to this day never had I cause to doubt her as a good girl. She declares that she was married to your son three weeks ago, when we had sent her for a change of air to her aunt, who lives at Sydenham."

The doctor grew a shade paler.

"Three weeks ago! My son was in London then. Good heaven, sir, he surely—the improbability—the—the——" Mr. Strangfield kept his glowing eyes bent on him. "For some time past," the doctor went on, "I have noticed a change in him, and his answers have been full of evasion. But if he were married," he cried, in his eagerness straining his head forward and leaning with both hands on the table, "would he abandon his wife and mysteriously depart as he has now done, leaving no hint behind him either of his motive or his whereabouts? Oh, Mr. Strangfield, that speaks for itself. That is a very persuading argument against your daughter, sir."

"It is that which has brought me here!" cried Strangfield, in a voice of thunder. "Has he gone? You answer yes. If he loved her well enough to marry her, he would not leave her. If he hath betrayed her, then have you his reason for flying!"

Dr. Shaw turned to pace the room. Light was beginning to dawn on him. It was difficult for him to bring his mind to believe that Cuthbert was guilty of a mortal sin; yet here was the father of the girl violent in heavy charges, so that the existence of the victim, at least, was an established fact by surest proof.

"As the husband of your daughter, he would not have left her," he said, speaking in a tone of pain and shame, and with something like horror in the expression of his eyes. "May God forgive him if he has brought disgrace upon the innocent! But, Mr. Strangfield, have not you approached your conclusion with extreme hurry? On the statement of your daughter, unsupported by any evidence, you convict her and my son. She affirms herself married; and, if this be so, it is most easy of proof. But, though the marriage cannot be proved, what impeachment should there be in the silence of evidence, unless you have testimony to satisfy you of their guilt?"

Mr. Strangfield picked up his hat and turned it about vacantly in his hands.

"I came here," he said in a low voice, "to find out if your son hath truly left you, as reported. If he be my daughter's husband, it shall be proved soon. Sir, I thank you for receiving me civilly, and bearing with me. For forty years have I dwelt in Greystone, and for all that time no man hath ever pointed his finger at me for any act of wrong. That my girl hath owned to a secret marriage is a bitter disgrace upon me, who have ever tried to teach her the hatefulness of deceit, as the pathway of one that forgets the Lord. If you have news of your son, sir, you will please to acquaint me with it, that I may sift this business to the bottom."

And turning abruptly he left the room, and in a moment the doctor heard the hall door closed.

CHAPTER XIII

THE DEACON'S CHARITY

"Sadness of every day, and all day long,
Spite of the summer glow and wild-birds song."
                                        —*Hon. Mrs. Norton.*

IN small towns news spreads quickly. It is an easy job and does not hinder business for the bareheaded tradesman to run into his neighbour's shop and deliver his bulletin or receive his mouthful. And idle people are never wanting in the market-places and ale-houses, and at sunny corners, to serve as tinder for the wild-fire of intelligence. So that from mouth to mouth a report goes, losing and gaining, in its wordy transit, until every house has caught its echo.

The news all over Greystone was that Dr. Shaw's son was missing. It was a theme to gather noteworthiness, from the prominence of the missing man's father. Three men had been impressed the previous night, and that was known—for two wives, with aprons to their eyes, had moaned their cruel severance everywhere; and Matthew Murphy's sweetheart carried evidence in a black eye of the fray that had ruined a frying-pan.

But where was Dr. Shaw's son? This was a gentleman no press-gang was likely to seize. Besides, who had seen him trepanned? Everywhere was it known that the rocks, the beach, and the country about had been searched by order of the doctor; and therefore was dished up a pretty mystery for the idle folks of Greystone to scratch their heads over.

But this was not all. With Cuthbert Shaw's disappearance was mixed up, in a way none of the gossips would have undertaken to define, the name of Jenny Strangfield. Who first coupled them in such a business was not to be got at, any more than you shall know, by looking at a blazing house, where the fire began. But go where you would, had you said, "They are talking about Deacon Strangfield's girl being concerned in old Shaw's trouble," some such an answer would you have got as,

"Ay, ay, so it is said, neighbour, and so it's likely to be; for she's pretty enough to turn a gentleman's head, and them as turns others as often as not loses their own over the job."

Mr. Joseph Skelton, another deacon of the Baptist chapel in George Street, a smack-owner, and the possessor of a sour countenance and a sing-song voice, was walking soberly down the High Street, revolving the various surmises that had been submitted to him respecting Cuthbert Shaw's disappearance by old Mrs. Gruff, who kept a snuff-shop at the corner of George Street, and sometimes went out nursing; when, having passed the market-place, he met Mr. Strangfield, who was coming from his interview with Dr. Shaw.

"Good morning to you, friend," said Mr. Skelton. "You look hot and troubled. This missing of Isaac Shaw's son is a strange thing to happen. Truly, of our common enemy, one may now say, with Bildad the Shuhite, 'His roots shall be dried up beneath, and above shall his branch be cut off.'"

"And was it not Bildad the Shuhite who said, 'How long will it be ere ye make an end of words?' Little things move the tongue of this town strangely."

"Well, well, pray the Lord for our integrity that the truth is not with the gossips," said Mr. Skelton, looking at Mr. Strangfield out of the corner of his little eyes.

At this, catching an under meaning, Strangfield stopped dead and confronted his brother deacon with his face of iron.

"What is the truth that touches our integrity, Joseph?" said he.

"Nay, nay, Mr. Strangfield, if it's a lie it'll reach you fast enough; and if it's the truth, then ye have no need to hear it from me," responded Mr. Skelton, lengthening his sour face and deepening his voice.

"Speak! speak!" cried Strangfield, impatiently. "If it's something you're ashamed to tell an honest man, name me the person who will give it to me."

"I am not ashamed to tell you; but, brother, please to remember, that 'in the multitude of words there wanteth not sin; but he that refraineth his lips is wise.' Now, as I would be wise, how should I talk?"

Strangfield looked at him with a quivering of contempt about his mouth, and was moving away, when Mr. Skelton, who was secretly athirst for news, cried out, "Well, then, Michael, be bold, for friendship's sake. They are saying that your pretty little daughter is in some way concerned with young Mr. Shaw's disappearance."

"They say a lie!" thundered Strangfield, turning with a furious gesture. "And give them the lie from me! And let whom it may concern know this, Joseph—by the Lord who hath made you and me, I will screw off that man's head who dares to use my girl's name in this business! Take that with you, as more news to spread."

And he marched off, leaving Mr. Skelton a shade yellower with—let us say, with pious consternation at such violent, unchristian wrath.

Mr. Strangfield went straight to his house, and stood a moment under the shelter of the leaves to wipe his forehead before entering. His wife, hearing his step, came out of the parlour, and looked at him in silence, too frightened to offer him any kind of salutation.

"Is dinner ready, Jane?" he asked, thrashing the dust from his shoes with a red pocket-handkerchief, and assuming an off-hand tone of voice, which was a lie in his wife's ear.

"More than ready, Michael. The bit of beef is baked to a chip by this time, I doubt; but if we eat it quickly, it may still be worth asking a blessing over. As to Jenny, now thou'rt in, I'll not wait for her."

"Where is she?" inquired Mr. Strangfield, looking at his wife with a frown.

"Why, she went out soon after you left the house, and Polly says she walked up the High Street. She's gone to get the news about her husband, I dare say. Dear! dear! to hear me talk of it in this easy way! But that must be because I have cried my heart dry."

Mr. Strangfield walked into the parlour, where the table was prepared for dinner; he held his face towards the window for a while, and then, turning round to his wife, who gazed at him from the doorway, not daring to ask questions, but too eager to hear the result of his quest after Cuthbert to divert him by calling to the servant, he said—

"Why do you speak of her husband? Do you *know* that she is married?"

"Do I know? It was she who said so. Oh, Michael, why do you look at me so wildly?"

"You do not ask me where I have been," he exclaimed, with a grim, fleeting smile. "That is strange in one so curious. I will tell thee, Jane—I have been to see Dr. Shaw."

"Up at the school-house!—a hot, long walk for thee, poor man. But I might guess the road you took by the dust on thy shoulders."

He continued staring at her, desirous of being questioned, with a look in his eyes as if he were drawing savage pleasure from anticipation of his answers.

He would not speak, and she must have news; so, very timidly—

"Michael, what hath Dr. Shaw to say about his son?"

"Ask me if he knows that he is married." Then, relenting under the twitch of pain in his wife's mild face, he cried out in a quivering voice, "Oh, Jane, this man swears that his son is not married—that neither by word nor look has he given him cause to suspect such a thing. And he asked me, *Would my son, if your daughter was his wife, leave her mysteriously, and without message or reason?* Such words he said. And he hinted at sin and conscience hurrying the scoundrel from the town!"

"Michael," said his wife, in a hoarse whisper, going up to him and putting her hand on his arm, "dost thee mean to say that—that——"

He looked down upon her with stony eyes; whereupon she half shrieked, "No, no! Michael, Michael, our girl is honest! Great Lord, did the vile schoolmaster charge my pure child with such a sin before her father, and no denial made him? Michael, didst thee let the foul old man say *that* of her? Oh, my pretty one! Oh, my Jenny! how can they think it of thee! how can they think it!"

"Do you call her pure?—she who, by her own confession, has deceived those who love her?" he exclaimed in a slow, bitter voice. "Since she has confessed to one sin, why shall not you believe in her deeper guilt, until she shall prove that she hath wronged us by deceitfulness only? It is good reasoning to declare that, if this man were her husband, he would not have left her without token of his going; and a truthful conclusion to come at, that having wronged her, and dreading my wrath and his father's, he has fled from the place and, like a sneaking coward, left her to bear her sin alone."

Dumbfounded, the mother listened; then, plucking up heart, replied, "Why do you doubt that she has spoken the truth? If she be married, she has not sinned as you say; and yet, though you know not for sure whether she be married or not, you condemn her as if she were a single woman that had fallen. Oh, Michael! thy heart is too hard. Though she be not married, yet why do you say that she hath sinned? Poor little one! must her heart be broken by her father?"

"It is her father's heart that will be broken by her!" he cried. "What did Joseph Skelton tell me just now?—that my girl is the talk of the town! Oh, fie! that you should excuse her!"

He walked hastily to the door, and, seizing hold of the staircase banister, stopped and looked back.

"Come with me to her bedroom," he said. "You shall bear witness."

"What to do?" replied Mrs. Strangfield, not offering to move.

"To get what truth is to be found in her letters, if she has any," he exclaimed. "I will sift this matter to the bottom."

His wife turned her back upon him, and he went upstairs alone.

"And now," says the Apostle, "abideth faith, hope, and charity, these three; but the greatest of these is charity."

And, wanting this, though a man bestow all his goods to feed the poor, and give his body to be burned, it profiteth him nothing.

But this was an omitted text from the glib category in Strangfield's memory. Texts that denounced those who opposed him (though equally applicable to himself), texts that enforced his own narrow exhortations, texts to cramp the large life of man into confined and shallow channels of prejudice, Mr. Strangfield had by heart. But texts to show weakness beautiful with humanity, texts to serve as crutches for halting virtue until the limp was cured, texts shining like mild stars in darkness to light the troubled soul unto the perfect day, were not to be found in his edition of the Bible—though, strangely enough, it was, word for word, yours and mine, reader.

And how should such a man better express his sincerity than by condemnation of his own offspring? Always, under crabbed piety, it is those that are at home with the teacher who suffer most. And hugging common vulgar passion (with prodigious reference to the world's judgment in it) as pious zeal, Strangfield fell to the dirty work of overhauling Jenny's bedroom for evidence to justify his base conclusions.

A little chest of drawers was soon ransacked, and pockets of dresses; and the rosewood desk, forced with a jack-knife for a lever, was promptly explored, and here was more than he wanted. A pile of letters, indeed, which no carrier had ever delivered, either; some of them illegible almost with stains of wet, which, in good truth, they could hardly fail to contract, seeing that the lovers' post-box was always the grass under the evergreens hard in the corner of the front garden, and close to the railing for accessibility from the roadway.

Drawing from his pocket the wooden case that contained his spectacles, and perching the glasses on his nose, Strangfield went to the window and began to read the letters. No tradesman guards his receipted bills more religiously than Jenny had preserved these precious missives. Folded most carefully were they, with sweet-smelling dry flowers among them, and held together with riband, and the dates in such accurate sequence as only love (after trade) would have patience to order.

A tender heart would have been moved by the pretty care and grave regularity of this preservation. Gentle thoughts of his girl's infancy, memories of her little form and tottering step, and the milky lisp of her tiny greetings, arise in the loving father's heart, when the life of the grown daughter takes momentous form, and the emotions that may shape her career are influencing her. But a sense of inflexible duty held Strangfield imperturbable. As he would have read a contract for building a lugger, so did he read these letters, waxing from the mild modesty of early love into the heedless poetry of passionate feeling. The dinner waiting below gave him no thought; he had no hunger, save for the knowledge of his daughter's guilt or honesty.

All these letters, with one exception, bore dates prior to Jenny's visit to Sydenham. In them he called her sweetheart and mistress; and the signature was always "Bertie." Many of them were hurriedly scribbled appeals for interviews. The one letter, written after the visit to Sydenham, was a passionate protestation of love, with a tender reference to deep endearments, and a bit of sly humour at the end, where pious Aunt Rachel and "the puritanical deacon of George Street" were spoken of as "people easy to hoodwink, because they imagined themselves so very keen-sighted." So from beginning to end of these letters was Jenny Cuthbert's darling, his pretty heart, his sweet girl, and the like; never once did he call her his wife, and there was no mention of marriage. Such are the trumpery accidents which produce tragedies.

Mr. Strangfield flung them upon the floor and went downstairs.

His wife had finished her dinner, and was coming away from the house door, where she had been standing a while on the look-out for Jenny, whose absence troubled her, though, for the girl's sake, she would not complain. Something like disdain was in her face when she looked at her husband. He could not have been guilty of more humbling meanness in her sight than to ransack his daughter's bedroom.

"The dinner is cold," said she, "and I have dined. If——"

"I have no appetite," he interrupted. "Let the wench clear the table."

He went to his armchair and seated himself in a sullen, rapt attitude, and never stirred all the while his wife helped the girl to remove the cloth. Then the poor woman, hardly knowing what she ought to do, was about to leave him alone, and was closing the door when he called to her. She came to the table.

"If you are taking her part," said he, in harsh, concentrated tones, "and justifying her conduct to yourself, tell me! that I may know how to address you."

"I do not take her part, neither am I against her, until I know the truth," answered the mother, firmly.

"The truth is in the letters you will find lying on her bedroom floor. Her sin is there, written by the hand of the villain who has brought shame upon us."

Mrs. Strangfield turned white, and grasped the table whilst she stared at her husband.

"Why do you say that, Michael? Is it so plain? Is it so plain?"

"Plain!" he cried, hoarsely. "What brains do you allow me, that I should not know the language of the paramour? Get upstairs and judge for thyself!"

"No, no! not if I died for refusing. Oh, Michael, art thou not headstrong in thy fears? If he be her husband, and loves her——"

But she faltered and stopped here; for what was to be done with that hard question—If he loved her, why had he left her to bear her trouble alone? and stammering a little, she went on—

"But you will not believe that she is his wife, and, 'tis easy, therefore, for their poor letters to make thee think they have sinned."

"Leave me!" he cried sternly, for he feared the anger which his wife's obstinate advocacy was kindling in him.

She went away quickly, smothering her sobs until the door was closed. Then, at her bedroom window, she planted herself to watch for Jenny's return.

CHAPTER XIV

THE EAST INDIAMAN

"Here's neither bush nor shrub, to bear off any
weather at all. . . . What have we here? a man or a
fish? Dead or alive? . . . A strange fish! Were I in
England now (as once I was), and had but this fish
painted, not a holiday fool there but would give a
piece of silver."—*The Tempest.*

AN hour before sunset an East Indiaman, of
the build and beauty familiar to students of
sea-pieces painted seventy years ago, was
some leagues to the southward of the Start,
under pressure of full and towering canvas.
She was one of five vessels, and carried the
commodore's pennant; for here was a little
squadron of peaceful merchantmen
undertaking a long and perilous voyage, with
nothing better to protect them against an up-
rush of enemy's ships than their own

carronades and the stout hearts that filled the forecastle.

The four ships, which had no need to check their weather-braces to let the commodore hold the van, were scattered to right and left upon the dark surface of the water, yet not so far but that a half-hour's sailing would enable them all to close. Such a majestical object as the foremost vessel looked, frothing the blue at her bow, and sweeping her stately spaces of white against the heavens, no pen could express. Indeed, there was in the ships of those times a magic that threw over the mind a spell such as the huge and iron shapes of our own age cannot reach to; something deeper and truer than the mere beauty and power we find in the witchery as it is reflected in the poetry of Byron, and the songs of Campbell, prince of lyrists.

At this moment some sailors, furling the awning along the tall poop, left to the nakedness of the sky a numerous company of passengers, and a charming picture of white deck, brilliant with colouring of female apparel, the gold and white of uniforms, the sheen of brass catching the ruby glitter of sunlight; the flash of glazed skylights, the trim coils of salt-white rope.

Conspicuous among the passengers was a black man, clothed with a mighty turban, in the midst of which flashed a jewel. He sat in state near the wheel, scarcely deigning to bend his red-brown eyes on the commander of the ship who was addressing him. At either elbow of this potentate stood two black attendants, inflexible figures of ebony. The rest of the passengers occupied parts of the poop at respectful distances from his highness, yielding him, with proper modesty, that regal environment of space which is one kind of sustenance of majesty.

"If you shall look dar," said the Indian, with a haughty nod of the head in the direction of the sea to the left, "you will see a black ting."

Captain Turbulent, a full-faced man, with legs curving outwards to as true an oval as the outline of an egg, looked hard at the water, but protested that he could see nothing.

"It is dar, I tell you," said the prince, and the jewel in his turban flashed like an angry beauty's eye as he gave his head a shake and pointed with his black hand.

"Mr. Mattocks," called the captain, "get the glass and sweep the sea to leeward on the port bow, and tell me if there is anything to be seen there, will you?"

The officer thus directed took up a telescope from the skylight, and began to work away with it.

"There's a ship's boat, sir, down there, about four points on the port bow," he sang out presently. "I don't see anybody in her, sir. It's a job to fix her."

"What I tell you?" said the prince.

"Let her go off a couple of points," exclaimed the captain, motioning with his hand to the man at the wheel. "We'll run down and see what it's like. Your highness has good eyes."

His highness smiled disdainfully, and without turning his head spoke some words in Hindustanee; whereupon one of the attendants vanished, and in a few moments returned with a jewelled hookah, which he handed to the prince on his knees.

Now, whether "his highness" was the correct term to apply to the Indian, Captain Turbulent did not positively know; it sounded well and felt safe, and that was the merit of it. The black man was prince of some territory to the north-ward of the Sautpoora mountains, and was now returning to his subjects after a voyage to London, where he had been enlarging his mind by visiting King George, the Tower, Change Alley, and more harmful places of curiosity. He was a profitable passenger, paying liberal store of rupees for accommodation, and exacting yellow satin hangings and royal immunity. All the way down Channel the lady passengers had been talking about the prince's jewels, and many a languishing look had the gem in the turban attracted, and the wonderful diamonds that shone like icicles in moonlight upon his black fingers.

The shifting of the helm brought the soft wind abeam, and the bubbles along the sides winked frostily as they swept past, and the wake of the ship went far into the dance of waters astern.

The boat was soon a visible object to the right of the crimson fall of sunshine on the sea, and one by one the passengers left their seats on the deck, and went to the poop-rail to look at her. Even his highness sunk his dignity for the sake of his curiosity, and commanded his servants to carry his chair to the other side of the deck, where he had the boat clear in his sight, whilst the attendants salaam'd to their slippers.

Mr. Mattocks, second officer of the *Elizabeth*, had ascended the rigging to the height of a dozen ratlines, and was covering the boat with his telescope.

"What do you make of her?" called Captain Turbulent.

"Why, she looks like a man-of-war's dingey gone adrift. I don't see any one in her, sir." Then a moment after, "Hallo! there's something dark in the bottom of her. I caught sight of it as she rolled this way. There again, sir!"

"Stand by to man the weather main-braces!" shouted the captain. "Let her go off another point, and pass her close—d'ye hear? But mind your helm, my man, and don't run her down. Put us that we may see into her."

Some of the hands came tumbling aft to the braces, and then a silence fell; for expectation was strong enough to keep even the ladies silent. No object that a ship can encounter excites more curiosity than a boat fallen in with leagues away from the land, for rarely does it fail to prove a witness to some tragedy; freighted, being ofttimes horrible with death or madness, or the gaunt agony of thirst; and empty, almost always a memorial of some great disaster, and pathetic in its loneliness.

In twenty minutes' time the boat was close ahead.

"Port your helm a trifle!" exclaimed Captain Turbulent.

As she swept past, close under the chains, the men forward, being those who had the first sight of her, cried out, and the cry came along the whole length of the ship with the boat, which, in a few minutes, was bobbing astern.

"Round with the mainyards! Aft here and lower away the cutter! Bear a hand, my lads, or we shall be overhauled, and that won't do!"

The ship's way was stopped; down splashed the cutter, full of men; the oars *cheeped* merrily, and with fine smartness the boat was laid in tow and brought alongside.

In the bottom of her were two men, one atop of the other, under the thwarts, and a third in the stern-sheets, his head back, and his half-closed eyes fixed upon the sky. The women sent up another cry when they saw them; but not the horror, but the pity of it went to the hearts of the men, for the dress of one of the lonely dead was an English naval officer's, and no more was needed to make feeling deep.

The women went away with their hand-kerchiefs to their faces when the bodies were reverently handed up the side; but his highness, though as aromatic as a drawing-room belle, had the soul of a traveller, and must abdicate his chair to see; and three black faces made the crowd around the hatchway motley.

The doctor, who had been roused by the steward from a nap, which he had been taking over a book in his cot, came bustling through the crowd, treading on the slippers of royalty with little concern, and even jeopardizing the delicate amber of the bejewelled hookah. Down he went on his knees and felt for pulses.

"Dead and gone!" was the laconic verdict of this juryman of Judge Death, letting fall the arm and head of the nearest of the three, a bushy-whiskered Jack, in life named Thompson. "See, captain, he has been in action. Look at the throat here; do you observe the small swelling? I should find a bullet there by probing for it."

He turned to the man in the officer's uniform, in life named Transom.

"Dead and gone too, captain. Here's cursed foreigner's work, depend on it. I see no wound. Ah! those fingers have been wanting a long time, poor fellow! Stay, here is a contusion behind the ear—no cutlass nor musket-stock produced that."

He rattled on, putting out his hand as he talked, and laying hold of the wrist of the third man.

Instantly, and in a changed voice, he called for brandy, and bade any man pull off his coat and roll it up for a pillow; and, with keen promptitude, was busy over buttons and chafing, and such working as skill dictated.

A spoonful of brandy swallowed (for twice as much ran on to the deck over the pale edges of the handsomest mouth man ever had) produced a sigh and a quiver of the limbs; and in a hurry, to the order of the doctor, was the body lifted and carried away to a cabin.

Then were the mainyards swung, and once more the great ship leaned her bow to the blue and drove a wilderness of foam towards the sun, whose lower limb was sipping the blood-red line of the horizon.

"One of them is alive!"

"Who is he?"

"He is not a sailor!"

"A mercy that such a beautiful face is not to be food for fishes!"

Such talk as this went among the people fore and aft, and his highness waxed wroth, and his eyes rolled like a truly noble savage's, because good Captain Turbulent had no direct answers to make him.

But there was no getting at the story that night; for the man, though brought to consciousness, was lying still and weak, and silent as a corpse, and, said the doctor to Captain Turbulent, "If you want him to die, go and make him talk."

Truly weak and still, and silent because of it, and for the first hour at least, even when he had opened his eyes and consciousness had shone in them, as near to death as ever he had been when the grape of the *Guerrière* was sweeping the deck of the little *Cleopatra*. All night long watch and watch was kept in his cabin, by order of the doctor, the steward and his mate taking turn and turn about, and with lemonade moistening his lips, and with spoonfuls of beef tea feeding him.

The rest and the food and the care were like a strong hand laid upon the shoulder of a man who walks towards a precipice, sluing him round and starting him back again to safety; for in the morning, when he awoke, he could speak, and his first question concerned his whereabouts.

"I'll go and tell the doctor you're awake, sir," says the red-headed steward's mate, whose spell it was in the cabin.

The doctor was with Captain Turbulent, arranging the funeral of Lieutenant Transom and the man-of-war's man.

"Dr. Cotton, sir, if they've come by their death by Frenchman, we'll bury 'em to a volley, sir," the captain was saying. "Sir, we'll make a state ceremony of it, for the glory of the cause and the satisfaction of our consciences, sir."

Here broke in the steward's mate.

"Captain, you had better come along with me," says Dr. Cotton. "He may have voice enough to give us his story, sir."

So they went together to where the sick man lay. But first some medical forms must be gone through, and when the tongue was inspected and the pulse felt, and feeble answers made, the doctor softly asked questions.

"Pray, my dear young man, who are your two companions, and how came you to be in this miserable plight?"

"They are both dead, sir?"

"Alas, yes—stone dead! and all their troubles over."

"They belonged to an English brig of war called the *Cleopatra*, and one of them is Mr. Transom, first lieutenant of the vessel."

"Dear me!—first lieutenant! Poor man! Promoted higher than any admiral now, sir. And the other man is a sailor?"

"Yes, sir," he said, in a feeble voice; and then rallying, and propping himself on his elbow to speak: "My name is Cuthbert Shaw, and I was impressed in error to serve on board the *Cleopatra*. We fell in with a large French frigate and fought her; but our captain was killed, with more than half our men, and a great number wounded, after a few broadsides, and we struck. It was a cruel fight, most unequal, and all chance for the brig was gone when her wheel was carried away. We made up our minds to be carried to France; but the Frenchman, who was some distance astern of us when we struck, and standing towards us, altered her course suddenly, and headed away to the east, under all the sail they could pile upon her broken masts. Mr. Transom believed that, from her superior elevation, she had sighted some vessel which was not to be discerned from our deck, and that she had hauled away for safety, as, in her crippled state, she would have to strike to any British vessel that might fall in with her. So hot had been the action, we had scarcely time to notice the condition of the brig; but, soon after the Frenchman left us, we found the hull settling under our feet. There was a rush for the boats, and most of the men got away in the pinnace and yawl, and Mr. Transom and I and the boatswain, who were left behind, had just time to scramble into the dingey and cut ourselves adrift, when the brig went down. It then came on to blow, and the boats got separated, and in the night the boatswain, who had been shot in the throat, died; and, within a few hours of his death, poor Mr. Transom died, quite suddenly, and I was left alone, without food or water, and God knows how many hours passed before my senses left me. That is the story, gentlemen;" and the poor young fellow dropped his head wearily on the pillow and closed his eyes.

"Bad news! bad news!" exclaimed Captain Turbulent, striking his leg with his fist. "An Englishman sunk by a Frenchman, by jingo! These are the chances that set the frog swelling to match the bull. Now, with Heaven's blessing, may froggee burst!"

"Gentlemen, please tell me where I am, and what ship this is?" said Cuthbert, in a faint voice.

"This is the ship *Elizabeth*, my lad, bound to Bombay, and we hope to clear the Scillies by sundown."

To the astonishment of doctor and commander, Cuthbert sat with a vehement movement upright in his bed.

"I implore you," he cried—"I implore you, in the name of God, to set me ashore on the English coast. I engage, gentlemen, that you shall not suffer for the delay, if money can compensate you. I have a wife who will not know why I have left her—you will save us both deep misery by landing me! I have strength to row myself ashore, if you will lend me a boat. I—I—— Oh, gentlemen, in God's name, do not carry me to India!"

The pen cannot put into these words the agony of voice that was in them, nor impart the pathetic force they took from his clasped hands, and pale and working face. Captain Turbulent and Dr. Cotton stared at each other. Their minds were slow at the digestion of facts, and it was very odd to them— extremely odd, indeed—that the salvation of this young man from death was not sufficing.

"As to setting you ashore, Mr.—Mr.—"

"Shaw," suggested the doctor, whose memory was good.

"Mr. Shaw, I do not see how that can be done. Indeed, with this wind it is impossible; and with any wind, sir, it would be a bad job for me to attempt, with a—a—damned black thief of a native prince to report me for delaying the journey. Besides, Mr. Shaw, there is a fleet of us, and I'm commodore, and

I give you my word, sir, if I stood in for the land, the rest of them would think themselves in duty bound to follow. No, sir, with Frenchmen about, my business is clear—a midship helm, Mr. Shaw, and the true course, sir."

"What you have to do," said Dr. Cotton, "is to write a letter and keep it by you, ready to put on board any homeward-bound ship we may come across. I'll answer that Captain Turbulent will help you in this way."

"Oh, to be sure. But to land you," exclaimed the captain, shaking his head, "against this wind, with that black rascal ready to swear me out of my ship—if you offered me a thousand pounds, Mr. Shaw, I wouldn't dare do it."

And, to save himself the pain of beholding Cuthbert's face, he quitted the cabin.

The doctor lingered to offer consolation and professional advice.

"A few months more or less of matrimonial life will not make much difference to you at your age, sir. You are not tottering on the brink of the grave—though, if you worry yourself, in you'll go, mark me! Botheration brings on fever, sir, and your pulse shows a constitution ripe for mischief. Keep to your bed all day, and console your mind with thoughts of the delight of meeting your wife in a few months, which pass quickly, sir."

And, with a kindly thump of the pillow, and a promise to look in on the patient in an hour, he went away.

The young fellow turned his face from the door, and sobbed aloud. But on deck all was bright and breezy; and under the blue of the windy sky, and over the long green sweep of water, went the stately ship, broadening, with every plunge and burst of foam, her distance from the English coast.

VOLUME TWO

CHAPTER I

MOTHER MEAD

"But so it was. And let the reader cease to wonder; for affliction is a divine diet, which, though it be not pleasing to mankind, yet Almighty God hath often, very often, imposed it, as good, though bitter physic, to those children whose souls are dearest to Him. "—WALTON.

IT had been a sudden sickness and a dreadful giddiness that had caused Jenny to sink on the floor, from which she recovered soon after her father had quitted the house for his visit to Greystone School. The wild distraction in her eyes had repelled Mrs. Strangfield, and for mercy and dread the mother asked no questions, but sat, silent and sighing, watching her daughter with piteous concern.

Then her duties calling her, and thinking besides that solitude would be precious to such bitter grief as Jenny's, Mrs. Strangfield gently left the room.

No sooner was she gone than Jenny started to her feet, and paced about as though seized with madness, with a frown upon her forehead, and her hands pressing tightly below her hips. Full realization of what had befallen her had come to her heart, and she was driven by intolerable agony of spirit. That Cuthbert had left her of his own will did not come into her mind. Belief in love does not fall dead in this way. And no one had yet suggested to her, as kindly solution of the mystery of his disappearance, that it might be he had taken a sudden shame of her as his wife and had left her, acting a sweet part up to the last hour—for men are shocking deceivers.

What, then, did she think? Why, that some accident had befallen him; and the idea that he might be lying dead in some hidden place so frenzied her, that, without consideration of her purpose, she fled upstairs for her hat and left the house to seek him.

She had wandered beyond the market-place, when her mind took a grasp of her intention, and that brought her to a stand. The mid-day sun beat fiercely upon the road, and held the pavements tolerably empty. But there were people in the shops, and they stared at her as she stood, perceiving which, she went down the street again, with her heart beating furiously over a new-born resolution to call on Dr. Shaw, and begin her inquiries after her husband at his own home.

But when she had got as far as the market-place, the fame of Mother Mead, as a gossip and teller of fortunes, occurred to her; and this because she saw the old woman's bent figure going at a hobble on the other side of the market-place. So Jenny, passing quickly through the stalls, intercepted the dame as she was turning into the court in which she dwelt.

Mrs. Mead was talking to herself in a loud, quavering voice, and so completely engrossed with witch-like thoughts—for what other thoughts could possibly visit such an ugly conformation?—that she did not observe Jenny, until she found herself stopped by the girl standing in front of her.

"Ah, Miss Jenny Strangfield—if that be your rale name, my dear! A hot marning, isn't it? with a power of dust for an old nose that finds snuff cruel dear. Why, your father is jest beyont—I am now from him—and Lard! his eyes are in such a blaze that my old skin cracked when he looked at me."

"May I speak with you in your house, Mrs. Mead? I am in great trouble."

At sight of the sad, sweet face, Mrs. Mead's ugly countenance underwent a kind of transformation. Her nose and chin did not, indeed, moderate their intimacy; but the blood-shot old eye took a sudden light of compassion, and a strange grin of good-nature overspread her face.

"Come along, my dear," she exclaimed, "if ye're not above being seen with sitch a scarecrow as me. Lard bless your heart! the truth's never hard to old ears that carries wool in 'em. When I was a gel—your height, my dear—I had a fine sweetheart. He coorted me in silk stockings, he did, an' that's as true as that this hand's atop o' the other. Ah, but it is, though. A handsome upright man he was, as iver you'd wish to see, but lost his head to a recruiting officer, and got killed somewheers wi' a furrin name. D'ye think I wur always shell-backed? My dear, I was as straight as you are at your age, though I never had your peach cheeks and pretty hair. Well, well, that old Goody Mead should be rattlin' about herself, when they say she knows no business but her neighbours'! Stoop your head, for 'tis an old-fashioned door, built afore palaces was known. There's a strong chair that'll hold thee and if I can comfort you, my pretty, I'll mop out my old heart to do it, I'll warrant."

They had arrived at a rickety old house, with a sitting-room very abruptly entered from the street. This room and a bed-chamber adjacent composed Mrs. Mead's dwelling. Overhead lived a tailor and his consumptive wife, and in a wicker-cage a thrush, that sang, peradventure, to prove that even abject poverty has its sweetness. But abject poverty was upstairs, and was no lodger with Mrs. Mead. How the old woman got money no one knew; but her two rooms were clean, the furniture decent, with a store of coal in the back yard, and tolerable cheer (as the tailor and his wife upstairs could vouch for) in the cupboard behind the chair which Jenny occupied.

Taking a seat opposite the girl, she ran her eyes over her from top to toe.

"Now, my child," said she, "what can I do? Is it your fortune you want told? Nay, nay, there's no physic in such stuff for rale trouble. It's good for foolish wenches whose brains are made o' ribbon, but not for the likes o' thee, dearie."

"I am in bitter trouble indeed, Mrs. Mead. Mr. Shaw, the son of the doctor, is missing, and I am mad to know where he is," said

Jenny, bending her pale face forward as she spoke.

"Likely enough, my dear—he had the most noble face that iver I see on a man. What was he to thee? Your answer shall be sacred with me. Speak the worst, if harm hath come to ye. You'll find Judith Mead dumb as your own heart."

"He was my husband," replied Jenny, in a voice scarcely above a whisper, for the secret was still so fresh that the revelation of it startled her to hear, though spoken with her own voice.

Mrs. Mead screwed up her eyes to look at the girl, until the upper part of her face was a mask of wrinkles.

"Your husband!" she exclaimed, in a tone and with a manner that would have made it impossible for a third person to know whether she believed the girl or not; for, as to Jenny, it could not occur to her that her word would be doubted. "Why, then, no wonder his going troubles ye."

"Oh, Mrs. Mead, why do you say 'his going'? He has not left his home, do you think? Is it not possible that he somewhere met with an accident? Or has his father forced him to leave? On Wednesday he promised me to call last night on father, and break the news of our marriage, for all this while was it our hidden secret. What should prevent him coming? Oh, Mrs. Mead, he loves me truly, and would be with me if he could come. Can he be dead? Oh, kind God! if I thought this I would kill myself, that I might be dead with him."

"My dear," said Mrs. Mead slowly, and reflecting hard whilst she spoke, "he is not dead. Folks do not die like this without it being known. Where could he die? Coming to call on father? Then his body would ha' been found—for the Lord knows they've bin sarching closely enough; an' unless he's gone up to heaven, clothes an' all, like the Prophet Elijah, you may be sure he's walkin' about on this world somewheers, hale an' hearty. Did they tell 'ee there was a press-gang here last night? But ye mustn't look to that. They'd never take a slender man like him. Billy Basings they forced away, but he's a strapping sailor. Mr. Shaw's meat for their masters, and the wagabone plunderers 'ud never burn their fingers on *him*."

She shook her head emphatically.

"He's your husband, is he, my dear? That's beyond doubt, I hope?"

"Oh yes, Mrs. Mead; we were married in a church in London three weeks ago."

"Ye're a soft little wench, and not larned in London ways. Are 'ee sure it was a church?"

"Oh yes, indeed—a large church!" exclaimed Jenny, gazing at the old woman with a new expression gathering in her eyes.

"Why, then, if ye knows the name, and got the bit o' paper they gi'es ye when folks are married——"

"I do not know the name of the church. I do not think my husband ever mentioned it. If any bit of paper was given to us he will have it. I was ready to swoon for fear, and took no notice of anything, so scared was I. But this I have," she cried, drawing out a purse with quivering fingers and showing a wedding-ring.

The old woman put it aside with a movement of her hand.

"You know if it be right wi' thee," said she "but the ring's only worth what it 'ud fetch as gold."

Something in these words, something in the irrepressible leer that weighted the old woman's eyelids, took Jenny's breath away. And then instantaneously there flashed upon her the sense and knowledge of the false and fearful position she was placed in by her husband's disappearance.

She started to her feet.

"Oh, Mrs. Mead!" she half shrieked through her pale lips, "is it possible that my words will not be believed? Great God! will it be thought that I am not Cuthbert Shaw's wife?"

And then recalling her father's iron nature, and his hard rejection of unsupported words, and his evil, unsparing habit of thinking the worst, her heart seemed to stand still, and she remained motionless and frozen, with her hands locked and her teeth clenched.

"Sit down, my dear, sit down, and do not run clane daft, for there's nothing heavy the matter yet," creaked the old woman, again inspecting Jenny closely, motioning her the while to be seated by arching her hands out of her shoulders like a rabbit's paws. "If he's your sweetheart, ye must have some faith in him, and maybe he'll be turning up in a day or two, and then the laugh'll be on thy side. Do ye hear?"

"He is my husband," said Jenny in a sobbing whisper, breathing quickly.

"Well, well, husband or sweetheart, if he comes he'll be welcome, won't he now, dearie?"

"My husband!" shrieked the girl, with a wild stamp of the foot. "Will it not be believed?"

"Why, to be sure it will. But see. I'm an old, lorn woman, who knows the world as thy father knows the Bible—all the harm of it, my dear; and if you was my child, this would I say, hold thy peace about your marriage until you can show proof, that Satan himself wouldn't doubt, that young Mr. Shaw is thy husband. What! will you make envious wenches and their flabbergoon mothers believe ye by saying, 'I do not know the name of the church where I was married, and I have no bit o' paper' (the Lard knows what them things are called) 'to prove that Mr. Shaw is my husband; and 'tis the truth itself that ne'er a living cratur', my own father not excepting, knew that I was Shaw's wife until this blessed day, when my husband hath left me to give the news o' my marriage alone!'"

She ceased leering shrewdly, with a forefinger against her nose.

The stunned look that had settled upon Jenny's face while the old woman was speaking, passed a moment or two after she ceased, and a strange and striking character was given to her beauty by an expression, which it seems absurd to describe as a mingling of despair and determination, yet which assuredly suggested both these qualities.

"I see that a great trouble is come upon me; but in the sight of God my heart is pure," she said, in a low but steady voice. "Mrs. Mead, speak to me honestly, and tell me what you think has become of my husband."

"My honesty won't ease you, my dear; and the Lard knows I may be wrong, though folks think that it's the devil as gives me wisdom," said the old woman, showing her fangs with a grin of ill-dissembled triumph; for in her own mind she had no doubt of the motive of Cuthbert's disappearance, and was flattered with the facile mastery that put her far ahead of the town's surmises.

"Pray answer me. I have the heart to listen to anything now, Mrs. Mead."

"Well," exclaimed Mrs. Mead, speaking slowly, intermitting her words for the sake of filling the spaces between with deliberate nods and shakes of the head, "they'll be thinking this of thee—that you are not married, and that Mr. Shaw hath left you to bear your shame alone. They'll argey that the son of th' old popinjay up at the school-house 'ud never match with Mike Strangfield's darter, and that he hath ruined 'ee with promises. And maybe they'll say that th' old doctor's in the secret, and hath got his son away slyly to save him from the deacon.

Unless you shall defeat the liars by sure proof of thy marriage, and that you must get about quickly."

Jenny stood looking at her with a steady, vacant gaze, as though she did not heed what was being said, and, with the same absent manner, was moving towards the door.

"How shall you get about it, dearie? You do not ask?"

"How?" exclaimed the girl, pausing. "If my husband does not come to me, I am quite helpless."

"Why, who should help 'ee but thy father? Let him go to work. He hath money and strength. If I was his wife he'd not sit idly cursing."

And at the notion of the deacon cursing, she set up a creaking laugh. But such advice was lead instead of life to the poor heart that heard it.

"Good-bye, Mrs. Mead," said she; "if you have news to comfort me, you will not keep me waiting for it?"

"Trust me! I'll do my best. But not come anear thy house, though I had young Mr. Shaw in my arms. I'm none so dear to th' deacon but that he'd bile me in his pitch-caldron, could he find a reason for murderin' me i' the Bible. As to thy mammy——But there, dear heart! if I have good news you shall have it quickly."

With pathetic effort to smile a farewell, Jenny left the house.

CHAPTER II

HER FATHER-IN-LAW

"Now, what could artless Jenny do?"—*Burns*

HER face like marble, but with no lack of determination in it, Jenny walked down the grimy court and crossed the market-place. She halted a moment to deliberate which way she should take to Greystone School. She chose the way of the sands, and down to the beach she went, with drooping head and frightened peeps at the people who passed her; for on her now was cruel sense of heavy shame, and the despair that bares the nerves of the heart for the sunshine and human eyes to torture.

Crossing the space of shingle on which lay the fishing-boats roasting in the sun, with hot smell of paint and tar exhaling, her feet pressed the hard sand, and the ocean lay close in a burnished, heaving sheet. And now, being clear of the street, the frown of deep and wondering sorrow settled again upon her fair forehead. What had imagination to say to her soul's cry for her husband? Peering into the caverns and hollows of the cliffs, with here and there a pause before the grand space of sea, with sad eyes questioning the lustrous depths, she toiled along the sands towards the ravine which led to Greystone School. The sun, standing in the south, left the sands shadowless; and at the mouth of the ravine or gorge or pass (these fissures have a dozen names), she seated herself for a little spell of rest, for nature was faint with fasting and the heavy load of trouble, and fierce pouring of the noontide blaze.

A pity now, if ever, that Echo was not the embodied spirit the ancients painted her; for, haunting the gloom and loneliness of these nodding heights, murmurous with the sea's wild moan, the nymph should have a whisper for the poor young wife to cheer her.

Her trouble was so new and strange that the wonder of it became as a dream, and she would start with a cry from the sense of madness impending.

Presently she began the ascent, hugging the steep side for the sweetness of its shadow, and passed the coastguard's hut, near which stood one of the 'prentices with a spy-glass. He stared hard at her, as the most timid man in the world would, so provoking was her beauty; and she was passing forward to escape his eyes, when a thought gave her courage to stop and ask a question.

"They have been searching here and all about for a missing man this morning, I have heard," said she. "Pray can you tell me if any discovery has been made?"

"You mean the master's son at the house yonder?" replied the man, pointing with his thumb over his shoulder. "Why, the fellow I relieved this morning told me as how some boys was gropin' about this way—skylarkin' a tidy bit, he reckoned, if the sarch was to be considered serious. I don't know much about it myself. Was he any connection o' yours, miss?"

"If he had fallen over the cliff," she exclaimed, "they would have been sure to find his body on the sands this morning, would not they?"

"I don't see nothen to prevent it," replied the man, tilting his hat over his nose to scratch the back of his head. "The neaps is on all this week; and if it was this way he fell, why, there he'd lie. Unless he took a jump—but even then he'd not come anear the flood."

"You have not heard that he has been seen? I should say would he be known to the coastguards?"

"I really can't answer that, miss. I was on duty at Caldpoint last night—a sight o' distance from this here station," answered the man, looking at her with an interrogative twist in the lay of his head.

There was no information to be got from him; so, with a timid "Thank you," she went on her way.

When she caught sight of the school-house the pulse of her heart grew smaller, and her feet dragged. To the nervous, modest girl, whose shy spirit all the might and fire of love had scarcely endowed with bravery enough to keep her bold in secret meetings with her own husband—whose coming to him was always a sweet scamper to his heart, and breathless concealment there until blushes waned under kisses, and courage rose to whispers— thoughts of an interview with the haughty little doctor, whose fiery prejudice had earned him hate and fame among the sect she belonged to—who had held her own Cuthbert in awe, and was always named by him with fear—was terrifying indeed.

But then, what would become of her if she had not spirit to push her quest into the presence of the one man who could, if he chose (as she believed), give her more information concerning her husband than all the rest of the town put together? Bravely she stepped forward under a supporting impulse, and walked firmly to the door of the house.

The servant who answered the summons happened to be a Greystone woman, and knew Jenny well by sight. Much surprised she looked to behold the daughter following the father so quickly, for the deacon had not left the house five minutes when Jenny arrived.

"Can I see Dr. Shaw?"

"Yes, miss, I think so," replied the servant, taking it for granted that Jenny knew her father had just called. "Will you walk in, please?"

Less impatient than Strangfield, Jenny waited until the woman came out of the study to request her to enter; and then, desperately gathering together her energies, she went into the room. Now, Dr. Shaw was at this moment vehemently pacing the study, and revolving, with mingled emotions of horror, doubt, and rage, the communication Strangfield had made to him. Five minutes is no time for such spirits as his to grow calm in; and, with a desperate frown upon his forehead, he was muttering eagerly to himself, and in a quite audible key, when Jenny was announced.

"Show her in!" he exclaimed, astounded, and rooted himself against the table, confounded by this utterly unexpected and entirely new condition of the trouble that had come upon him.

The strange, pale beauty of Jenny's face, and the hint of pride and the sorrowful dignity in her manner which were there, through her hard and violent effort after courage, made the old man stare at her with unaffected surprise. Then, with an elaborate old-fashioned bow, he saluted her, and, coming round the table, placed a chair.

She addressed him at once in a sweet, plaintive voice, fixing her sad eyes on him.

"I have to beg your pardon for calling on you, but I am seeking my husband, whose home is here. They tell me he is gone; but I cannot believe that he would have left me without sending me a message; and, in my sorrow, whom should I come to but my husband's father?— though indeed, indeed, nothing but my misery would have made me intrude upon you."

"No intrusion, Miss—Miss Strangfield—at least, ahem! I am so much taken by surprise, madam, so little qualified at this moment to—to——"

The old gentleman smothered his incoherence with another bow, and, pulling out his snuff-box, looked shyly and frowningly upon the floor.

"It should have been Cuthbert's duty to tell you we are married. I knew he had not done so, for last night he was to have seen father and broken the news to him; but he did not come, and this morning they say he is gone. Oh, Dr. Shaw! can you tell me where he is? Do you know? Have pity on me, sir! Without him I am very, very lonely; and if he does not bear witness to what I say, I—I——"

The poor girl broke down, biting her lip to subdue her tears, lest the sight of them should anger the old. gentleman.

"I positively assure you that I am as ignorant of his whereabouts as yourself," he replied hastily, that she might not labour under a wrong impression one moment longer than he could help. "His ungrateful conduct has wounded me to the heart. All last night I sat up waiting for him, not doubting that he would return. But—may I ask you if you are aware that your father has just left me?"

She shook her head.

"He and I have been discussing the subject, and I can only trust," continued the doctor, "that, to my son's unnatural conduct to his father, he has not added a deeper, a more unpardonable, an inexpiable offence."

"I am truly his wife, sir."

"Truly! Pray forgive me. I may lay rough fingers on a wound my heart would choose they should touch tenderly. But let me ask you—when were you married to my son?" said the doctor, forcing his voice into a tone of suave composure; for emotion could not be permitted to qualify his dear delight in asserting his elegance and breeding.

"Three weeks ago," replied Jenny, anxiously, with her heart beating painfully; for she feared the next question.

"He was in London three weeks ago. He went for a little holiday, as at that time I suspected his depression, or absent fits, were owing to the monotony of our scholastic discipline. Were you in London then?"

"No, sir; I was at Sydenham, stopping with my aunt Rachel. I met Cuthbert, by appointment, on a Wednesday morning at the bottom of a hill on the road to Dulwich, and there we took the coach that passed; and afterwards, when we reached London, he put me into a hackney-coach, and we drove to a church where we were married."

The doctor applied a pocket-handkerchief to his forehead.

"A strange rascal!" he muttered to himself. "I had never given him credit for so much duplicity." And then he sighed and looked through the window, and, recollecting himself, forced his voice into suavity once more, and said—

"I represented to your father that nothing could be easier than to prove your marriage. If—as I do not doubt," with a bland wave of the hand, "you are my son's wife, I—I scarcely know whether there be cause to offer you my congratulations. Since he has played his father a vile trick, there is nothing to hinder him from deceiving you. But each to his kind: you to your father, to whom you are accountable, and my son to me—when he chooses to return."

His whole manner had changed with these words, and he addressed her with an icy hauteur of gaze.

Jenny looked at him fixedly for some moments, with a wonderful gaze of mingled consternation and disdain, and rose.

"I did not come here in expectation of finding sympathy or kindness," she exclaimed, with a bitterness that took a keener acidulation from the very beauty that should properly have failed to warrant it. "You know whose daughter I am; and what you think of my father Cuthbert has often told me. I have called to know if you can give me tidings of my husband. Doubt my honour as you please, sir; but, in God's name, answer me my question."

"I have answered that question," he replied. "Many of the elder boys of the school and several men were despatched by me this morning to search the shore and the neighbourhood; and likewise are inquiries still being made in places beyond Greystone. If I obtain information, be sure that I shall cause it speedily to be conveyed to you. Should he ever return," he continued, in slightly deepened tones, "this trouble he has brought upon you is an account to be settled between him, and me, with an adjusting he will not relish."

She was standing near the door, and he was raising his hand to pull the bell; but she had not done with him yet. The change in his

manner from blandness to hauteur, from a
kind of tenderness, at least, to a demeanour of
blank indifference to her sorrow, deepened
her doubt of his sincerity. A simple, country
girl, reared by plain, outspoken parents, and
habituated to the blunt expression of a com-
munity whose business was to ponder the
path of their feet, and whose boast was that
their eyelids looked straight before them, she
had no cultivation to take at its worth the
glaze of breeding with which men like Dr.
Shaw overspread their manners, however
excited by emotion; and, failing to find in this
old man any such sorrowing after his son as
should prove him honest to her own mourning
heart, a feverish suspicion that he was
holding back the truth seized her.

"You can tell me, sir, that he has not left me
for good! Say some little word to give me hope!
For *his* sake, Dr. Shaw—he loves me truly!"
she cried, with her hands clasped.

The doctor was affronted by her doubt of
him, for it was plain in her recurrent appeal.

"I have answered that I am as ignorant as
you—perhaps more ignorant," he said,
frowning at her.

"Last night," she continued, too bitterly
yearning after hope to be abashed by his
manner, or even to heed the cruel

suggestiveness of his words, "he was to have seen father. This he promised, and I was to watch for him at my window. Oh, sir, he would not have bid me wait for him had he meant to deceive me; for, indeed, he loves me fondly. A gentleman from this school, who called on mother this morning, said that he had seen him leave your house in the evening; and to father he was coming—oh, be sure! Who stopped him, then? Was he followed and set upon? If he had died, or by an accident been killed, his body would have been found. Do you know where he is? Tell me, sir! The Lord God, who hears me declare it, judges me; and before Him I swear thy son was my husband!"

Now, but for the continued and affronting suspicion informing the girl's words, this piteous appeal, taking tragic pathos from wild dry eyes and outstretched hands and shrill intensity of tone, must have roused the doctor though his heart of flesh had been as hard as a pet prejudice. But he was so extremely mortified to find his word—*his* word, too!—doubted by this wench, that anger came down on all kindly stirrings with a weight of lead, and false perceptions pricked him. For who was this woman but pig-headed Strangfield's daughter? And might not all this pother be a mere trick of the enemy—a plot, speedily hatched out of Cuthbert's strange disappearance, to mortify the dignified, cultured, well-bred foe of Dissent, and champion of orthodoxy and divine rights?

He rang the bell.

"A direct answer has been given you," he said, "and you must excuse me for declining to continue this conversation. I trust, madam, for your own sake, that you will be able to establish the fact of your honourable connection with my son."

And, with dislike and contempt on his face, he made her a short bow. Without another word she passed through the door which the servant held open, and left the house.

CHAPTER III

HOME AGAIN

"That which is crooked cannot be made straight: and that
which is wanting cannot be numbered."—*Eccles.* i. 15

SHE walked slowly down the hot and dusty
road towards the town. Now, far more keenly
than before her visit to the school-house, did
she feel the bitterness of her trouble. The
sense of her loneliness was intolerable. She,
whose beauty had always won love for her,
whose gentle life no frown had ever darkened,
who was dear to all who knew her for the
sweet goodness and soft charms of her
character, had, in the space of a single
morning, been rudely repulsed by her father,
whose severity was never before hard to her;
had brought tears from her mild mother's eyes
and reproaches from her lips, and challenged
disdain and doubt from the father of the man

who was dearest of all earthly things to her divine and helpless innocence.

What had been her sin? That, loving well, she had confided wholly, betraying naught but her candour, which her father should have been merciful to, seeing that what was deceit to him, was the expression of beautiful allegiance to her husband.

Along the dusty road she went—the high crops motionless on either hand, the land around (in sheen of silver barley and yellow wheat, and the lustrous green of meadow-grass) trembling in the steam of the sweltering earth—and felt a homeless woman, unloved, and sinful too.

She came at last to the shadow of the wayside trees under which she had met Cuthbert; and here, with no eye to see her, and passionate memories crowding piteous misery into her aching heart, she stopped and flung herself upon the grass, and tried to relieve her burning eyes with tears.

A long while she lingered here, dreading to return home. Strange it was to behold her looking up and down the road and quickly around, as though she waited for some one who should now be with her. Then she cried to herself, "Be calm! be calm! think of thy dear one's words, and put them together with what thou hast this day heard, and strive to know where he is and why he has gone, and if he will return." So, knitting her brow, and clasping her hands upon her knees, and bending downwards her tender, troubled eyes, she essayed to reason as a lawyer might. But to the poor heart the mystery of her bereavement was as a blank piece of paper, and all her hard thinking could make her sure of nothing else than that she was very lonely and helpless.

Time passed rapidly and unheeded, and the shadows of the trees had grown well into the road when she rose to her feet, disturbed by the town clock striking the half-hour after three. The thought of meeting her father was almost unbearable; yet home she must go, for where was other shelter for her? Before this time her fear of the deacon was in his anger, when he should learn that she had deceived him by her secret marriage. Nothing more had her innocence then to dread; though enough had been here to furnish her with dismal contemplation and trembling apprehension, and an insupportable yearning for the permanent companionship of her husband, that discovery might never catch her without the prop of his love and presence at hand for her weakness. But now her husband was gone, and, by going, had left her exposed to dreadful suspicion. He was gone, and she was left alone to justify her purity, to encounter the wrath of her father, stirred to his deepest heart by infamous doubt.

What, then, was she to do? for when she fell to consider how she should prove her marriage, she found another blank as maddeningly perplexing as Cuthbert's disappearance.

She well remembered the marriage-morn: how, with a faint voice and pale face, she told aunt Rachel she was going for a walk, and bade her not be surprised if she delayed her return, for she loved the pretty scenery around, and to linger among the trees.

She well remembered the beating of her heart when, at the bottom of a deep and shady lane, she beheld Cuthbert waiting for her, and how she had nearly swooned when he hailed the passing coach to Southwark, and handed her into it.

Likewise she well remembered how they had emerged into a crowded street, along which he had hurried her into another street, where he called a hackney-carriage, and they were driven down interminable streets at which she never glanced, for her white face was hidden on Cuthbert's shoulder, and she had needed all the cordial of his constant, passionate, reassuring whispers to save her from fainting.

And how at last the carriage stopped before a church—a gloomy, heavy City edifice—so that it seemed to her they had to grope their way along the avenue of high pews to the altar-railing, where speedily a thin voice read the service that made her the wife of the man at her side.

The acted portion of it all was a vague memory; her love for the man who had induced her to secretly wed him was only reality.

Four o'clock was chiming when she reached home. Long before this had Mrs. Strangfield grown weary of watching at the window, and with deep anxiety had gone to seek the girl in the town. Polly was singing in the kitchen as she scrubbed the floor, so that Mr. Strangfield in the parlour did not hear Jenny enter, nor her light footstep as she went upstairs.

At her bedroom door she halted, with such a shock of surprise and consternation as the sight of a dead man might have produced on her; for all about the window the floor was littered with her husband's sacred letters, heedlessly tossed and lying open, with their riband-bindings among them.

She well knew whose hand had done this; and, recovering herself, entered the room, closed the door, and removed her hat, moving softly, and all the while looking at the letters.

This done, she knelt down and gathered together the precious missives, pressing them often to her pale lips, and narrowly inspecting the carpet for bits of the dry forget-me-nots and other fragments of flowers which had fallen from the letters under Strangfield's angry handling of them.

Scarcely had she replaced the papers in her desk when she heard her father's steps on the stairs. He entered his bedroom, but speedily emerged, being struck, perhaps, to find Jenny's door closed.

He turned the handle sharply, and exclaimed—

"Ah, you be here, then! Your mother has gone to look for you. You are well practised in treading softly. Where have you been?"

"I have been to the school-house to seek my husband," she answered, returning his stern gaze with a look of despairing resolution.

"And you have not found him?"

"No, father, no!" she replied, with a shriek in her voice.

"If he be your husband, why has he left you?" he said, speaking as a judge might in preface to condemning a man to death.

She shook her head and locked her twitching fingers, no longer meeting his eyes, for the bitterness in them was insupportable.

He approached the bed and leaned heavily upon the frame of it.

"Woman! in my heart you are condemned for treachery to me and your mother. Yet I have said to myself, in the words of the Preacher, 'Be not hasty in thy spirit to be angry!' and now, if you find me so, you shall rebuke me. Jenny, for what you have this day told your mother, I hate my own flesh that you should be a part of it. Yet I will be merciful. You shall prove to me that your sin is not the dishonour of your parents' name, nor the destruction of your soul in the eyes of Almighty God. Do you heed me? You shall prove this."

She made no answer.

"Speak!" he cried. "Show me how this may be done."

She looked at him with terrified eyes, for no courage that she had could combat her instinctive fear of him. He waited for her reply.

"Tell me what I am to do, father; indeed I will obey you. I am truly his wife. God, who hears me, knows that I am not speaking falsely. With this ring he wedded me, father."

And with trembling hand she sought in her pocket for her purse.

"Nay, nay, I have no wish to see it. Such a matter signifies nothing. Better tricks than such tokens cannot fool old eyes. Tell me where you were married."

"In London, father."

"Ay, in London. At what church?"

"I do not know the name; it has slipped my memory. Or my husband never mentioned it," she replied, with an expression on her face that should have told her father to press her no further.

"By whom were you married?"

"I did not see—I was frightened. The church was dark, and I did not lift my eyes, and we were but a moment signing our names."

A look of savage incredulity—the scepticism of a man stirred to the most hidden and deadly forces of his nature —shot into his face. He gazed at her for some moments in silence, and then, in a voice that, for the hollowness of it, sounded as though it rose from under his feet, said—

"It is as I before said—you remember nothing. But their wedding is a thing all women remember; and it is strange you should so soon forget yours, when your mother will tell you everything that befell on her wedding-day, twenty-three years ago. Would you know the church if you saw it?"

"Yes, father, I—I think so—I do not know, father."

"To-morrow you and I will go to London," said he. "Make up a little box of things, for this business may keep us. In the morning, at seven, we start. Be in readiness!"

Without another word he left the room.

She leaned against the wall near the window, and her heavy eyelashes drooped over the sorrowful beauty of her eyes. So standing, and with her graceful profile taking a delicate transparency from the light shining through the window, and the soft fulness of her perfect form ripely figured on the white ground of paper that supported her, never more lovely had she looked; and the shimmer of her yellow hair was as the trembling of evening sunshine upon water.

Deep grief is always quiescent, and the deepest grief was shrined in this gentle woman. That she was not guiltless only made her sorrow the more moving. She had erred in deceiving father and mother, in privily and without home's blessing undertaking the sacred obligation of marriage. Yet how hardly was she dealt with! how cruel the interpretation of a deed of faithful love! And why had Cuthbert left her? How bitterly hard that any act of *his* should be beyond the skill of her heart to construe! Yet her glorious fidelity could not hold him faithless. All the reasoning of her brain was but a cobweb under the sweeping hand of instinct. Living or dead, he was her husband, and loved by her as never man deserved; and that he did not come to her was fate's cruelty only, and for him her heart held no reproach.

In this wise thinking, with an impulsive movement she drew forth her purse and slipped her wedding-ring on; kissed it wildly, and, with a quick toss of her hands, fell with her face upon the bed, weeping bitterly.

This posture was she in when her mother entered the room. The poor woman ran to her quickly.

"You have come back, my darling? Where hast thou been all this long time? Jenny, do not cry so—my heart will break if you grieve in this way. Has father been saying unkind things to thee, my pretty? Come, come, it is not all hopeless yet. Truly I believe that Mr. Shaw is thy husband; and be sure, be sure he will return, for no man with his beauty is heartless, and he would not have married thee, Jenny, to leave thee in this way!"

She raised the girl from the bed and led her to a chair, and, kneeling by her, pillowed her head on her bosom.

"Oh, mother, is it not too cruel that I should lose my husband and be doubted by father? To-morrow he means to take me to London to show him the church; for he will not believe me without dragging me a weary journey. And God knows what I shall do when we reach London, for I do not remember the name of the church, nor the street where it stands, and I have told him I was too scared to take notice. And would not a young girl like me be frightened, mother, in that great place, and acting wrongly, although I was with my darling?"

"To-morrow does he take you to London! Oh, what a strange, hard man! Why, all day you will be travelling; and cannot he see that you have no strength!" cried Mrs. Strangfield, rising from her knees; and, with a hot, indignant look, she swept out of the room and went to her husband, whom she found in the act of quitting the house.

"Michael, I must speak to thee. What are you going to do with Jenny? If you break her heart you will kill us both, and that indeed you are doing!" she cried shrilly.

With his hand on the latch of the house door, he stared at her with contemptuous sternness; then with a stride made for the parlour, and closed the door upon them both.

"Jane, subdue your voice, and speak to me respectfully. You are the girl's mother, and I will listen to you; but I am her father, and mine is the name she has blasted. Do you heed that? It is Michael Strangfield's daughter whom the people are talking about. Remember this, and now say your mind."

"For shame! for shame! to speak of her as having blasted your name!" replied Mrs. Strangfield, quite unable to control her voice. "Hath she not told you that Mr. Shaw is her husband? The wedding-ring is now on her finger—as good a ring as this—and if she be not an honourable wife, then my name is my father's. What! you would take the poor heart to London, when she declares that in her fright she took no notice of the street and church! Would not a stout spirit be scared by what she did, with thee, as her father, to terrify her conscience? Why, myself, when you are hazing me with your strong voice, lose my head and know not what I am about. And shall our little wench have stronger brains than her mother—at a time, too, which makes the best of women tremble and keep their eyes down in modesty and awe, though their parents are with them and kind friends to give them heart for the journey? For shame, to doubt her! What think you is her sin? Great Lord! that a religious man should have no charity for his only child! Would you break her heart for the sake of your neighbours? Yes, yes! I believe thee wouldst! But what will killing her with cruelty do for thee? It will leave thee a lonesome man, scorned by all good fathers, for that you showed your pretty one no mercy, and denied her love and compassion when her heart was sore, and she had no power to prove her innocence!"

"Understand this!" he shouted with fury, and his eyes in a blaze; "if she says that she knows not the church wherein she was married, nor can show it me, nor the book wherein their names should be written, nor the man that married them, and hath no more evidence than a ring which a crown-piece will buy for any harlot, I'll know her for what she is—and no tears from her, nor insolence from thee, shall change me!"

She held out her hands in the attitude of one fending off an attack.

"Never could I have believed it of thee, Michael!" she said, in a voice of indescribable reproach, and turned to leave him.

"Stay!" he commanded, "Before you go, give me your reason for opposing me."

Too insulted by his words about her child to confront him, she replied, "She has not the strength to travel to London; and why would you take her there? She tells thee plainly she will not know the church, though she see it, and its name was never mentioned to her by Mr. Shaw."

"You believe her!" he said, with deep-toned sarcasm.

"As I believe in the Lord!" cried the mother, eagerly turning her swimming eyes upon him.

"You shall credit her if you please but your faith in her innocence does not purify her. Give me proof of her honesty, and, though I scorn her for her deceit, yet you shall see me use her gently. Am I to stand still under this shame that has come upon me and mine, and make no effort to clear it away, that our light may shine again before men! She does not lack strength to seek her husband, and since noon has she been wandering in the heat.

Though we had to travel a thousand miles for proof of her honour, would the journey be too long? Let God forgive her for sending me in my old age from my home, to clear her name of foul suspicion—if it can be done! Go now and repeat my words to her, and let her be in readiness to start with me at the hour I named. No more!" he cried, with a stamp of the foot, holding up his hand. "Too much have you already said. Bid her keep to her room, for I'll not meet her this day."

And passing his wife, he flung open the door, and left the house.

"The Lord have mercy upon him, and forgive him his sins!" moaned poor Mrs. Strangfield to herself.

Not immediately could she return to Jenny. She had bargained on controlling her husband, by her appeal, from taking the girl to London; and, being defeated, wanted time to recover her heart to meet the poor child. Her husband's austerity was, indeed, an old knowledge of hers, and his violent prejudices and the inhuman hatred of wrongdoing that shuts the gates of mercy on the fallen. Was it not Dr. Shaw who had described him as one of a class of men who, professing to loathe the emotional pageantries of the Papists, and the smaller displays of the Established Church, were, nevertheless, those who had kept alive, to a period within living memory, the monstrous superstition of witchcraft, and hanged old women on the evidence of crazy wenches—who had made of Dissent a bitter fountain, to drown out of the Christianity of the land all charity; denying to others the liberty they themselves took, and stretched into trespass; degrading human nature by a sombre scepticism of human goodness; and squeezing the large and lovely religion of Christ into a narrow funnel for their own and sole decanting into salvation?

Mrs. Strangfield had read the printed lecture with such mute remonstrances and ineffectual plungings of wrath, as an honest wife should feel when her husband is heavily dealt with; but now, as she stood pondering over Michael's cruel theory of his girl and his unfatherly severity, and harsh resolution to purge himself of dishonour in his neighbours' eyes, if he broke Jenny's heart for it, she could not help recalling Dr. Shaw's lecture, and thinking that the schoolmaster had a tolerable idea of what he was speaking about, after all. She heaved a deep sigh, and wiped her moist forehead. Was religion, she wondered, given to us that we might always carry grave faces, always be quoting Holy Writ, always rebuking mirth; that we should have no forgiveness for sin, and no mercy for error which is not sin, and no tenderness for the child that had stepped out of the hard dry road of life to pluck one of the few flowers that bloom on the wayside, but must not be gathered without our leave? She was a good Christian herself, punctual in her devotions, versed in Holy Scripture, and leading a blameless life; yet sometimes, God forgive her! had she owned to her secret heart, that if she had her time over again she would not marry Michael Strangfield.

Jonathan Grouse the barber, whom Michael called a sinner, and wholly damned, loved his children, nevertheless; and when his eldest girl Susan was betrayed by a marine, he wept over her and took her to his heart, and spent a month's earnings to hire a coach to drive her to the church, when he got her honestly married.

Well, the Lord forbid that she shouldn't think right, if she thought at all; and if Michael was only a little softer, all would be middling well with her—perhaps. But to think of poor Jenny upstairs—whose only sin was that she had married a gentleman's son slyly,—driven to it by father's hate of Dr. Shaw, which was a most irreligious sentiment to begin with—abused and wrongly suspected, and now to be dragged away to London!

She must have a good cry before she went to her; and cry she did, heartily, thinking all the while of the proud position she might hold as Cuthbert's mother-in-law—the envy of all tattlers—if Michael would only take things quietly and leave her to manage a bit.

CHAPTER IV

A BITTER RESOLVE

"Twin-souled she seemed, a two-fold nature wearing,

Sometimes a flashing falcon in her daring,

Then a poor mateless dove that droops despairing."

O. W. HOLMES

NIGHT is the bitterest time for sorrow. Something there always is in the day—in the activity of cloudy sunshine, or the waving of trees, or the going to and fro of men and women, and the sound of their voices—to pluck grief as it were by the sleeve, and compel it from fixed contemplation. But the stillness of night gives subtlety to thought, and quickens the madness which despair truly is: for what are the stars but funeral lamps in the eyes of the mourner, and each passing wail of wind a voice of the eerie sympathy that cheers not?

All the evening Jenny had remained in her room, and had but now, at this hour of ten, which was even tolling, said good night to her mother, parting with her after a long and close embrace, and with a prayer that God would bless her for her love. Then did she lock her door, and sit and listen; and presently heard both father and mother come to their bedroom, and the murmur of their voices.

In those old times there used to be in fashion a little travelling-box, light to carry, with a strap across the lid that the arm might sling it, and much used by country folk; so that when in London a girl was seen equipped with one of them, she was immediately set down as a wench from the provinces, and Lysimachus's thoughts fell busy.

One of these boxes stood on the floor, and the packing of it, with many a long halt for a sobbing fit, and active protest and hopeful reassurance, had been Mrs. Strangfield's occupation for a part of the evening. Presently rising, Jenny went to the box and tried its weight. Light enough it was with a single change of apparel only; yet she took a turn with it about the room (treading on tiptoe), as if to make sure that it was not a burden above her strength.

She was restless, and could not remain quiet. Now she would draw out her purse and count the money that it held; now she would approach the glass and gaze at the spectral, mournful beauty of her white face; anon, and with no more sound than a mouse creeping, she would pace the room; until the fever in her waned, and the passionate spurring of thought ceased to lacerate and drive. Whereupon she extinguished the light, and took a place at the window, and surrendered herself to contemplation of the stars.

Manifestly she meant to take no rest that night, or was very long in going to it. Her window overlooked the High Street and the dark shadow of the market-place. The moon was crawling out of the sea at the back, and casting its sickly yellow film upon the highest points of the cliff, and the oil-lamps of the town burned steadily up the slope, till the abrupt gloom of unlighted houses and the land about was a space of black between them and the stars.

Perfect stillness there never is at the seaside; there is always moaning on the beach, and a delicate seething among the motionless folds of the air. Yet there was very nearly a perfect stillness now: no tramp of foot in the street, no distant rattle of wheel on country road. In those old times, Greystone went to bed early, and, like a man without care, fell asleep at once.

One would have had no need for sharp eyes, to look at Jenny's face and know her as a girl on the eve of some wild business. To-morrow morning was she to be carried a long and sorrowful journey by her father; and when in London, from church to church they were to wander; and all the while her heart was to burn in the fire of his wrath, and her sacred purity to be blackened by his thoughts of it. A whole week, and more days yet, might pass in the search, and every disappointment would be an extra weight to strain the tension that must end in breaking her heart. Her ignorance of matters which, had she but foreseen all this, would have been easy to learn and remember, was so deep, that even her mother had groaned over her that evening. The very neighbourhood wherein Cuthbert had hired lodgings during his holiday in London she did not know; she had never had occasion to write to him. He had come to Sydenham and met her by an appointment planned before they left Greystone; and all their arrangements were verbally concerted, with never a hitch of weather to disappoint them, and that was why no letters had passed.

So, then, the London parish in whose church they were united was unknown to her. No light could she give, beyond taking God's holy name in witness that she spoke the truth, which only her mother believed.

But the uselessness of the journey, and the fear of her father's anger if failure should attend their search, were not the first causes of her present resolution. Pride wounded to death, an exquisite sensibility torn and bleeding, a high and noble innocence scarlet under contumely, and mad to veil its injuries in a place where she should be unknown; the trembling womanly fear of the poisoned tongue of gossip, and the despairing sense that the home in which she was born could not contain her whilst her father's frown condemned her as a criminal, and his bitter face showed him poisoned by the moral atmosphere which he mercilessly believed she exhaled around—these were the main determining influences.

That night, she resolved, would be the last she should ever pass in the old wooden house. Call her mad if you please—and few such desperate resolves but have madness at bottom; but there was courage too, a virtuous audacity, and of a most womanly sort, acting without reflection; that is, influenced by the present that was driving her, and taking no thought of the future upon which she was rushing.

The church clock was striking the half-hour after eleven, when with a shiver she rose from her chair at the open window, and, stealing to the bedroom door, opened it noiselessly, and listened. The deep breathing in the adjacent apartment where her parents lay, the fall of an ember in the kitchen grate, the loud ticking of a clock, were the only sounds audible.

Leaving the door ajar, she put on her hat, to which a veil was attached, threw a shawl over her shoulders, and raised the little trunk. There was clear moonlight abroad now, and light enough reflected to give distinctness to all objects in the room. On tiptoe she descended the staircase, and, the better to make her exit soundless, went through the kitchen. There was moonlight shining through the dusty scullery window, and an old cat lying on the kitchen table mewed tremulously as she passed. This plaintive cry, rising out of the dead silence, smote her nerves wildly. With shuddering fingers she touched the animal's head, and then could she have broken forth into wild weeping. In a few moments she had lightly drawn the bolts of the back door, and stood in the moonlight.

The night was soft and sweet with dew, and the mild stars shone lustrously. Now was it that the cool air, and the deserted length of the High Street, and the black shadows of the soaring town, brought to her an unutterable sense of homelessness, and the chill and terror of the lonesome state. She came round to the front of the house and under the gloom of the bay tree, paused and reflected, not daring to lift her eye to her parents' bedroom window.

A rough programme of her actions had she formed, and when in her room had felt she had endurance enough to compass it fully. But the long and lonely night-walk meditated seemed now beyond her strength, although she was sustained by a wonderful spirit, and, in the heat of the fever in her blood, and the despairing passion of dread which the shame and horror of her father's suspicion had excited, was capable of effort that should seem independent of mere physical force.

Suddenly she heard the tramp of a man's heavy step, and the figure of one of the four watchmen who guarded the little town (chiefly in armchairs, and asleep over tobacco-pipes), holding a lantern which flitted in his grasp and illuminated his long grey coat and the folds of his cap, stalked solemnly out of the shadow of the market-place through the moonlight in the High Street, and passed away, raising a melancholy cry in his passage for the edification of all listening night-caps.

She crept softly out of the darkness, and crossed the road and went up the street, hugging the shadow of the houses. When abreast of the market-place, again was she seized with a numbing sense of helplessness, and a great agony of spirit. The sympathy of a human voice—some one to tell her story to and take advice from, she wanted; and, perhaps, the very last person whom it would have entered her head to apply to under any other circumstances, she now resolved to seek.

This was Mrs. Mead, who had shown her some kindness that morning, and the sort of sympathy that was not likely to thwart if it did not profit her.

So she flitted like some restless spirit through empty stalls and vacant, silent gloom, and hesitating a moment before Mrs. Mead's door, knocked lightly.

Although there was no light in Mrs. Mead's window, the old woman was not asleep, having not two minutes before Jenny's arrival extinguished her tallow candle and got into bed. The truth was, that at nine o'clock that evening had come Mrs. Basings, her niece, moaning over her husband's loss; and, to comfort her, Mrs. Mead had gone to the expense of a half-pint of gin, over which the two ladies had sat until after eleven. Hearing a sound that resembled a knock on the door, the old woman lifted her ear out of the pillow and listened, questioning whether it was Mrs. Basings who had returned or the tailor overhead, who had an evil trick of pacing his room when he should be asleep. After a little interval the knock was repeated, and there being no mistake about the noise this time, Mrs. Mead, greatly wondering, darted her withered legs out of bed, struck a light, swathed her old form in the counter-pane, which she plucked from the bed, went to the door and opened it, holding the candle over her head.

To an eye unprepared for such a spectacle, a more terrifying object of ugliness than this old woman could scarcely have presented itself; the coverlid gave her the look of a corpse in a winding-sheet, and the twisting shadows thrown upon her face by the flare of the candle-flame in the draught of the narrow passage struck a most unearthly vitality into her features.

She instantly recognized Jenny, and uttered a cry of astonishment.

"Michael Strangfield's girl! At this time o' night! Seekin' of me, too! Lord, Lord! what is the matter?"

"Let me come in and speak to you, Mrs. Mead," said the girl in a hollow whisper. "I am leaving father and mother for good, but have no strength to walk all the way to Winston without a living voice to give me a word of comfort and advise me."

"To Winston! This time o' night! But come in, come in!" cried the old woman, lowering her voice with involuntary relish of this new mystery that had come to her very door, and looking backwards at the staircase to make sure the tailor was not listening. And, in her hospitable and inquisitive eagerness, she put out her hand to draw Jenny by the arm, whereby she let go of the coverlid and down it tumbled on the floor, and left the old thing staring like Philosopher Square in Molly's attic.

But this was a mishap easily remedied. She was soon decent again, and promptly closed the door.

"Leaving father and mother for good!" said she, leading Jenny to a chair, and pushing the candle close to her that she might see her face. "Whativer are you doing that for?"

"Because father suspects me of speaking falsely," answered Jenny; "and I cannot bide with him to be thought sinful, and spurned at by the people."

"And for that you are leaving home!" exclaimed the old woman, who showed no symptom of sleepiness. "And you are going to Winston? What to do there, Miss Jenny?"

"My cousin, Bridget Lloyd, lives at Marples; and the coach passes Winston at eight in the morning. To Marples I am going, to ask Bridget to give me shelter until I can find my living."

"Well, indeed! And do ye mean to walk five mile to-night? Why, ye says t' coach doth not pass before eight, and where will ye stay till it comes?"

"I have not thought," answered Jenny with a heavy sigh. "But I will not stop in Greystone to be mocked. Oh, Mrs. Mead! to-morrow morning father would take me to London to show him the church where I was married, and this I cannot do. What then will he think? But it is not only because I cannot prove myself my dearest one's wife that I am leaving home. Because father thinks me a wicked sinner and a liar I am running away, and because all the town who have not a father's heart for me will think worse things of Jenny. Oh, may God lend me wisdom to know the right thing to do, and forgive me the sorrow I this night cause my mother!"

She bit her lip cruelly to restrain her tears, for she feared the sight of them would move Mrs. Mead to hinder her desperate resolution.

"Before you move a step, or say another word, ye shall have something to mend your spirits with," said the old woman, briskly, and entered her bedroom, whence in a few moments she returned, with a gown and shawl on, and, going to a cupboard, produced a little flask of cherry cordial, of which she obliged Jenny to swallow a glassful.

"It is a strange thing for you to do," said she, resuming her chair, and twisting her scant grey tresses into a knot at the back of her head. "Doth your cousin, Mrs. Lloyd, know you are coming to her?"

"No," Jenny answered. "I did not make up my mind to leave home till father told me to get ready to quit for London with him in the morning. I should fear to be with him if we could not find the church. If he does not think me truthful, then I am a sinner to him, and not fit for his house; and that is why I am leaving him for ever!"

Her eyes flashed as she spoke, and the hard look of her mouth might have reminded Mrs. Mead of the deacon at his sternest. But the anger melted away, and she cried piteously, "You will tell my poor mother that you have seen me, and why I have left her? Father's harshness to me is breaking her heart, and what will she do when she finds her pretty one gone?" and she paused again to battle with her tears.

"Miss Jenny, if ye are wise, ye'll go home," said Mrs. Mead, nodding her head. "Why, what'll folks say, when it's known you've roon away? Sure enough they'll call ye a guilty wench, and you would not like that."

"They will call me that if I stay—why should they not, if father thinks it?—and never could I go into the street, nor meet human eyes, with this shame upon me!" she cried, despairingly.

"It's hard to know! it's hard to know!" groaned the old woman. "Would ye wish your mother to hear where you are?"

"No!" she answered quickly. "So that I am living and with friends, as you must tell her, Mrs. Mead, she will not despair. But no one must be told where I am—no one, Mrs. Mead. Promise me that! Swear it!"

"I'll swear it if you please, Mrs. Jenny," replied Mrs. Mead, sympathetically giving the girl her wifely prefix. "But before ye make me take an oath, just think awhile. If I swear, they may drown me and not get the truth. Suppose Mr. Cuthbert——"

"Ah!" exclaimed the girl, with a short, passionate cry, "if *he* should come—why, why, Mrs. Mead, you would tell him *instantly*; he would be eager and mad to find me, and I to be with him. O heavenly Lord! if Thou wouldst but give him to me now!" she cried, raising her clasped hands, whilst her voice died away into a soft, exquisitely musical plaintive note.

"I don't like this business—truly, I would rather have no hand in it," said Mrs. Mead, slowly turning her face from side to side. "Thy father would come and burn my house down if he knew I had helped you to leave the town."

"You need not help me. I will go away now, Mrs. Mead, and leave you to your rest."

"That you shall not!" cried the old woman, jumping up and laying her skinny hand on Jenny, who had risen. "Sit down, sit down, my pretty. Why, how long will it take ye to walk to Winston? Two hours, will it? And so you shall come to the village at three i' the morn, and have five hours to count the daisies in afore th' coach comes! Sit down! sit down! Ye'll not leave this house yet a bit, I'se warrant!"

"But I will be on my way before the light comes and the people are up," answered Jenny, still standing.

"So ye shall, but not afore the light comes. Sit, mistress. Lord save your heart, 'tis easier nor standing, and I for one niver can think on my feet. No-wheers like bed for thinkin', say I, and then ye're flat. Ye'll be changing your mind, I doubt, if ye'll sit and ponder."

"Do not say that, Mrs. Mead. I have already left home, and it is as bad as if I were a thousand miles off. I will not go back, indeed. Bid me good night, and be sure my heart is warm to thee for thy kindness."

"Ah!" cried Mrs. Mead, forcing her, but not untenderly, into her chair, "ye come from an obstinate father, and argiments, as I've always said, is wasted on sitch. If ye mean to go, I'll not stop you—and who should know best but you? But the job needn't be worse nor it is. I'm one," said she, going to her cupboard, as loves crature comforts. Crature comforts," she continued, producing a couple of cups and saucers, a loaf of bread, some eggs, and a strange-looking vessel of tin in which was some tea, made precious by the price of it in those days, "is a true woice of consolation to the afflicted, to my way o' thinking. Niver did I attend a buryin', or go a-nursin', or help to lay a body out, but first I laid in a meal o' food. Niver doth the mind do duty on an empty stomach. If it's but a crust o' hard bread and a spoonful o' gin, let me have it, I says, before I go to work. There's no sperrit in fasting."

And so she rattled on, in a subdued voice for fear of disturbing the tailor and his wife overhead, all the while kindling a fire, and preparing the table, and ceasing her gabble only to go and draw a kettle of water from some back place.

Jenny watched her with heavy, dreamy eyes. There was no desire for sleep in her, no feeling of weariness, no pang of abstinence, though but little food had passed her lips since the day before. An unnatural excitement sustained her, and rending emotions of pride and despair, which would have made the softest bed that ever a queen slept in a couch of iron and pain to her irritable nerves. If ever suspicion of her error in quitting home fugitively, under a burden of dreadful doubt of her purity, flitted across her mind, she knew that the step she had taken made her impulse irremediable.

With stolidity pitiful to behold in lovely eyes, and a face hard with misery, gleaming marble-like in the poor rays of the candle, she watched Mrs. Mead as she pursued her hospitable labours, listening to her quaint discourse with an inattention which was often abruptly illustrated by sudden glances at the window, upon which the night still lay black.

There was a despatch in the old woman's method of going to work, and a quiet, too, were it not for the subdued, eternal cackle of her tongue, that would have made a sick man love her. She produced another candle and brightened up the room, and presently the kettle was blowing out its filament of steam.

"Now, mistress," said she, "here be a dish of tea which all Chaney, where the herb grows, as I've heerd, couldn't match. Just a shred of bread, with this fine new butter, 'll give that egg a relish as ye'll niver cease to remember. Come, come! sin' we mun both keep awake, there's naught like tea—or tay, as my mother used to call it; and that's the right word, though in these queer times a body hath no liberty. Well, will ye not laugh over this feast some day? I reckon Mr. Shaw'll make ye see a joke in it, for I niver knew a blue eye like his that didn't mean a merry heart; and this will I say of your husband, mistress, that since the days when poor Will Hacket coorted me i' silk stockings, I've niver seen a prettier lad than Mr. Cuthbert Shaw. Crack the egg, my dear, an' if ye shall tell the inside of it from cream, I'll swallow the shell. It's middling late for supper; but as thy father once said to me fifteen year ago, when I loved a bit o' riband as has no relish now, we're all artificial cratures—which is the Lord's truth. Why shouldn't a body eat i' the middle o' the night as well as the morn? Come, come, make a beginning, or I'll not go along wi' ye."

"But I do not want you to come along with me, Mrs. Mead. Indeed, I should not allow you to leave your house after keeping you from your bed—no, truly; though I love you dearly for your kindness," exclaimed Jenny.

"Do you think I should let a pretty young woman walk alone to Winston at this time o' morn, with her box and her sweet face to court ivery smock she may come across?" cried Mrs. Mead, poising a saucer on a level with her nose, and straining her eyes at Jenny over it. "What is a summer's morning walk to me? If I can't hinder thee from leaving home, I'll see thee safe in t' coach, anyways, and that'll be something for me to tell thy mother."

The need of companionship was strong in Jenny. All the way to Winston, with a long waiting for the coach, was a weary undertaking, and what society should she have but bitter thoughts? Besides, a little touch of comfort there was in the feeling that her mother would know that no harm had befallen her, if Mrs. Mead gave the story so far as her promise of secrecy permitted. But there was that in the old woman's face which helped Jenny to prompter acceptance of the offer than otherwise her sweetness would have sanctioned. Mrs. Mead was clearly determined, and ready to quarrel, that her will should have its way. So the lonely-hearted girl, with the saddest smile on her white face, went up to the dame and thanked her with a kiss upon the ripples of her forehead; and had she been a man, a favour more delightful the old woman could not have made it seem. But oh, what a contrast when the faces were together!

Now slowly, as they sat in these small hours—outside, the solemn stillness of the night, and within, no sound but the humming of the kettle to thread the melodious complaining notes of the girl and the creaking tones of her sympathetic listener—the faint and mystical light of the new day, creeping from the infinite abysm into the towering chambers of the western heavens, stood palely on the window-glass, and little twitter of birds broke abruptly from invisible places.

Until the light had broadened, Mrs. Mead refused to heed it; and Jenny, with her back to the window, and telling the long story of her love and marriage and sorrow to her companion, did not see it. Then the girl pausing with feverish eyes, after words of bitter wonder that Cuthbert should have left her, and a wild cry that he might not be dead, Mrs. Mead held up her finger.

"Mistress," said she, "before it is too late, think well of what you are about to do. Hush! If ye were my own child I should not say more to thee."

"I have thought! I have thought!" moaned Jenny, rocking herself to and fro. "My cousin Bridget will give me a home; and she and her husband only shall know my story. But what will the talk be here, whether I stay or go? Never could I stir abroad, and at home my father could not bear to look at me. Should God send my husband back, then father will hang his head to think of the wrong he has done his girl. And thou shalt tell mother where I am. But, until Cuthbert comes, I will keep hidden. I have sworn it to myself; and if I should be forced to stay here, I would kill myself—indeed I would!"

"Well, truly!" muttered the old woman. "To see your beauty, like a kitten's, and such soft smiles as ye greet with, who'd think ye had so much spirit? I don't say ye aren't right. You're taching some folks a lesson as 'll profit 'em; and when you're righted, the people here 'll make a queen of ye—see, now! Doth not the Lord say, 'It is not meet to take the children's bread, and to cast it to dogs'? Yet his own child's bread hath your father taken, and niver are dogs wanting when there is a crust to gnaw. Turn your head now, my pretty. Do ye see it's day?"

With a sharp glance at the window, Jenny jumped from her chair.

"I must go quickly," she cried. "There will be people abroad, and if I am seen they will run to father."

"There'll be no one abroad for another hour yet—not aven the market-folk," replied Mrs. Mead. "But I'll not keep ye scared."

She fetched her shawl and bonnet from the bedroom, and whilst she put them on she said—

"There's Sally Walker, as kapes the Greyhound at Winston. I nursed her mother, and was at her funeral; and niver doth Sal come to Greystone without droppin' in to see if Mother Mead be still alive. We'll have her up, mistress, though she be snoring, and she shall give thee a couch for two hours' rest. For d'ye think you're made o' wire and parchment like me, that you can sit through a whole night without a nap? At seven there'll be summat to break thy fast wi', I'se warrant—if I kill one o' Sally's pigs myself, for the daintiness o' chitterlings. Then unto the coach ye'll get, and may the Lord send ye happiness!"

So saying, she laid hold of Jenny's box, and with muffled tread, and without speech, they both of them went into the grey morning light.

CHAPTER V

THE EMPTY BEDROOM

"In marriage blessynges are botte fewe, I trowe."

Chatterton

A LITTLE before six in the morning a ray of bright warm sunshine, like a golden wand projected from the window, having crept gradually along the wall, smote Mr. Strangfield between the eyes as he lay asleep in his bed, and awoke him.

Looking upon his watch, which hung at the side of the bed, he rose, without disturbing his wife from the deep sleep into which she had fallen scarce an hour before, after long and weary wakefulness. The weight on his heart and the languor in his limbs he knew how to account for by remembering what had happened yesterday, and what he had felt;

but never before this morning had old age, or rather the sereness that comes before the branch lies naked against the sky, made itself so sensibly apprehensible as an influence of weariness.

Not without pity which, even, should not find the lines of stubbornness repellant, would one have beheld the worn, handsome face: there was an ashen greyness over it that developed the care and the pain and the age, as the photographer's chemical calls forth the picture on the plate; the white in his hair looked plentiful, and the bristles on his chin were white, and the lustre of his eyes faint. One might have said that he had aged ten years since the morning before; but then, to be sure, men who are growing grey never look greyer than when they leave their beds.

He had almost finished dressing himself when his wife awoke, and, after the first bewilderment, asked him the time.

"There is an hour before the coach starts," he said. "See about getting the breakfast ready. I shall be in the yard until the half-hour; and get you to Jenny, that she may not keep me waiting."

Saying which he left the room, wearing his yesterday's bitter face, which had come to him with the first words of his wife,

No sooner was he gone than Mrs. Strangfield quitted her bed, and went to the door to call Jenny. The room used by the girl was to the right of the room occupied by the husband and wife; the door of it stood open, and that was something to wonder at if Jenny were not downstairs. Into the room walked the mother, and all she saw was a bed that had never been slept in.

Now for some moments this was a sight with a significance not to be realized.

She went to the bedside and stared at it, and then round her, with a slow slipping of her head on her neck, like a ball on a pivot. Presently on the bed again she fixed her eyes, with all the blankness of the frost-white counterpane reflected in them.

"What trick is she playing me?" she cried to herself, but in a clear, strong voice. "Jenny!"

And all about the room she went, probing and peering like a faithful dog sniffing for its hidden young. Until it came into her head that her child had run away; on which she fled from the room with a shriek.

That shriek brought forth the trollop Polly, who beheld her mistress clinging to the top rail of the banister, motioning with her hand.

"Lor, missus, what is it? For mussy's sake, mum, don't look so scarifying, mum! Oh, missus, what ha' yees seen?"

"Tell your master to come to me," exclaimed Mrs. Strangfield, in a choking voice, and she went reeling into her bedroom, and sank upon a chair. But up again she must jump in a moment, and run into Jenny's room, and in the centre of it she stood looking around her with rolling eyes. She was too frightened for deliberate search—even a direct clue she would not have heeded. With both hands pressed upon her heart she stood. Was it that the sorrowful girl, mourning her cruel bereavement, and the dishonour done her by her father, and dreading the journey, and the object of the journey that morning, had not chosen to rest; that all night long she had kept her vigil, and now was gone forth to cool her burning eyes against the soft wind blowing from the sea? Was it so? Ah, pray God! And the mother, with moving lips, drew to the window, and sent her startled gaze over the summer scene of swelling cliff, and folds of houses standing with shine of gold under the meek sweetness of the morning blue.

Mr. Strangfield came upstairs, and from the landing called to her. She ran to him, crying, "Michael, see here! Our child hath not slept in her bed! Where is she, do you think? Oh, if you love your wife, run to your men and bid them seek her. For God's sake do this, Michael,— *now!*"

He went past her without answer and entered Jenny's room. If amazement or pain were in him, it was veiled by a heavy frown.

"Silence!" he cried, as his wife began to speak. "Before we judge her, let us know what she has done. It is no sign that she has run away from us because she has not slept in her bed. Has she not acted more crazily than to stay awake in her clothes all night? Look about you and tell me what things you find missing."

"Nothing, Michael. Oh, my heart, yes! Where be the little trunk I packed for her last night?"

With wonderful quickness she flung open the door of a closet, and then searched beneath the bed. Next she uttered a sharp cry, and leaned against her husband. He led her not untenderly to her room, but his own steps were weak and shaky, and his face as white as a dying man's, which made his frown a black shadow upon his forehead.

"We must have patience yet," he exclaimed, drawing forth his watch, and speaking with his eyes bent down upon it. "She knows at what hour the coach starts, and if she be not guilty she will be here. Get thyself dressed, and let the breakfast be ready by the half-hour. She may return, and then what will it be that her box is gone? Bear up, for in half an hour great changes come. I will wait for thee and her in the parlour."

He went slowly and painfully downstairs, and stood at the window whispering to himself, which was a strange trick for an obstinate, hard-headed man to fall into on a sudden.

In a short while Mrs. Strangfield came from her room, and stood at the doorway watching him in silence. She sighed heavily; but as though he heard neither her step nor her sigh, he did not turn his head; and with a fear of his stern, unbending silence on her, she went away to the kitchen to help Polly to get breakfast ready.

"Polly," she whispered, "didst thee see Miss Jenny leave the house this morning?"

"I? No, indeed, missus! Be she gone, then?" said the girl, with her hair all feathery for lack of brushing, and the end of her nose black from frequent strokes of her bare arm.

"Hush, silly wench! Why do you shout? She hath not slept in her bed, Polly. Oh, God! if she be run away from me!"

"Roon awoy! Why, missus! whativer would she be doin' that for?" said the slut, craning her neck out of the collarless rim of her frock.

"Stir the fire, that the eggs may boil. Never do you talk but that you stop your work. Cannot you use your hands and tongue together? Hold your prate! As sure as thy nose is as black as thy master's boot, I'll be packing thee to thy mother for a slovenly fool!" cried Mrs. Strangfield, in that phase of grief which admits of easy supervention of irritation.

The time was passing quickly. It was five minutes after the half-hour when breakfast was put upon the table, and Mr. Strangfield drew a chair for himself, and began to eat with the gesture of a man who forces himself to do something he abhors. Not a mouthful could the mother swallow; her gaze was for ever upon the open window, and her ears pricking for every little sound.

But expectation was wrought by fear into insupportable pain at last, and unable to endure the hard silence, she cried out—

"Michael, she doth not come!"

He looked at her vacantly, aroused by her speech out of deep thought, and pulled out his watch. He rose from his chair instantly, his whole manner changed, and he exclaimed—

"It is too late for the coach. Now what do you say to your girl's honesty?"

Under the crushing bitterness of the tone in which these words were delivered, and the dangerous passion which his smouldering eyes showed to be burning in the heart of his iron will, Mrs. Strangfield sat for a space motionless. Her husband's personal challenge of shame and stubborn wrath, and the remorseless severity of his ashen face, took her for the moment from thoughts of the girl whose chair was vacant. But it is the Lord's will that in a woman's heart the mother should always triumph over the wife and on a sudden her manner changed from rigidity, and the stupefaction of fear, to eager agitation—to a restless working of mouth and eye, to a wild hurry of emotion over her face.

"Oh, Michael!" she cried, "where do you think our child is? Why should she not be here? Did you say anything to her yesterday to scare her? Last night she kissed me sweetly, and thanked me for my love, and she would not break my heart by leaving me! Oh, Michael, what didst thee say to her?"

"I said no more than bid her be ready for the coach at eight o'clock this morning," he said, speaking with difficulty through the tension of his lips. "What is there to fright you in this? Could you not have guessed that if she had sinned she would not go with me to London? Would she rush upon her own conviction, silly woman?" He added, in a faint voice: "What heavier blow than this could come upon a man? I would sooner see her dead. And after all these years—in this little town where we are honoured —how will some people scoff to hear that pious Michael Strangfield's girl—"

"I'll not hear thee say it!" shrieked the mother, raising her hands to her ears. "Michael, will you not go and seek her? Shall we stand here wickedly raging at the poor heart that hath been driven from our love by our sorrow and your anger, when every moment is taking her further from us? Oh, husband, think of our pretty one—so tender, so gentle, Michael—sitting wearied by the wayside, weeping and calling upon death, and thinking there be naught to love her but the gracious Lord who is in the sky! Dost thee not see her? If she had gone twenty miles I would walk to her! I would—I would!"

In a paroxysm of grief and love she ran towards the door. But her husband came after her hastily, and his hand fell upon her shoulder.

"Where would you go?" he said.

"To find my child. Michael, let me be. I will not be hindered!"

He drew her back from the door and closed it violently.

"Listen to reason, woman!" he exclaimed, controlling his voice with an effort that discoloured and convulsed his features. "You run mad easily, and madness is on you now, and in this temper you are not to be trusted abroad. What will your sorrow do but publish our shame? At thy time of life to chase a phantom! Such is your child now; for where is she gone, and what road will you take? Oh, fool! to let love blind thee to the curse that God has set upon our foreheads! You have suckled vice, and I have loved it and caressed it, and now it has brought shame upon us and left us! The will of the Lord of Hosts be done! But this is my death, Jane——Wife, this thing has put ice in my heart—I am cold here."

He stopped short, with his hand upon his breast, shaking his head slowly, with his frown gone.

"Sit thee down, Michael. My poor man! This is cruel hard upon us both! What have we done that God should take our only one from us? Sit thee down. Why do you pluck at your shirt?—your hand is all of a shiver."

She pushed a chair under him and he sank into it, and faintly beat with his fingers upon his thigh, looking downwards with a sideways droop of the head.

He rallied presently, and gazed at her wistfully with a softened eye, as she stood before him with averted face silently crying.

"Am not I wise, Jane, to restrain thee from running into the town to seek the girl? 'That which is crooked,' saith the Preacher, 'cannot be made straight: and that which is wanting cannot be numbered.' If she come not back of her own accord, is it meet that her mother should bring her? Not with my leave shall you do it. And if she come, I go! for this house will not hold us two. Hush! I'll not hear you. Your love is a mother's, and I say, God help thee! but if she were twenty times my child, the hem of her garment should not touch the sole of my boot, so hateful hath her sin made her in my sight."

He spoke with subdued energy—as a man in an illness might, indeed; and though bitter and shocking as his words were for his wife to bear, yet his broken aspect, his ashen face, his drooping head, the senile twitching of his fingers, the dulled gleam in his eye, were sights of pathos to modify pure maternal anguish with wifely yearning and a dim dread not yet definable.

"You will not think her honest!" she moaned. "You will not believe that fear has driven her forth. If she is ignorant of the church wherein she was married, and hath no memory to help thee to find it, would she not think with terror on the journey and fly rather than take it with you who are so stern to her? Oh, Michael, it drives me mad to stand here and think of her as a lonely, helpless wanderer."

"Why do you say that? Has the man no friends, or means, to give her shelter? How know you that her flight is not a scheme to join her lover who is in hiding? Does she lack cunning? Do not seek her! I would lock thee in thy bedroom rather than that this last disgrace should come upon us!"

She answered him not a word, but leaned her forehead against the edge of the high mantelpiece, and thus stood in silent anguish.

CHAPTER VI

PROOF POSITIVE

"If I meant anything now let me die;
I'm blunt, and cannot fawn and cant, not I,
Like that old Presbyterian rascal, sly:
I am, you know, a right true-hearted Tory."

JENKYNS

DOWN the familiar road which we have traversed before in our visits to Greystone School, there was coming at this hour, and walking with brisk steps, which ever and anon shot up a twirl of dust, no less a personage than Dr. Isaac Shaw. With brisk steps he was coming; yet he was a man on whom dignity sate as a habit, and never could he bestir himself to a degree that should deform the ramrod erectness of his mien, and impair the pompous amplitude of his reedy frill.

This was an uncommonly early hour for Dr. Shaw to be found outside his school; for here was not a man to be courted from discipline by the sweetness of early morning air. Once, hearing the chime of a church clock, he stopped to uproot his watch from the band of his breeches; and then he went forward again, with a well-mannered whirl of a silk pocket-handkerchief over his face, and a tender drag at his back hair.

As he approached the bottom of the hill and neared the houses, his step slackened and took yet a more dignified moderation of gesture. A woman on the other side of the street dropped him a humble curtsey, which he acknowledged with a salutation of such largeness and elegance as placed the superiority of his breeding above all doubt. The big signet-ring glittered on the finger of his right hand, and in the suave and cleanly circumference of his face scarcely a hint was visible that he carried a real trouble in his heart, and was bent on one of the most distressing missions which fate could have forced his pride upon.

When at the bottom of the street, he paused a moment to inspect the wooden house of the shipwright, which looked shyly towards him through its green drapery.

The glorious expanse of lustrous sea was a background to make a lively picture of the building.

In the yard men were busily hammering at the growing frames of the vessels building.

To the right the grey beach sloped into the white lip of the water, and sweet smells of resinous wood, the dust of pine, and shavings of the homely elm, were blown softly upon the doctor's nostrils in the salt wind coming lightly from the sea.

With an uneasy glance around him, such as a man might cast who wishes to effect an object without detection, the doctor crossed the road and knocked hurriedly on the door of the wooden house.

There are many kinds of bad servant; but the worst kind of servant is the servant who keeps you waiting on the door-step.

Had this door flown open under the doctor's hand, uplifted to catch the knocker, still something of promptitude would have been missing. For nothing was plainer than that Dr. Shaw had no wish to be seen standing on that threshold.

At last came Polly, and saluted him with a dirty stare.

"Does Mr. Strangfield live here?" asked Dr. Shaw, holding that it would be a little too condescending for a man of his dignity and station to appear to know so humble a fact.

"What do 'ee say?" cried Polly.

The doctor repeated his question in a loud, imperious manner.

"Ay, do he!" replied Polly, evidently astounded at his ignorance. "Are ye in want of him?"

"I wish to see him; show me in," exclaimed the little man, with a frown.

The girl made way for him to pass, and for love of his frill gave him a wide passage; closed the door with turgid attention to the catch of the latch, and left the doctor planted against the wall, to escape all touch of her, whilst she went to announce him.

Mrs. Strangfield came hurrying out, with a wild look of sorrow in her face, and her eyes sore with weeping.

But at sight of the fine frill, and haughty mouth, and twisted forehead, and silk waistcoat, God bless her! she curtsied to the ground.

Salaaming was a great business in primitive days, and thought highly of.

Sir Peter Macsycophant made his way through life by bowing, as he admitted to his nephew.

Every boy was taught to make a leg, and do it properly.

Mrs. Strangfield's curtsey made Dr. Shaw a pliable thing.

"I have the pleasure, madam, of addressing——?" And the doctor made a bow that twisted his figure into a note of interrogation.

"My name is Mrs. Strangfield, sir. I know you to be Dr. Shaw, and may God send you have come to bring us tidings of our girl!" replied the poor mother, in her tearfullest voice.

"I am here on a very special errand—one that concerns us all closely. If your husband is visible I should be glad to see him."

"Oh yes, sir, he is in this room; pray walk in, Dr. Shaw," said Mrs. Strangfield, wondering that her tearful face should provoke no expression of concern from the doctor, and herein exactly showing herself to be her daughter's mother; for on the very previous day had not Jenny herself fallen into the same wonder over the little man's glazed manners?

He followed her into the parlour, and within a pace of the door stood to deliver his cool, collected bow to Mr. Strangfield, who half rose from his armchair to return the salutation.

"Good morning to you, Dr. Shaw. Pray take a chair, sir. This fine weather is very promising for the farmers, and there be talk of a grand harvest this year," said the shipwright, remaining half risen out of his chair until the doctor was seated.

Mrs. Strangfield looked at her husband with an expression of helpless, eager despair. How could he talk of the weather; how could he receive the doctor's visit so easily! Why did not he ask him at once his object in calling? Great Lord! how did he know but that the schoolmaster was come with shocking news of Jenny? Bolt upright she sat, with her hands tightly clasped.

"I am out betimes this morning," said Dr. Shaw, with a short glance around the homely room. "But then, Mr. Strangfield, from your occupation I naturally conceived you an early riser, and my duty would not permit me to delay my visit."

"Had you come two hours ago you would have found me risen," replied Strangfield, who had gathered his forces together for this unexpected interview, and was now again wearing his hard face and speaking in his stern, deep tones.

Indeed, it must be said that the deacon's antipathy to the doctor was like the smear of a branding-iron on the withers of a weary horse. The pride of both of them, and their common dislike, were better than a film over the eye of their minds to prevent a clear sight of each other's thoughts. Not for worlds would the doctor let the Baptist deacon know that deep trouble was in him; not for worlds would the Baptist deacon let the doctor know that a breaking heart beat in his breast.

So, with demeanours to ensure reciprocal repulsion, they fell to their talk, without heed of the mother's desolate, pale face, and the anguish of expectation in her eyes.

"I am here, Mr. Strangfield, in compliance with my promise to give you all news at the earliest opportunity that should enable you— to use your own words—to sift this business of your daughter to the bottom," began the doctor, pulling out his snuff-box for no other motive than to toy with it. "Strange things come to pass in this world, which truly is much smaller than we can get to conceive it by estimate of geographical mensuration; and I apprehend," said he, with his suave smile, "that our respected neighbours will be not a little surprised to hear of visits exchanged between Dr. Shaw and Mr. Strangfield, whose strong objections to the schoolmaster's theological opinions are tolerably well known."

Strangfield looked at him keenly under his frowning eyebrows, and appeared about to speak, but dismissed his thoughts with a wave of the hand, and sank back silent.

"Oh, Dr. Shaw!" cried the mother, incapable of holding her tongue, however awed by the cold fencing between the men, "I wish that difference of religious notions was all the trouble 'twixt you and Michael, sir. Your name hath a sorrowful sound in it to my ears, God knows; and this morning hath made it more bitter than my heart well knows how to bear." And she hung her pale face to hide her tears.

"Jane!" exclaimed her husband, sternly, "there is no need for thee to put in. Dr. Shaw is here to give us some news; we can await his leisure. Keep thy tongue quiet. It's a sign of a light head to fret over the past. Whom to upbraid we know; but Dr. Shaw hath no hand in our grief."

"Madam," said the doctor, haughtily, not to be mollified by the deacon's admission—for the manner was offensive, though the words were kindly—"between you and me there should be silence in the matter of reproach. If you have to mourn over a daughter's deceit, I have to lament a son's folly. And there I stop; for the world shall judge who is the greater sufferer."

Neither husband nor wife answered him.

"Mr. Strangfield," he continued, turning quickly upon the deacon, with the sudden contrite air of a man who feels that he is wasting valuable time, "I have left my home early this morning expressly to bring you two items of news, one of which should properly be delivered by me only. First, as to my son's disappearance:—

"There came a man to my house late last night, to inquire after me. He was a man belonging to the Preventive Service, and he said, being at an ale-house in the town not two hours before, there were persons there talking over the disappearance of Dr. Shaw's son, and likewise the impressment of three men out of Greystone on that night or thereabouts, as it is concluded, of my son's going. Now, it is very exactly known that three men were impressed; for no other man is missing, unless it be my son. This coastguard sat considering what he had heard, and, taking particular note of the conjectures concerning my son thrown out by the gossips, he came round to my house (having finished his glass, and being off duty for the night) and asked me if it were true that I had a son who was missing. I replied that I had, and wondered he should not know it, for I conceived it was every man's talk in this district. However, I was sure the matter was news to him."

"Now, he said that, having heard that only three men were kidnapped, and being satisfied upon this point from what the fellows in the room told him, his reason for calling upon me was to state that on that night, when the press-gang was ashore, he was on duty with another man at the hut that stands to the south, upon the cliff near my house, and at the head of the pass that leads to the sands. It was a windy night, he said, and his mate had gone half a mile along the cliff, to look at that curve of sand where some smuggling was done last Christmas, as you may remember, sir. There was moonlight abroad, and, riding clear of the breakers, though mightily tossed by the inshore seas, was a man-of-war's boat, which my man, about whom I am telling you, knew to belong to a brig-of-war that had that morning dropped anchor off the town."

"Now, whilst he stood in the shelter of his hut, he saw a crowd of the boat's crew coming along through the dusk, and among them walked three prisoners; and on the shoulders of two of them a fourth man was borne, bound like the others, but plainly insensible. The Preventive man stood forth, and some of the men-of-war's men called a greeting to him as they passed. Indeed, he was as near to them as yonder window is to me, and could not, therefore, mistake what he beheld. Most solemnly does he swear that there were four men pinioned, and not three, as the town's gossip would show; and that of these four, who were clearly kidnapped men, as he might judge, one was carried; and though a confusion of shadow was cast upon them all by the hurrying of clouds over the moon, and the unequal and swerving steps of the men, yet is he positive that the carried man was young; and such description does he give me of him as leaves me in no doubt that the figure on the men's shoulders was my son."

He told the story in an equable voice, and on pausing extracted a pinch of snuff from his box; but the quiver of his nostril proclaimed a hard struggle with emotion, and it was easy to see that his application to his snuff-box was a stratagem to drop his eyes, and an excuse to hold his peace for a moment.

Mrs. Strangfield was about to speak; but, with an imperious gesture of the hand, her husband silenced her.

"This coastguard's tale seems a likely one, sir, and makes the riddle of your son's disappearance easy," he said, with his hard eyes fixed upon the doctor. "It is a pity there is but one witness."

"But one witness may rescue a man from damning dishonour, though there be no other evidence to prove his aspersers liars!" exclaimed the doctor, lifting his head with a flashing glance.

Mr. Strangfield met his gaze with a faint contemptuous smile.

"These coastguards," he said, "like other men of their condition, are fond of a glass, and the hope of earning a shilling will make them smart at inventions. One may be sure the man did not leave the school-house unrewarded."

The skin about the doctor's eyes tightened, and an expression of unspeakable contempt settled down upon his face.

"This is not the first time, Mr. Strangfield, that I have experienced your qualifications to render yourself offensive. A man so sceptical should surely possess a judgment above all chance of blundering."

"Dr. Shaw, I am a plain man, with little knowledge of fine words. Your tale may be truly believed by you, but it doth not satisfy me. Your son has acted the part of a villain, sir, and nothing that does not prove him a villain in every step of the vile wrong he has done me and mine will I credit. Tell me rather that, having betrayed my child, he has meanly fled to escape my vengeance, and has put any rascal upon lying on his behalf!"

He was white with his passion, and as he grasped the arms of his chair, the veins of his hands stood up, black with the energy that swelled them.

In the contempt and dislike with which Dr. Shaw, after a slight backward push of his chair, surveyed him, there seemed positive cruelty; for no insolence that Strangfield could be guilty of, could in a humane man's eyes qualify the moving influence of his deep and passionate emotion.

"You are pleased, Mr. Strangfield, to call my son a villain. This did you term him once before. But my memory is not keen, and I should be glad to hear again your reasons for abusing him."

"Oh, Dr. Shaw, my husband is beside himself this morning," wailed Mrs. Strangfield. "Our poor——"

"Silence!" thundered the shipwright. "It is to me this gentleman speaks. Leave me to answer him. Whatever may be your true purpose in calling upon me this morning, my own judgment upon it I will give you, and let the question you have now asked me find you a reason for what I shall say: that the father of a villain who has ruined my child, and brought desolation and shame upon an honourable home, must perforce be too much like his offspring not to have a relish for the wound his son has inflicted, and a pleasure in fingering it for the sake of his curiosity. Hold! you are not yet answered. Do you think I am to be touched by your sneers, man? You would teach all those with whom you have to do to look down upon me, and such as me, as despicable men, holding a humble faith that makes your flaunting religion keck; and that your son hath ruined and disgraced any one of us, should give you no more concern than the scourging of a negro gives the white ruffian who looks on at the whipping! Is that it? Why, sir, be satisfied with your son's work: but you shall not stop me from calling him villain! You would know why? Look at my wife yonder. Is there no answer in her face? Look at this hand. Never did it tremble as now it does. I am aged a score since yesterday, and that is thy son's doing. No!" he shouted, in a strange shaking voice, "I'll not put my dishonour again into words. Sir, I wish you a good morning."

He rose from his chair and stood upright, with his hand extended towards the door. His wife sat in a crouching attitude, hugging herself. Dr. Shaw did not offer to move. His face was pale, but otherwise his manner was collected. He put his snuff-box in his pocket, and, drawing forth a pocket-book, he extracted a paper, which he held in his hand whilst he addressed Mr. Strangfield.

"Sir," he said, in a slow, deliberate tone, "throughout my life I have ever striven to act the part of an upright man, resolute in the vindication of things I hold to be just and true, but always ready to acknowledge my errors. Through haste and surprise and disappointment which, in imitation of your own admirable candour, I shall be at no pains to dissemble, I have fallen into a grievous error: that of misjudging youthful folly and calling it sin; that of repelling with rude doubts the pleadings of helpless innocence; that of denouncing my own flesh and blood as a monster of vice when he was not at hand to justify himself. But, sir, the God who rules over us is the Vindicator of the just, and last night I humbled myself before Him with gratitude and remorse. I beg you to be seated. I came to you with two items of news. One I have related, and the other I will now relate, in mercy to you who, by desiring me to leave the house, would be entailing upon yourself the endurance of a grief greater, *in spite of my theological opinions*, than I could wish you to know."

Mr. Strangfield continued standing, leaning heavily upon the back of a chair and looking down with a scowl upon the doctor. Mrs. Strangfield, in a half-risen posture supporting herself with her hand upon the table, stretched eagerly forward, her eyes fixed on the paper in the doctor's grasp.

"Last night," continued the doctor, "after the coastguard left me, I reflected upon his story, and felt persuaded that the riddle of my son's disappearance was solved. But, though there was a melancholy satisfaction in detecting the means by which one portion of the mystery had been brought about, the boy's honour still remained befouled by the charges that had been made against him by you. It was clearly my duty to leave no stone unturned, either to prove that he was actually your daughter's husband, or that their connection was sinless, and the affirmations of your daughter the delusions of an ignorant loving woman. This morning, I should have taken the coach to London, and remained in that city until every vestry had been searched by persons I should have hired for that purpose, and every clergyman and dissenting minister officiating called upon. But I have been mercifully spared a duty which, at my time of life, would have made heavy demands on my strength. Before retiring to rest, I entered my son's bedroom. Up to that moment, beyond a cursory inspection of the room, I had made no close examination of it. But I felt that it would greatly facilitate my project if I could obtain some clue to the name or neighbourhood of the church where they were married and I further remembered that he had written to me one letter from his lodgings, though I could not find that letter, and had no recollection of the address upon it. I found his desk in a drawer, and had no difficulty in opening it by a bunch of keys of my own. Sir, among letters of his mother, most tenderly preserved, and letters signed in your daughter's name, I found this document" (holding it up) "carefully sealed in a sheet of paper, on which was written *Jenny Shaw*; and I also found," continued the doctor, drawing from his side pocket a small sheepskin volume, "this little diary, some passages of which, sir, I will take the liberty to read."

There was breathless silence between husband and wife whilst the doctor turned the leaves in search of the entry he proposed first to read. Mr. Strangfield never shifted his posture nor moderated his frown; but over his wife's face was creeping the illumination of an expression of joy pathetic to behold, in the growing gladness of her eyes and the faint parting of her lips.

The doctor read:—

" '*April* 3, 1806.—I am bewitched by Jenny Strangfield's beauty. It is a fortnight ago since I first addressed her, and to-day we conversed like old friends. Strange that anything so sweet and gloriously feminine should be found among the hard conditions and rigours of the sect of whose prejudices her father is the most acid exponent hereabouts.'"

The doctor turned the leaves slowly, skipping evidently much that was too personal for himself to read aloud in the presence of the deacon with relish.

" '*May* 20.—To-day I told Jenny I loved her. She believes me; and well she may, for truly is she dearest of all earthly things to me now. "You should not love me," she said; "for what would thy father say to hear that thou art in love with Michael Strangfield's girl?" What wonderful tenderness her voice gains from use of that quaint, old-fashioned *thee*-ing and *thou*-ing!'"

"Why do you read such stuff, sir?" cried Mr. Strangfield, with an air of sullen impatience. "You have something to prove by producing that book. Come to it—or leave it, if it be as I think—for you shall not dangle our dishonour in our face, sir. By God! your cool recital of your son's infamy shall not drive me mad!"

His face was again dark with passion, and well might the violence of an emotion that could force an oath from Strangfield startle even the imperturbable Dr. Shaw.

"I must detain you another minute," said the doctor, curling his lip, whilst he rapidly turned the leaves of the diary, " and then I am done. Here is the one entry that concerns you:

" '*June* 18.—This day I was married to Jenny Strangfield at the Church of St. Matthew, Dane Street, London. Have I, as her sweetheart and husband, acted wisely for my darling by this secrecy? I will have no fear, but thank God humbly for His precious gift. How timid she was! All the way from Sydenham she scarcely spoke; and her hand was as cold as stone in mine as we went into the church—a gloomy church indeed, with a mistiness all about the altar, as if the fogs of winter had not had time to escape. How much happier and easier to have been married in the dear old church at Greystone, with her father and mine to give us a kindly word. But it is the mother's kiss my darling must most miss. Love shall atone, my little wife. Good night—good night!'"

Mrs. Strangfield started up with a wild, loud laugh.

"Oh, Michael!" she cried, in an eerie, jubilant voice, raising her clasped hands above her head, "did not I tell thee our only one was pure? Oh, Dr. Shaw, he would not believe her! He is a stern father to the dear heart. He turned from her, when she wished to kiss him, and to me hath called her a vile name—and, O God! he hath driven her from us. She is gone away from her home, sir! This very morning we found her gone! Oh, cruel! cruel! He would not let me seek her—and now where is my innocent lamb? Is she dead of a broken heart? Oh, my pretty one! why did I bear thee for this sorrow? Better had we died—better had we died, than lived to see this bitter, wicked time!"

With the joyous look fled from her white features, she dropped her face into her hollowed hands and broke into piteous sobbing.

With laborious roll of the eyes, which had a vacant look under the darkness of the hanging brow, Mr. Strangfield gazed from her to the doctor, from the doctor to her; and he made a picture of a strong man smitten with a great and deadly fear, or a man whose brains are crazing under the apprehension of an unspeakable grief: for so he looked.

But obstinacy is an instinct—for qualities are drooping and dying when instinct is still a flourishing force—which will survive many shocks, and give battle amid the languors of dissolution and prompt the last breath; as who that has attended the dying but knows?

Though the diary furnished evidence which ninety and nine men of a hundred would have yielded their judgment to in calm certainty that the truth was at last made plain, it was evidence that could not despatch the stubborn shipwright's conviction. With a slow smile, so full of anguish that all sarcasm was lost in it, and holding firmly to his chair that the giddiness in his head might not cause his body to vibrate, he waited until his wife had drowned her speech in sobs; and turning to the doctor, who had now risen, and was looking at him with a gaze of steady contempt and dislike, he exclaimed, in a thick and struggling voice—

"Who is to prove to me that the characters in that book be your son's writing? If my girl's chastity be broken, stronger cement than that'll be needed to mend it. And until I am better assured that your son path acted honestly by my girl, not ten thousand times the number of his pretty words shall stop me from calling him villain!"

"Read that!" said the doctor, and he thrust the paper he held into the deacon's hand, and took up his hat and made a step towards the door.

Mr. Strangfield, still wearing his painful smile, opened the paper with a shake of the head and looked at it vacantly, holding it at a distance from him, as a man might who scarcely deems the thing he is asked to read worth the trouble of spectacles.

"Michael," cried his wife, "your glasses are in your pocket. Read it quickly, husband, for my sake—or give it to me! I will read it aloud."

She went towards him, but with a faltering gesture he warned her off. Then slowly, with stubbornness in every move of his arm, he drew out his spectacle case and put on his glasses, and went round to the other side of his chair, which was nearer to the window, to read.

They could not see his face, for it was towards them, and he held the paper before it. A whole minute passed; then said Dr. Shaw, in a whisper, pitying the agony of the poor mother, "Madam, your daughter is lawfully my son's wife: that is the certificate of their marriage."

But she made him no answer, for she was watching her husband. How long he was mastering the contents of the paper! Suddenly his tall figure swayed; from side to side it went, with something of the rhythmical action of a pendulum.

"He is dying!" shrieked the wife, and bounded forward; but too late to break the fall of the man as he dropped with a crash, the full length of him, upon the floor of the parlour.

CHAPTER VII

THE GREYHOUND INN

"Jog on, jog on, the footpath way,
    And merrily bent the stile-a;
A merry heart goes all the way,
    Your sad tires in a mile-a."

Winter's Tale

THE sweetest hour of the summer day is when the silver sun looks to be risen as high as tenfold its own glorious circumference above a level line of land; when all the dews are not yet drunk by it, and thin vapours still hang crisply over the meadows; when the ringing joy of the lark courts the eye to the blue heavens, and winged aromas come nimbly flying, and the heavy grain-fields salute, with rich and stately swellings, the splendours of the young day.

Through a fruitful land, bounded by blue hills, in places dark with the soft grouping of trees, and here and there a break of lustrous water, went the white level road that led to Winston; cornfields to right and left, and tracts of vivid green soaring, and the bland eye of the ocean shining betwixt the two tall heights of cliff.

Along this road, with steps that offered no defiance to time, walked Jenny and her old companion, and the movements of Mrs. Mead showed, at all events, that if the sun had overtaken them unduly, the fault was the girl's.

How otherwise should it have been? To weariness of mind the halest body will succumb, and two whole nights had Jenny passed without sleep. Her feet dragged heavily; the glare of the sunshine, which no veil could exclude, and the drowsy kissing of the air, which would not be denied, put weight into her eyelids and on her lips. Though but half the distance was compassed, she had lost all power of speech, all heart to give effort to her tongue. The very faculty of thought was numbed; and drearily, with piteous hanging hands, and slow mechanical gait often stumbling among the ruts that scored the road, she trudged at the side of the old woman, who frequently had to slacken her pace that she might not leave the girl behind.

Now, no old woman was ever better qualified to prove that two persons are not needful for talk than Mrs. Mead, who could sustain a conversation whilst there was a listener, and often without; as witness her frequent chats with herself. But she, too, had been awake all night; and, to speak the truth, a light box will become no mean weight on an ancient arm when carried for above an hour. Moreover, bones of which age has turned the sap into powder, and made brittle as a spear of ice hanging down from an eave, abhor every road that jolts the frame, and threatens the feeble sinews of the ankle; so that by this time her dry tongue had rattled off all it was now disposed to coil to; and in perfect silence they advanced, the old woman busy in her mind, though where her thoughts were confined might positively be known by her deliberate looks at the girl.

At last, coming to a turn of the road—a truly magnificent bend of lofty hedge, with golden monuments of hay behind, and a rich, cool orchard beyond, again—there appeared at the very bottom—or end of it, rather, for level as a river it ran just here—a grey stone front with ivy grandly endowed, and further on a row of little cottages, with a church to the right of them, pointing a flaming apex to heaven.

"Here we are, dearie!" exclaimed Mrs. Mead; "Winston at last! And the Lord bless it for coming upon us just when I'm beginning to think thy box here hath some pounds o' lead at the bottom on't."

"Let me carry it now," said Jenny in a painfully languid voice.

"No, no. I'm still good for that bit o' distance. D'ye see that board hanging up yonder? That's the Greyhound; an' if there be no fire i' the kitchen that'll bile us a dish o' tea, Sally'll have no more o' my love, though it bain't six o'clock yet, if the sun don't lie."

By the village clock it was a little more than half-past five, but to both of them the drag had seemed to occupy a long morning. Yet the villagers were awake, and at work; smoke was circling into the blue air out of chimneys; hens, freed from the servitude of a night's cooping, pecked in the roadway; here and there a woman scrubbed the stone step of her door, and already stood a market-gardener's cart at the ale-house facing the Greyhound.

A little inn was the Greyhound, to take the eye in a picture as a sweet bit of rustic painting, for simplicity inimitable. With low, cleanly windows down almost upon the road, permitting a glimpse of snug and pretty rooms within, and an overhanging storey framed in delicate Gothic angle, the woodwork chocolate-coloured, and a door, half made of glass, partially screened with red baize, furnishing, through a shining space, hospitable hints of crystal for lips of thirsty men, and little brass-bound mahogany barrels, and the blush and glow of flowers intermixed from the wilderness of walled garden at the rear. The building stood looking up the great highway, of which the road from Greystone was but a vein or tributary, so to speak. From the upper windows of this inn, the highway could be followed, rising and falling in a white line, until to right and left it vanished in a tiny thread of white among the blue shadows. This was the great road to London from the south-eastern coast of England; and the coaches that ran upon it were, by Greystone travellers, met twenty-one miles onwards at a famous ancient city, to which they were borne by Mr. Franklin's coach, chosen often in preference to this stage of Winston, as it saved a walk or the hire of a hackney-coach, and was a pleasant ride.

Paying small heed to the scrutiny of slow eyes at the windows and doors of the cottages,

Mrs. Mead, preceding Jenny, led the way to the door of the inn, and, finding it locked, put down the box and pulled the house-bell hard.

They had not long to wait. A servant, newly risen, came to the glass, and after a prolonged stare at Mrs. Mead's features, opened the door.

"Tell Mrs. Walker that Judith Mead is come from Greystone to see her. And take this here box, and lead us to a room wi' chairs in't, whiles our legs have life 'em, if ye don't want the job of carrying of us," exclaimed Mrs. Mead. And the girl, thus admonished, ridding the old lady of her burden, conducted her and Jenny into a parlour to the right of the bar.

With a groan of weariness the old woman tumbled herself down upon a chair, and Jenny sank languidly upon a sofa.

"Well, if ever I should ha' believed Winston to be so far!" exclaimed Mrs. Mead, lifting her bonnet off her grey hair and throwing it upon the table.

"How do ye feel, dear heart? Tired you look as niver I see the like; but I have promised thee a good snatch o' sleep betwixt breakfast and the coach-hour, and that ye'll git. And here is Sally, whose mother I remember as the prettiest-waisted wench i' this part o' the country. Don't curtsy to me, my dear, for my bones'll not allow of my rising. How are ye— how are ye?"

She addressed these words to a stout, kindly-faced young woman, who had come suddenly into the room, and now stood staring at and curtsying first to Jenny and then to Mrs. Mead.

"Sally," continued the old woman, "we have walked all the way from Greystone to get a sup o' breakfast afore t' coach starts. What have ye got i' the house to comfort th' inside of an old friend—and a lady, whose beauty should make ye proud to sarve her? Speak out, my love, and niver fear to name thy choicest. Is it a pretty slice from a tender side o' bacon, with the eggs which the hens are now singing over, and a pot o' thy best tea, wi' cream to give it a dainty colour? That will do— that will do, Sally; but I'll not gi' ye a farden for it all, if ye don't make the saucy wench, as ogled me through your glass door, brisk in cooking of it."

"What ! Mrs. Mead? Who'd iver ha' thought of seeing you this time o' marning!" cried Mrs. Walker, in a rich, clear voice. "Where be ye going by t' coach? Not to Lunnon, at thy time o' life! Well, well! only last night did I say to Roger, 'Next time thee goest to Greystone, see

that ye fill the biggest basket wi' the largest
gooseberries for Mrs. Mead, that she may
know Sally is alive and wishes her health.'
How strange, now! An' it's breakfast you're
wanting at once? That you shall have, an'
quickly. Hi! Martha!" she called at the door;
and a voice answered, "Here I be, missis!"
"Run out and bring in what eggs ye can find,
and first set the kittle on; and if ye stay
talking with jackanapes Johnny, I'll know you
by my clock, which I'm looking at now! There's
breakfast for two to get, and if your shoes
hinder ye from running, toss 'em off!"

She looked back into the room with a merry
laugh, which died away on her catching sight
of Jenny's face, for the girl had lifted her veil.
Observing the change of expression in her
friend's face, Mrs. Mead frowned knowingly
upon her, with an extremely suggestive shake
of the head, and then begged for the loan of a
pair of slippers, which Mrs. Walker
immediately went to procure.

"Now, mistress," said the old woman, in her
kindest manner, and hobbling over to Jenny,
"ye must make yourself comfortable here, and
there's no reason agin it. A better-hearted
young woman than Sally there is not in this
world. Niver you heed her if she look at thee.
It will be your beauty that fetches her eyes

and nothing else; for this is a house of call, and them who kapes such houses soon loses all curiosity. You shall breakfast and then lie down for a mossel o' sleep. Why, my dear, what beautiful hair is yours! 'Tis like putting one's hand on feathers, and just the colour o' the hair o' some of them drawings ye see on church windows when the sun shines through them."

This bit of praise was provoked by her gentle removal of Jenny's hat; then she slipped the shawl off the girl's shoulders, and knelt down to take off her shoes and chafe the little feet.

Grief and fatigue are by no means such conditions as beauty covets for their physical gifts; yet it was a question if Jenny's loveliness was impaired by the whiteness of her face and the languid droop of her eyelids, and the mournful set and curve into which sorrow had twitched the sweetness of her mouth. Her hands were folded wearily on her lap, and her wedding-ring glistened.

"How kind and good you are to me, Mrs. Mead!" she said. "If ever my darling comes back to me, how will he love and bless you for our goodness to his wife! If I could get a little rest first, I could eat some breakfast; but, indeed, I do not think I could swallow food now."

"Well, perhaps ye are right," replied Mrs. Mead, thoughtfully, still on her knees, with Jenny's foot in her hands; "food will not do ye much good while your fancy's agin it, and your head is aching for sleep. Ah, here is Sally. Thank ye, Sally. I'll put 'em on in a moment. Why, they're your husband's, I declare! Lard, is my foot as big as all that!"

"Anyways, they'll fit thee, Mrs. Mead," exclaimed Sally, with her merry laugh, dropping the slippers on the floor; "and a slipper's a poor job if it don't fit loose."

"Now, see here, Sally," continued Mrs. Mead, rising off her knees with one of those involuntary groans which old folks like her will send up over any harsh exercise of their bones; "this lady wants some sleep, and I'll thank ye, my dear, for the loan of a quiet room for her, where the drawn blinds'll make her poor eyes think it night."

"If ye'll come with me, ma'am, I'll lead you straight to such a room as Mrs. Mead asks for," said Sally with a curtsy, giving Jenny the "ma'am" on account of her wedding-ring, which the quick eye of the woman spied instantly.

With a feeble smile of thanks, Jenny slipped her feet into her shoes and, taking up her hat and shawl, followed Mrs. Walker out of the room, and Mrs. Mead went creaking after them.

Now, though Mrs. Mead had represented Mrs. Walker as hardened into incuriosity by her calling as hostess, the truth was Mrs. Walker was still, and was ever likely to remain, a thorough woman in respect of inquisitiveness when any real object of curiosity came under her attention. To this quality, which after all is harmless enough when it prompts honest and kindly hearts, Jenny was indebted for the promptness with which she was conducted to a bedroom and made comfortable in it; for Mrs. Walker was very anxious to have Mrs. Mead alone, that she might hear all that was to be told about this beautiful young girl with the wedding-ring on her finger, and what part in the mysterious little play Judith herself was taking.

"There," said the old woman, when Jenny had stretched her length upon the bed and her hot forehead pressed the snow of the pillow—"there," said she, pinning the curtains together, so as to effectually darken the room, "now ye'll think it's night; and a good two hours you've got, and every inch of it must be sleep wi' ye."

"Give me a kiss before you go," whispered Jenny, putting up her lips.

The old woman bent her furrowed face over the girl; and, as she turned away, the notion struck Sally that all three of them were in a very fit state to cry.

Gently they quitted the room, and closed the door upon the girl.

"Niver was creature born more sweetly lovable than that dear heart," exclaimed the old woman as she hobbled downstairs, holding on to the banister. "Do ye know, Sally, that she is Mike Strangfield's darter, the Baptist deacon—him as talks o' hell-fire as coolly as thee talkest of thy big gooseberries?"

"Ye dunno say so! Well, now, thought I whin I see her, 'Missy, I know thy face.' What, in the name o' goodness and mussy, brings her to Winston this time o' morn?—and she a wife, as any creature might see with one eye by her ring, not to speak of her pale face, poor thing."

"Is this the room I came out of? Yes, there's my bonnet. Now, Sally, no word dost thee get from me till my breakfast is gotten," said Mrs. Mead, sitting herself down; "and then maybe I'll make your eyes big, and give ye a secret worth all that iver you did hear sin' ye left your mammy's breast."

Such a promise was sufficient to put alacrity into a doll. Off went Sally, and in ten minutes' time a good repast was smoking under Mrs. Mead's appreciative nose. Yet, though the old woman did good justice to the sweet country food, there was a contemplative manner about her, a thoughtful hesitancy, an absent glaring at nothing in particular, the while her old jaws kept her temples leaping, that indicated a mind in labour.

Mrs. Walker, who breakfasted with her for company's sake for her husband had gone to Marples and was there stopping—watched her anxiously and spoke seldom, until breakfast was done; and then Mrs. Mead, with a little thanksgiving to the Lord for her meal, folded her hands and told Sally all about the cause that had brought Jenny to Winston.

The mighty master Shakespeare, who knew all things, among his other knowledges had infinite perception into ejaculation, and of its value was so exquisite a judge that never does astonishment in his pages weary.

This Shakespearian gift might have seemed Sally Walker's now; for to give you in their full abundance all the ohs! and the ahs! the well, wells! the lawk-a-daisies! the dear heart alives! the I nevers! and the eloquent ejaculations of her eyes, and the simpering wonder of her mouth, which her tongue and face delivered while Mrs. Mead related Jenny's story, would fill a chapter; and yet they gave the old narrator delight, and so fed her imagination and inspired the excitement of deeper amazement, that truth halted in her rear, and the old thing fibbed poor Jenny into something beyond the dreams of romance.

Why, put a cup of tea into the hand of a woman aged threescore and ten, and show me what shall stop her cackle if it be not a bow-string! Were her old bones to be rattled all the way from Greystone to Winston merely to bring the truth? Since she had earned the shame of a gossip, let her enjoy the bliss of gossiping, at least. Her story took an hour to relate by the clock and when she had made an end, what had been hot on the table was cold; the sun had come round into the window to look at the prater, and the cool breeze of the dawn had been smothered in the sultry arms of a burning morning.

"Now, my dear," said she, "I want you to go upstairs and look at the girl to see if she sleeps—for how it may be with the wenches of this age I know not, but wheniver *I* was troubled, as a young un, I niver could sleep.

Don't come back now and tell me she's awake. If you do ye'll spoil a good scheme."

Mrs. Walker went away softly, and, after an absence of five minutes, returned with the information that Jenny was in a deep slumber.

"But law, dear heart alive! what a beauty she is! More lovely than a picture! And there she lies, with her left hand agin her chin, just as if she had fallen asleep kissin' her weddin'-ring. Poor dearie! I never liked the look o' that Strangfield, somehow. Wood's all very well to build ships with, but when I see a man's face made of it, it don't seem to take my fancy much."

"Sally," exclaimed Mrs. Mead, clasping her hands in her lap, and frowning portentously on her, "can 'ee keep a secret?"

"Why, as niver you could believe of a married woman."

"What's the true hour for the coach to some to thy door?"

"Eight o'clock; true as a hair, if there bain't no accident."

"Sally, I'll tell 'ee what it is: Mistress, upstairs, mustn't go to Marples. I argeyed wi' her last night when she come to me. It's only her fear o' the neighbours as makes shame of her business yet; but if she roon away and come back no more, what'll the town think?"

"Well, now you speak it, Mrs. Mead, I'll be plain. If I did not hear thee say he be married, I'd niver believe it, for her laving home."

"There!" shouted the old woman; "have I lived all these years i' the world to be taught wisdom by a wench? With might and main I argeyed, and, like her father, she looked at me, and that was the good I did. I told her I didn't like the business, and would have no hand in it. Yet, see what good natur' is, and what long journeys it putteth old people upon! But to Marples she'll not go with my leave; and if the coach don't wake her, she shall lie till it's gone."

"And what then will ye do, Mrs. Mead?"

"What then will I do? Ah, an' ye would like me to speak quicker nor I can think. Oh, Sally! thou art a cormorant for news! Sitch gluttony! Well, well!"

Sally laughed, and, looking at the clock, exclaimed—

"If she sleep for another half-hour she'll not get to Marples this day."

There was a pretty long silence whilst Mrs. Mead reflected.

"I see what I mun do!" she cried out at last, with great vehemence. "Her mother must know where she is—for here she'll be all day if she don't wake for the coach; and that'll be my dooty. Let folks speak ill of me then! Is there iver a cart goin' to Greystone? Thee must find out. I'll not walk it."

"Tut, tut! Johnny shall drive ye in the van. It's big enough to hold thee!" replied Mrs. Walker.

CHAPTER VIII

ALONE

"This trick may chance to scath you. I know what:
You must contrary me. Marry, 'tis time."

Romeo and Juliet

UPSTAIRS lay Jenny, in the deep slumber which profound weariness in youth begets; the solemn sleep that, like death, smooths the countenance into an expression for which human knowledge has no definition. Without a stir in her she lay, and the mysterious sweetness of her face was a sight for love to look upon with fear.

Suddenly she started, and awoke with one of those quick leapings from sleep which the sleepless soul will force the body into, and sat erect, with a frown of bewilderment, and her beautiful eyes alarmed and eager. She had no watch to tell the hour, but upon the carpet lay a streak of sunshine, and the mellow glory of it was a hint to draw her quickly to the window.

The sun was high, and a splendour as of noontide upon the land. In sure belief that she had overslept the hour for the passing of the coach, she took her hat in her hand and went downstairs. The first thing she beheld was the big Dutch clock just beside the door; the hands of it pointed to the quarter past ten, so that Marples was not to be reached that day without posting.

With her eyes fixed upon the clock, she stood on the last step of the staircase, and her baffled intentions plainly showed in the wonder and embarrassment of her face;— until Mrs. Walker threw open the glass door of the bulkhead dividing the passage from what would now be termed the bar, and, dropping her a little curtsy, hoped that she was the better for her rest.

"But I have missed the coach, I fear," said Jenny, "if that clock be right."

"It is right enough, ma'am. But Mrs. Mead is in the parlour, and will tell thee how this happ'd, if she be not sleeping," replied Mrs. Walker, with something like a look of contrition on her face, if it were not nervousness.

Without further words, Jenny pushed open the parlour door, and there, sure enough, at full length upon the sofa, was Mrs. Mead asleep. With her head on one side, dropped clear of the bolster, her mouth open, and one honest leg revealed to the knee (a queer muddle of wrinkled stocking; for what hose would fit such a shank?), she lay; and such deep-toned snoring came from her, such writhings of sound, and steady pouring of groans, as kept the two glasses, that touched one another upon the table near her head, jingling as though a waggon were passing.

But Jenny was in straits which would not permit of tender thoughtfulness. She wanted to know why she had been allowed to miss the coach, and what she was now to do. And so gave Mrs. Mead a push, which set the old woman talking in her sleep. "Ay, ay, thee need'st not bother—the Lord love 'ee—an' it's as true as this hand—yaw!"

"Mrs. Mead! Mrs. Mead!"

The old woman opened her eyes, stared at Jenny, lifted her head, gave a terrific yawn, and, planting her loose knuckles into the network about her eyes, exclaimed, in a smothering voice, "I've bin asleep, I do believe!"

"Mrs. Mead, it's a quarter past ten, and the coach has been gone this long while. Oh, why was I allowed to sleep! I shall not get away this day; and here must I stop, for I have not money enough to hire a post-chaise!" cried Jenny.

"Sit down, mistress, and think a bit before ye quarrel. For maybe I'll be showing ye that it's no fault o' mine ye've missed the coach, and then how sorrowful would your heart be for being angry with Mother Mead, who loves you," said the old woman, continuing to rub her eyes until all the sleep was squeezed, out of them. "Sally, Sally!" she squeaked; and on Mrs. Walker running in, Mrs. Mead exhorted her to procure breakfast at once for Jenny, and to look in upon them again presently, which was as good as saying, "Don't listen now, at all events."

"You must not think I could be angry with you," said the girl mournfully, "but it is a sad thing for me to lose the coach; for I hoped to be with Bridget this day, and in a quiet place, where I could think how I am to act in the future."

"And what's to stop you thinking here?" exclaimed Mrs. Mead. "Isn't it quiet enough?—for hours together ye shall hear no sound but the hens talking and scraping in the road. Besides, it's nearer thy home nor Marples. And Jenny, Mrs. Jenny! I'll own to thee it's my fault ye missed t' coach; and it were my wish ye should. What did I say to 'ee last night? Dreadful scandal will follow you when folks hear you have roon away, and I *will* not help thee to be foolish."

Jenny looked at her with astonishment and fear. Whatever force the objection might still possess, she thought that Mrs. Mead had put it aside for good and all when she offered to walk with her to Winston.

"Give yourself time to think," continued the old woman. "If ye should have a mind to return to your mother, 'tis an easy walk from here; if you will still go forward, then the coach will be at this door to-morrow morn. But ye be taking a mighty step in quitting home without iver letting a cratur' but me know where you've gone. It's because I love you that I've let you miss the coach, and given you a whole day for reflection wi' thy home close at hand."

"My mind is quite made up," said Jenny, moving restlessly about the room. "I will not return home."

"Well, that you say now, but by-and-by you will be thinking another way."

"I am grieved to have missed the coach, but I am not angry," she went on, in a subdued but firm tone. "It will be dull work for me here all day; for I suppose you will return to Greystone?"

The old woman nodded. Jenny looked at her hard.

"Mrs. Mead, be frank with me. What do you mean to do? Shall you tell mother where I am?"

"I'll not answer ye," replied the old woman, rather sulkily, not liking Jenny's sharpness.

"You have sworn to keep my secret," said the girl, reproachfully.

"Suppose the first man I met in the street should be Mr. Shaw?" cried the old woman in a shrill voice.

Jenny turned to the window and looked through it in silence.

It was a long way to Marples, and but one coach to it, and that was gone. The next town was eight miles distant, and she shrunk from the long walk and the notion of her loneliness when she should. arrive at it; for she had no friend there, and the curiosity and staring of the people at any inn she might enter would be hardly less galling and painful than the frowns or averted eyes of people in Greystone. Yet, her mind being resolved never to return to her home, where basest thoughts were held of her, she had a dreadful fear of meeting her mother, who would surely follow at once, if Mrs. Mead proclaimed her whereabouts. How would she be able to resist her mother's passionate supplications and reproaches—those appeals to a love which, God knows, was never so strong as now, when she thought of her mother's cherishing sympathy, and the tears she must surely have wept over her pretty one's empty bedroom?

"See now, my dearie," said Mrs. Mead, mildly; "will ye let me judge how to act for you? If you were my child I could not wish you better than I do; and thy fame, which must be the dearest thing a woman hath, is my reason for hindering your journey this day. Neither you nor me knows what is being said i' Greystone, and things may hap to-day to make 'ee thankful you had not all the way from Marples to come. Bide here while I go to Greystone. I'll find out about thy mother, and how she bears thy going, and what is said of thee, and all that should be known. And to-night will I return with what news there is; and it shall either be that you return to thy home again, or go straight on into the world, as shall seem best on what report I bring you."

If Mrs. Mead had said this at first, Jenny would have understood her motives. But, says an ancient adage: "When you hear an old woman talk straight, you shall see your cow walk on its hind legs."

"There may be good sense in what you say," replied Jenny, who had turned from the window and stood with her fine eyes fixed on Mrs. Mead; "and here will I stop till you come back. But, truly, I do not know that any news you could bring should take me home again. For when father misses me his anger will be terrible, and not to save my life would I face him without proof that I am an honest girl."

At this moment Mrs. Walker came in with Jenny's breakfast. She chose to prepare the table herself, that she might have a good sight of the young wife; for Jenny was a wonderful heroine in the hostess's eyes, and created a chance for imagination to chew upon that deserved to be made much of.

"Your papa is known to me, ma'am," said she, curtsying, in token that the breakfast was ready. "I heerd him preach a sermon once—nay, it weer a lecture, as I remimber—in St. Martin's Hall, down Beach Street, in your town. He hath a strong voice, and is a fine man, as I think. Is he quite well?"

With a sad smile Jenny answered her; and as she seated herself at table, Mrs. Mead asked Sally about the waggon that was to carry her to Greystone.

"Johnny shall put the horse to when it pleases ye," replied Sally.

"The sooner the better," said the old woman, striving to catch Jenny's eye, that she might bestow a knowing look upon her. "The mistress here will stay till I return, and you will do your best to amuse her, Sally."

"Well, she shall do as she please, and heartily welcome indeed."

"See that her dinner be choice. I've praised your cooking, so ye'll not make a lie o' my words."

Jenny looked up with a smile, and Sally burst into a laugh.

"Did ye iver hear such an old chatterbox, ma'am?" she cried. "There niver was the like of her tongue. When my husband finds me stubborn, as sometimes he should, God bless him, for the good it does, he allers says, 'Sally, if ye don't mind me, I'll go fetch Judith Mead.' That's because he knows Mrs. Mead could talk a deaf man into hearin', and make a blind man leap o'er a ditch."

"So ye see, my dear," said Mrs. Mead, with exquisite complacency, "that though I've lived all my life at Greystone pretty nigh, ye must come to Winston to get a good character of me. Now, Sally, get thee gone to thy man, and let him bring the waggon round. And bid him put a bit o' hay for me to sit on i' the bottom, for I know what thy road will do for waggon-wheels; and if jump I must, let me fall soft, for thy mother's sake."

The so-called waggon was a small metamorphosed cart, with a canvas hood, and wheels stout enough to support a house. In ten minutes' time it was at the door, and on the near shaft of it sate, with his hobnail boots within a foot of the road, a sour-faced man, who sucked an inverted pipe, and doggedly combed horse-flies off the rough hide of the horse with a whip.

Sally came into the parlour to announce it, and Mrs. Mead at once got up and put on her old bonnet and shawl.

"I shall find ye here when I come back?" said she, interrogatively, holding Jenny's hand.

"Yes, I will wait for you," replied the girl, wearily, with the now familiar absent look in her eyes.

The old woman hobbled out of the room after her friend, and with a hard expression of misery on her face, Jenny went to the sofa and leaned her head upon it.

Beyond the uneasiness inspired by the delay in her wished-for distant removal from the town in which, as she believed, her name would be on every tongue, coupled with base suspicions of her purity, she felt no great disappointment; to her tired heart one place was as good as another. So languid was the movement of her mind, it had scarce power to take cognizance of its own desires. The one deep yearning for her husband was with her always; but, like a familiar ache in the body, habit had already induced a kind of insensibility to it. Of resolute contemplation she found herself incapable. Sudden agonizing throbs visited her when she thought of her mother, and the dreadful dishonour that had falsely and cruelly come upon them all. But there was the merciful assuagement of a torpor, created by acute mental suffering, upon her; her fears and doubts were involuntary instincts disturbing the brooding haze of bewilderment. Quite motionless she sat, an uncherished lovely form, with the stupefaction of heart-breaking grief in her face, and the muteness of death in her eyes.

CHAPTER IX

MRS. MEAD RETURNS TO GREYSTONE

"Here comes the lady—let her witness it.

Othello

"I KNOW I'm doin' right. Niver could I hold up my head if they got saying it were Judith Mead as helped Michael's girl to roon away and leave her character behind her," said Mrs. Mead to herself as the waggon drove off; and upon a loosened truss of hay she sat, right in the centre of the vehicle, staring out of the shadow at the pretty little inn that was dropping behind.

It was eleven o'clock, and the sun hot indeed; and the shagged forefeet of the horse struck out of the road a very fine dust, which, mixing with the hot air that passed through the hood of the cart, seemed to increase the temperature by many degrees.

Mrs. Mead loosened her bonnet-strings and opened the neck of her dress, and looked hard at the back of the head of the sour-faced man, whose canvas cap was a trifle below the level of the front board of the cart. But there was something so stolid in the manner in which he took the jerks of the vehicle, letting his body hop with a savage indifference to the value of elastic adjustment, something so obstinate and morose in the mat of black hair that hung upon the collar of his coat, that even Mrs. Mead was repelled, and held her peace.

For the space of ten minutes, and a trifle faster than a snail carries its shell, they jolted along the road, when suddenly the cart halted.

"Missis!" shouted Johnny, without turning his head, "ye doan't moind stoppin', do ye?"

"What for?" cried Mrs. Mead, starting out of a reverie, and gazing eagerly at the canvas cap.

"What for?" replied the man with sour disdain. "Do ye thinks I'se carrion-mate, to be toorned into woorms wi' bloudy flies? I'm a-goin' to git down."

"And what's to become o' me?" exclaimed Mrs. Mead, standing erect in the cart, at the risk of a fall if the horse moved.

"Doomed if I know," answered the man, dropping slowly on to the road; "an' doomed if oi care, missus. Fourteen shellen' and sixpence a week'll not pay me to kape flies fat!"

Not without horror, induced by the violence of his adjectives, the solemnity of his movements, and the mysteriousness of his motives, did Mrs. Mead survey him. He stood in the road, laboriously groping in his pockets, and, after endless search, drew forth a large red pocket-handkerchief, which he opened and held up and eyed all over; he then took off his cap and placed it between his knees, threw the handkerchief over his head, put on his cap again, and sluggishly recovered his seat on the shaft.

"Now, missus," said he, "they may bite thee if they're wanten' more groob. Hold on, or ye'll roon a moocker!"

He struck his horse over the tail, and Mrs. Mead had barely squatted herself down when they were moving again.

Without further stoppage they arrived at the top of the High Street of Greystone.

"This'll do, mister," exclaimed Mrs. Mead, who had no opinion of Johnny as a driver, and was weary of the jolting inflicted on her, and the miserably slow way they made; "ye needn't go no further."

Johnny, however, refused to take any notice of her request. There was an ale-house some distance down the street, and not until the waggon was abreast of it did he cry, "Whoa!" Then, dropping from his perch, with a trifle of briskness in the action, he came round to the back of the cart and said, "Ye can git down here if ye loike."

The old woman scrambled down as best she could, and Johnny looked on with a grin at her boots. Then correcting his smile, as she faced round upon him, he said—

"This here's the Wheatsheaf, and the flavey in the liquor is as foine as though 'twar all roon stoof."

"Ye're welcome to drink as much as iver they'll trust ye with," replied Mrs. Mead, tartly.

"Aren't ye goin' to stand summat?" cried the man.

"Yes, half a pint o' vinegar, if ye're good to drink it," answered the old woman.

"Go along, or I'll git ye drownt for a witch!" shouted the disappointed Johnny; and off she went, chuckling audibly.

Not ten yards, however, could she go without meeting an acquaintance. Who should this be but old Mrs. Bruff, going to her snuff-shop in George Street, with her dinner in a paper parcel.

"Good mornin', Mrs. Mead. How are you? 'Tis an age sin' I seen ye my way. What nasty weather is this! I cannot walk for the cling o' my clothes; and as to the flies—well, I reckon we must be 'Gyptians, to desarve sitch a cuss," said Mrs. Bruff, a corpulent old woman, quite as aged as Mrs. Mead, but looking a deal younger.

"I'm middlin' well, thank 'ee, Mrs. Bruff. As to comin' your way, what hath snuff to say to a lone old cratur' that counts her valley in fardens? The flies, they do tickle, truly. Them and the dogs knows what's good," exclaimed Mrs. Mead, with a glance at the paper parcel. "And doth not the parson say that prosperity draws strange things to it?"

"Ye're allers quizzing, Mrs. Mead. Prosperity, indeed! Five and fourpence was my airnings last week; scarce three loaves in it—thanks to them wagabone French, as it's a mussy for them I ain't a man."

"Well, and ye give me no news? That two gossips should roast i' this heat with nothing to say! But they're wonderful liars i' Greystone," said Mrs. Mead.

"News—to *thee!*" cried Mrs. Bruff, with a ludicrous toss of the head. "Why, here I stand for the truth; for, as you say, they're dreadful liars i' Greystone."

"The truth o' what?"

"But you know!" exclaimed Mrs. Bruff, looking at her old companion with absurd incredulity in her face.

"I do not know," replied Mrs. Mead, with the eagerness of a born gossip. "I am this minute arrived from Winston, and if anything hath happ'd I'm as strange to it as a unborn infant."

"Why, then," said Mrs. Bruff, speaking slowly, and with evident sense of superiority, "it's everywheres towd that Mike Strangfield's wench hath run away for shame o' the wrong done her by Dr. Shaw's son. But that's not it, neither. Not twenty minutes since, I met Deacon Skelton, who says to me, 'Is it true, Mrs. Bruff, that my brother Strangfield is dead?' 'The Lord forbid!' I says. 'I hope not, Mr. Skelton.' 'I'm afeard he is, then,' he says. 'Jim Mason,' he says, 'him as keeps the Blue Posteses, had the news from Tom Raffles, as is cousin to the Strangfields' servint; Polly her name is. She was sent for the doctor, but came fust in a fright to her mother—who's kept her bed sin' April, poor wretch—an' says that Strangfield's fell down in a, fit, and's a dead man.' 'Lord bless me, sir!' says I."

"That's news indeed!" exclaimed Mrs. Mead, very pale, and catching up her dress. "If it's true, it's as strange a wisitation as any that iver I read of in Holy Writ. Good-bye to ye. You've put me in a hurry, Mrs. Bruff. Lord save us! what wonderful things happen in this life!"

She was limping rapidly away before Mrs. Bruff could return her farewell.

She was too experienced a gossip herself to believe in the accuracy of any story related; but then, likewise, she well knew that almost never does any story get abroad without foundation. They may say there's a flame where there is only a spark; but, be sure, there is fire of some kind.

Hastily down the street she went, as one with a purpose; but when she came to the market-place the speed of her hobble slackened, she changed her mind, and walked through the stalls towards her court.

There were a dozen stalls in the market, variously furnished; but after ten in the morning little business was done, and at this hour of Mrs. Mead's passage through them, their keepers hung lazily among the shadows, talking one to another, while the women knitted or rocked their babies, or, by a new arrangement of fruit and flowers, made a new picture of their wares.

To each and all of these people Mrs. Mead was as familiar an object as any of the pillars that supported the roof of the market. With nods of the head, and amiable answers, she passed them; until, arriving at the stall that directly faced the court where she dwelt, she stopped to ask a large, bony woman, with a beard, and bare red arms like a smacksman's, if it was true that Michael Strangfield was dead.

"That I can't tell 'ee, mistress," replied the woman, in a hoarse voice; "there's summat wrong there. If he's dead, I'll treat myself to a dram. An on-civiller brute niver looked a female i' the face. Him it wur as swore me into the stocks two months ago come to-morrow."

"Ay, ay, for bein' in liquor—which was harder upon thy boy Joey than thee."

"Niver was the like o' that lie told sin' Sandy Thomson swore Micky Forward's life away, an' himself the thief! Me in liquor! Ail my drink is water, wi' a drop o' milk in't at the best."

"Well, kape to that, an' the deacons will do ye no hurt," replied Mrs. Mead. "Can't ye gi' me no more news o' Strangfield?"

"No more than what I've said," answered the woman, sullenly. "D'ye want a pretty cowcumber for three-ha'pence? Here's some here as'll suit your gums."

"Give me two an' I'll pay ye twopence," exclaimed Mrs. Mead, with a languishing look at the vegetable.

"I'll gi' ye three for sixpence," said the woman.

"Who's to ate of them? Two for twopence, and here's the money."

"Ye knaw how to profit from hard times! If thee wast a parson or a Frenchman ye'd do no worse," grumbled the woman, handing the cucumbers to Mrs. Mead, who paid the twopence, and walked off.

Arrived at her home, she washed her face, brushed her hair, dusted her bonnet and shoes, and, glancing at her cupboard to make sure of a bit of dinner to be cooked on her return, she sallied forth once more, and walked direct to Strangfield's house.

No outward and visible sign there was of anything being amiss. The men were at work in the yard, and there was an occasional laugh among them as their hammers flashed in the sun, and the saw grated out its harsh song. The loving creepers framed the windows with their peaceful leaves, and the hens crooned in the dust of the path that went between the house and the tarry palings of the yard.

Mrs. Mead knocked softly, and, with an uneasiness bred in her by the dislike bore her by the Strangfields, kept herself close, that she might not be spied by any sideways glance from the window. No one responding, she knocked again loudly, and presently the door was opened by Mrs. Strangfield herself.

The desolate white and grief of the poor woman's face was indeed something heart-moving to behold. The utter forlornness of the eyes, the piteous droop of the mouth, the dishevelment of hair and attire, which into grief throws a violent dramatic element, were beyond expression. She looked at Mrs. Mead, while the old woman bobbed a curtsy, as a person to whom everything that offers has a meaning cruelly hard to master.

"God forbid, mistress," said Mrs. Mead, "ye should think I am come out of evil curiosity. They say the deacon hath been stricken ill, and positively would I know this from one who hath the truth."

"Why do you come here for news? This is a house of mourning now. I am a desolate, lonely woman. Heaven help me!" replied Mrs. Strangfield in a broken voice.

"So, indeed, ye be, if it is only for your daughter's leavin' you," said Mrs. Mead, with deep compassion. "But what hath happ'd to the deacon? For the Lord's sake let me hear it of you, ma'am!"

"He hath been struck with paralysis, and lies dying and calling for his daughter. That is the truth. And now must I go to him, for your knock has brought me from his bed, and the maid is away on an errand, and I am alone in the house."

She spoke with the stolidity of exhausted grief, and was stepping back to close the door.

"Stay!" cried Mrs. Mead; "I bring thee news of thy child."

The mother wheeled round with a shriek, and with both hands seized her arm.

"What of her? Is she living?"

"Living and well. Not an hour ago I left her."

Mrs. Strangfield had no words. The sudden dispersion of the fears that had torn her heart was a moral convulsion that deprived her of speech. She stood, with her fingers clutching hard the old woman's arm. Then incoherently she spoke.

"Sweet girl! How hath she been wronged! My pretty one! Alive, indeed, and I have been praying for thee. Oh, what a sorrow to befall the pure in heart! God forgive us!"

She drooped and leaned towards Mrs. Mead, and brought up the old hand to her mouth and kissed it, weeping the while such tears as only mothers weep.

"Alive and well!" she burst out again. "Dear heart, to bring me such tidings! Come in, come in! God is good to send thee! Dear heart, what joy you give me!"

With drops trickling down her furrowed cheeks, Mrs. Mead suffered herself to be drawn into the house by the passionate mother.

"Quick, now, dear friend!" cried Mrs. Strangfield, feverishly. "Tell me where my girl is! Is she in Greystone? . . . Oh, my poor heart!"

"She is at Winston, at the Greyhound there, and you mun go and fetch her, and tell her what blow hath fallen on thee, or she will not retoorn. Oh, she is bitter—and rightly so!"

quavered the old woman, in a voice strangely composed of indignation and sympathy. "Niver, she swears, will she come to her home again, to be despised and thought vilely of. For her dying father she may come—but you must fetch her, mistress."

"Come! Oh, she will come when she sees my face, and hears that her father lies moaning for her. Besides, hath not Dr. Shaw proved her a married woman? Ay, this very morning, Mrs. Mead, he came to bring us written proof of my Jenny's marriage with Cuthbert Shaw! But how can I leave my husband?" she cried distractedly. "The doctor says he must be watched. And how can I fetch my Jenny and be with my poor Michael?"

"Well, well! truly proved married! And she hath told no lies, then?" gasped Mrs. Mead. "The Lord forgive ye all for the pain you have given her. What didst thee say?—thy husband wants nursing? While ye're gone I'll watch by him. I've nursed a many i' my time. Hath he his mind?"

"Yes; he lies still—he has no power in one arm and he groans sadly. He calls for Jenny, and—— Oh, Mrs. Mead! if I am not quick he may never see her again in this world. Dear Mrs. Mead, since you will stop, run up to him now, dear heart, while I get my bonnet. I will be very quick. Do you mind, I have courage to be quick since she is living. Straight up, Mrs. Mead, to the right. Stay, I will show thee. Oh, God grant him a little life!"

She ran upstairs swiftly, yet with light feet, and Mrs. Mead went laboriously, quivering and stumbling after her. Outside the door quite clearly was the groaning of the man heard. He lay on his back, looking towards the wall, and in the gloom of the room his face was scarcely distinguishable from the pillow for the whiteness of it.

With a finger on her lip, Mrs. Strangfield motioned to Mrs. Mead to take the chair by the bedside; and, nimbly apparelling herself, she came to the old woman's ear and breathlessly delivered instructions. They were simple enough, and to Mrs. Mead's discretion was left the explanation of her presence if Strangfield should observe her. But truly there seemed little chance of this: never once, since lifted from the parlour floor and laid upon the bed, had he stirred, and that should be over three hours. At regular intervals he groaned, and as his wife glided out of the room he called for Jenny.

CHAPTER X

JENNY AND HER MOTHER

"She keeps unbroken
The bond which nature gives."
LONGFELLOW

JUST out of High Street, not a stone's throw from the church, lived Mr. Franklin, who owned the Swiftsure coach that plied between Greystone and the old city on the road to London. Mr. Franklin, was the owner of some hackney-coaches as well as the Swiftsure, and a large stable of horses, and out of his special traffic a comfortable living did he get; for in those days balls and routs were no uncommon things on country sides, and relations were often visiting each other with equipment of luggage; and Franklin was the only hackney jobber in the district.

He was a pudding-faced man, and shaped like a ball in that part of his body which the band of his breeches circled; and he stood, with his legs wide apart, sucking a straw at the gateway of his yard, wherein, under sheds, stood his rolling stock, when Mrs. Strangfield breathlessly came to him, and besought him, with clasped, entreating hands, instantly to order out one of his coaches, that she might be driven to Winston.

Now, fortunately for her, Franklin was a prompt man; and reading urgency in the poor woman's desperate face, he gave a shrill whistle, and out from a little office tumbled a knock-kneed ostler.

"Number Two, Jeremy, and Sarah's your gal. Let Thomas scrape hisself, and tell him the leddy's waiting," said Mr. Franklin; and with despatch that would pleasure this electric age to experience, a coach rattled up to the gate.

"To the Greyhound, at Winston, as quick as ever you can gallop," cried Mrs. Strangfield; and in a trice the heavy-wheeled vehicle was scattering loungers in the roadway on to the pavements, and making the shop-windows clink to the thunder of its progress.

Still, it was a half-hour's drive, and a terribly hustling one; the ruts sweating steam from the horse, and proving honesty in the traces. Yet the flight of an eagle would have been a snail's pace to the impatience of the mother, who, in her eagerness to recover her child and be back again to her dying husband, sat in a frenzy.

At last the village hove in sight: a little row of cottages swept by, and the coach came to a stand in front of the glass door of the Greyhound Inn. The man descended from the box of the coach, though already she was spraining her wrist in desperate efforts to open the door for herself; and no sooner was she liberated than she flew—into the arms of Sally, who, having caught sight of the coach from a window, was running to the door.

"Are you the mistress?" said Mrs. Strangfield, in a wild way.

"Yes, I be, ma'am," replied Sally, with a civil curtsy.

"Is there a lady here?"

"Ay; an' you be her mother, I reckon."

"I am her mother. Take me to her at once."

Though Sally had been fortified with a dozen scruples, they would have been helplessly swept away by the peremptoriness of this command.

"She's just where Mrs. Mead left her, ma'am. This way, please;" and she went to the parlour door and threw it open, saying, "Here be thy mother, mistress."

Jenny was standing at the window overlooking the rich green space of garden at the back of the house. With a stupefied face on her she turned, and a cry left her lips, and she stepped back a pace when her mother rushed to her. Then, like a flash of light, at the sight of the beloved face, an impulse of love and joy leapt up in her; and in close sobbing embrace were they locked as Sally, looking away from the sacred sight, closed the door upon them.

"Oh, Jenny, why are you here? why didst thee leave me?" cried Mrs. Strangfield, relinquishing her daughter to gaze at her, with eyes in which rapture and sorrow were strangely blended. "Never was mother's heart wrung as mine was when this morning I beheld your bed untouched, and you were not near to answer to my call."

"I could not stay. Father would have taken me to London to-day; and see what a mad journey it would have been, and how cruel my ignorance would make him!" the girl said, pushing back her hair, and standing in a half-defiant, half-drooping posture before her mother.

"Thy father! Oh, Jenny! not only is it my love for thee that has brought me here in mad haste—thy father is dying! Ay, he may be dead before we can return to him!"

"Dying! . . . Mother, what do you say?" said Jenny, taking, so to speak, firmer hold of the floor with her feet, and frowning, whilst a sickly hue of pallor overspread her face.

"Oh, Jenny! for the sake of God who hath brought me to thee, put on your hat and come with me quickly. I tell you your father is dying—he fell to the ground when Dr. Shaw brought him proof of your marriage with Cuthbert. Dost thee not know that the doctor has proved thee his son's wife? Ah, my poor heart, how should she know!—and that the cause of thy husband's missing, as the doctor believes, is that he was seized by the press-gang and carried away to sea! Down thy father fell, and we bore him to his room, and the surgeon fears for his life; and all the while he lies groaning and crying upon thy name. '*Bring Jenny to me! bring Jenny to me!*' he moans. My pretty, come quickly, or you'll see him no more in this world."

The girl stood transfixed and overwhelmed by her mother's news. Then you could have seen her battling with the rush and surge of tumultuous emotions a whole minute ere she spoke.

"Do you tell me that my darling is carried away to sea?" she said, in a febrile whisper.

"'Tis what his father believes."

"And that Dr. Shaw hath proved me his son's wife to my father?"

"Yes, indeed. He came with a paper, and the sight of it hath killed thy father. His heart is broken for the wrong he has done his only one!" wailed the mother. "Oh, Jenny, do not delay! There is a coach at the door. Make haste to put on your hat. You would not let him be moaning for thee in dying sorrow, and not come!"

She looked at her mother with a wonderful expression of troubled amazement and incredulous horror in her eyes, then took up her hat, and in a few minutes was ready to depart. As she left the room, she met Mrs. Walker, into whose hand she slipped a guinea, giving her a sweet, strange smile as she did so, but quite powerless to speak.

The woman, much affected by Jenny's munificence, put the little trunk into the coach, and low and numerous were the curtsies she dropped as it drove off.

The rattle of wheel and window, if not a prohibition to speech, was a decided obstacle to the hearing. But Mrs. Strangfield had too much to say to hold her peace. With her child's hand locked in hers, she poured her heart into Jenny's ear, and all the story of Dr. Shaw's visit told her, and the medical man's judgment on Michael's condition, with whatever else that her head was giddy with—sometimes reproaching and sometimes breaking into passionate exclamations of rapture, which thoughts of her husband would inevitably choke; silent scarcely ever, and of the matter of her volubility leaving Jenny, amid the roar of the coach, in possession of but very small fragments.

And the girl?

Her father knew at last that she was honest, and for a brief while had exultation, of the kind that enflames the madman's eye, swelled until it had sickened her heart with the force and fulness of it. But the emotion died under the heavy droop of humiliated honour. She had won back her name, but what had the victory cost her? Her husband was gone, her father was dying, her heart was wounded and bleeding badly. To her very mother her instincts moved rebelliously, for even in *her* implicit faith had been wanting; and as perfume is got from flowers by crushing them, so surely had the girl's heart been cruelly used, that the truth might be torn from it.

The bitter passion of shame that had driven her from Greystone revisited her again when the coach entered the High Street, and she leaned back and involuntarily drew her veil over her face. The mother noticed the action, but had no sympathy to comprehend its import. To *her* belief it was fear of father that had caused Jenny's flight; and now that home was near, the dreadful terror that Michael was gone into eternity without forgiveness from the child he had wronged, dried up the wife's tongue and held her solemnly mute.

She stopped the coach at the corner of the street, that the jar of the wheels might not penetrate the resonant wooden house, and alighted with her daughter, and both of them went quickly in.

"Mother," whispered Jenny, standing in the passage as a stranger might, "I will stay here till you have seen him."

"In the parlour, then, dearest, and rest thee. Oh, Jenny, pray God to spare him! He is thy father."

Softly the poor woman climbed the stairs, and Jenny went into the little room which, in all her life, she had vowed never again to enter. Speculating she stood, wondering how it had befallen that her mother had come so speedily, and if Mrs. Mead had arrived straight from Winston to break her promise; with an undercurrent of breathless expectation in her mind, quite apart from her other thoughts, that amid her conjectures held her listening painfully and drawing the air with labour and short struggles.

Then through the doorway came a whisper—"Jenny!"

She went out, and on the stairs she saw her mother, who for despair could only beckon or toss her hands. She followed Mrs. Strangfield upstairs, with a creeping chill over her limbs, and the sensation of a thousand quivering fibres in her body.

In the bedroom, near the bed, were two figures, whom she could not immediately distinguish for the feeble light in the chamber; but she speedily found that one was Mrs. Mead, and the other the doctor—a square man, in a long-skirted coat and buckles on his shoes, and a brown wig glossily shining over a face whereof the pensive concern was as clearly a part as any lineament.

Both figures drew away when mother and daughter came into the room. Mrs.

Strangfield went to the bedside, and, bending over the motionless form upon it, said, in a whisper of exquisite sadness—

"Michael, Jenny is here. Wilt thou speak to her?"

For some moments there was no answer. At last, in a faint, hoarse murmur, the dying man said—

"Let her take my hand and kiss me. Jane, thee knowest that I cannot move."

The girl went to her father, and put her hand into his and kissed his forehead.

"Jenny, my little one," he murmured, "thee didst wrong to trick me. Of old did the prophet chide, saying, 'And thou saidst, I shall be a lady for ever: so that thou didst not lay these things to thy heart, neither didst remember the latter end of it.' But thy punishment has been sore, my poor one. By thee am I condemned, whom I condemned. I was a liar for speaking what, in my wrath, I believed the truth; and it did nearly break thy heart, poor wench, as mine is broken!"

No pathos the meaning of his words had could equal the deeply moving effect given to them, by his speaking with his head turned away, all power lost, life ebbing from him as surely as the shadows cast by the sun were slowly circling to the east, whence darkness comes. She hung over him with dry eyes, for the grief in her was too deep for tears.

"Father," she whispered, "I wronged thee by loving secretly; but has not my husband's going wrung my heart with punishment enough? Truly I was innocent of worse sin than deceit; and now that you know I am innocent, and bear with my kisses, I could be happy to die."

No answer did he return, and he began to breathe heavily; on which the doctor came gently to her, and would have led her from the bed; but the father had a grip of her hand, and she would not disengage his hold.

Said the mother, in a feeble whisper—

"Is there no hope?"

The doctor shook his head, and let his chin fall on his breast, and stood quiet, with his hands clasped.

No more was said.

What was killing him, God knows! Not paralysis only, nor yet a broken heart. Yet visibly was he dying, and the difficult breath grew slower and weaker; and within an hour from Jenny's return to her home, the breath in him was gone, and the body growing cold. He passed away, amid a deep stillness in the room; and Jenny herself, who was near him, knew not that he was dead, until a strangeness in the hold of his fingers made her shriek out.

Thus did it come about; and the mother and daughter wept in each other's arms, while the doctor glided noiselessly from the house, and Mrs. Mead tenderly closed the dead man's eyes, and veiled the marble silence of his face.

CHAPTER XI

IN THE CITY

".... This soul hath been
Alone on a wide, wide sea;
So lonely 'twas that God Himself
Scarce seemèd there to be."

COLERIDGE

NOW, it was just five months after Michael Strangfield had departed this life, which brings us into the sloppy, inglorious month of November, that there hung over London, close down to the streets, a yellow fog.

So thick was it, that a man, standing still in any thoroughfare, found life strangely converted into a mere pulsation of phantoms; a brief emergence and abrupt vanishment of figures—of men and women and horses—

silent for the most part with the bewilderment of the shroud of fog.

All about the Monument, and where a maze of streets meets, to pour their crowds towards London Bridge, the fog was thickest, smothering the business of the hour, as though the heavens had come down upon mankind in the form of a feather-bed. Here were many vehicles at a standstill, and voices belonging to invisible creatures went through the fog, with the clang of bells and stamping and slipping of iron-shod feet.

A hackney-coachman, swathed in a mass of capes, and looking, with the immense white shawl around his throat, like an artichoke trimmed with sauce, suddenly brought the horse he had been pulling and hauling at to a stand, and, slapping down his whip on the roof of the vehicle, leaned over and shouted into the window—

"There's no movin' agin it. You can git out or sit vere you are; but here I stops!"

And, saying this, he recovered his upright posture, and with great deliberation folded his arms under his cape.

The individual thus addressed, protruding his head through the window of the carriage, took a despairing look at the blank scene around, filled with outlines which grew defined or vanished, as the folds of the fog circled or released them.

"Whereabouts are we, coachman?" he called out.

"If I knew I'd go ahead, and blow the odds!" replied the man.

But the gentleman inside was clearly too impatient to behave sensibly; for, catching hold of a travelling-bag, he jumped into the middle of the fog, and, giving some money to the coachman, went steadily in the direction to which his nose happened to point; and, luck being with him, he came to the pavement.

He asked a man the way to Cornhill. "Straight on," was the reply. And after twenty minutes of bumping and groping, and when he had measured some two hundred yards, the fog lifted, the whole space and scene around cleared, and with a rush and a shout London went to work again.

It was a short walk to Cornhill. Looking carefully from side to side as he went, our friend arrived presently at a passage, on which, amid other names, carefully indicated by a pointing hand, was the scroll, "George Hunter and Company, Second Floor." He mounted the gloomy staircase, and reached a landing of four doors, on one of which he knocked.

Behind a tall, long desk were several clerks writing by lamplight.

"I wish," said the gentleman, "to see the principal—the owner of the ship *Elizabeth*."

At the sound of that name the whole of the clerks looked up like one man and stared at him.

"Certainly," exclaimed one of them, jumping up. "What name, if you please, sir?"

"Mr. Cuthbert Shaw."

The clerk passed into another office, and in a moment returned and requested Mr. Shaw to walk in. This was done by passing round the desk; and Cuthbert, followed by the eyes of all the clerks, entered a large office, where at a table sat two elderly gentlemen.

One of them, a grey-haired man with spectacles, immediately rose.

"Mr. Shaw, I think the name was?"

"Mr: Cuthbert Shaw."

"Pray take that chair, sir. My partner, Mr. Atkinson. My name is Hunter."

He resumed his seat, looking inquisitively at the brown, though emaciated, face of the young man.

"It is possible, Mr. Hunter, that you may have already been apprized of the loss of your ship the *Elizabeth*, off Cape Palmas?"

"Yes; but only one week since, by the third mate of the vessel, who was rescued from a boat, with four companions."

"I was on board the *Elizabeth* when she was wrecked, and am only just arrived in London."

"Cuthbert Shaw? I do not remember the name in the list of passengers," said Mr. Hunter. "I will refer——" and he was about to summon a clerk.

"You will not find my name in your list. I was rescued by the *Elizabeth* in the English Channel last July, a day or two after she sailed from the Thames. I was on board an English brig of war called the *Cleopatra*. She engaged a French frigate, and was sunk by her. Some of us got clear of the sinking hull by means of the boats, and, on the following day, the *Elizabeth* came across the boat I was in and took me on board.

"Permit me to continue my story, and relate the object of my visit. My time is very short in London.

"All had gone prosperously with the *Elizabeth* until we were drawing near the latitude of the Gulf of Guinea; when, one

Friday evening, a furious gale set in from the west. It obliged us to run before it, and for a whole day we were driven helplessly; but, on Saturday night, the captain, not daring to run to the westward any longer, hove the ship to, in doing which she was struck by a sea that swept away the galley, stove in the bulwarks, and carried some of the men overboard. At the same time we lost one of our masts.

"Gentlemen, you will probably have received a full account of this disaster from the mate. It is enough if I tell you that, on the Monday morning, finding the ship leaking beyond our power to keep her afloat, the men took to the boats; but I was in feeble health, and, in the selfish rush, I was beaten down and left insensible, and for a quarter of an hour I lay: when coming to, I found there was another man left on board—one of the Indian prince's attendants. I sprang up, and hallooed after the boats, which were sailing rapidly away—the gale had broken on the previous afternoon, and the sea was comparatively smooth, if I take no account of the heavy swell—and then, perceiving that the ship was rapidly sinking, and the occupants of the boats either did not or would not heed me, I prepared myself for death—which, God knows, at that time had no terrors for me, for

I had endured more than many hearts could have stood without breaking under."

Observing the pause, Mr. Hunter produced a bottle of wine from a drawer and filled a glass for the young fellow. With kindly eyes and much sympathy he encouraged him to proceed.

"Gentlemen, whilst I stood awaiting the moment of death, which I conceived inevitable, the Indian, appearing to observe me for the first time, rushed up to me and, with many wild gesticulations and unintelligible words, dragged me to the stern of the vessel, where, to my joy, I saw a small boat suspended. She hung by ropes at the head and stern, and I motioned to the Indian to slacken the left-hand rope whilst I released the other, by which means we got the boat down upon the water without capsizing her.

"No sooner was she afloat, than the Indian sprang over the taffrail and swung himself into her; and, dreading that he might leave me to my fate, I followed him hastily, and cast the boat adrift from the ship, which, twenty minutes after we had quitted her, sank.

"From this point my story is a mere commonplace narrative of suffering, with one strange feature in it. Our boat was without sails. The other boats, having the advantage over us in size and sail, soon vanished upon the water-line."

He glanced at a timepiece, drank his wine, and continued, speaking quickly—

"There was a small quantity of fresh water in a beaker in the boat's bows, but no food of any kind. In the night, which was very calm, with bright stars, I fell asleep; and when I awoke, my mouth being parched, I went to the beaker, but found it empty. I knew that the Indian had drank the water in the night whilst I slept, and, in my rage and agony, I could have murdered him; but the wretch fell on his knees and so piteously moaned to me in his native language, that my fury was sobered by the fear and despair in his face, and in my misery I sat down and wept. Observing my anguish, the Indian crawled over to me on his knees and kissed my feet, and then, pulling out a package from his breast, he placed it in my hand and withdrew to the bows of the boat. Scarcely knowing what I did, I thrust the package into my pocket, and instantly forgot it in the sufferings of thirst which tormented me. However, some relief I obtained by sousing my shirt in the sea and wearing it against my skin; and likewise I chewed a piece of leather from the sole of my boot, which kept my mouth moist.

"Four days passed, in sufferings I need not describe, and on the fifth day the Indian fell crazy, and, leaning over the side of the boat in a manner that nearly overset her, he drank the salt water greedily as a sheep would, with his mouth upon it, which brought on a black vomit, and towards the morning he died. Not until the evening of the sixth day was I rescued by a small schooner from Pernambuco to Portsmouth, blown by the gale that had wrecked the *Elizabeth* many miles out of her course, who on sighting my boat bore down and picked me up. That was on the 12th of September, as I was told—for I had lost all reckoning of time—and four days ago I arrived at Portsmouth. So this brings me to an end of my perils, gentlemen; and now will I state my motive in calling upon you."

He put his hand in his pocket, and held it there while he spoke.

"You of course remember that an Indian prince sailed as passenger in the *Elizabeth*?"

"Certainly."

"He was reported on board the ship to be possessed of very valuable jewels."

"We will give you the appraisement in figures—£170,000."

"I have explained to you that my fellow-sufferer in the boat was one of the Prince's attendants. The parcel he placed in my hands contained precious stones, which a jeweller in Portsmouth valued at £63,000."

"He must have stolen them when the ship was sinking," said Mr. Hunter, quickly.

"No doubt, and by so doing saved them. Here they are, in the wrapper in which they were handed to me."

Saying which, he placed the package on the table. Mr. Hunter took it up and opened it, and his partner drew close to him; and when the gems lay exposed, his eyes glistened in the light of them.

Splendid stones some of them were, truly: diamonds chiefly, with the lustrous red of rubies intermixed, and here and there the mild shimmer of a pearl. It was hard to tell whether the gems had been extracted from settings or gathered loose as they were; but an ignorant eye might know their preciousness.

"Well, Mr. Shaw," said Mr. Hunter, placing the open paper carefully on the table, with a gentle setting of it towards Cuthbert, "these stones are unquestionably your property, and well may you hold them, in compensation for the sufferings you have undergone."

"Well, sir, it comes to this: if they were not on that table, they would be at the bottom of the sea."

"Quite so," from both partners.

"Now, gentlemen, you cannot tell me that the prince is alive?"

"That is beyond our power, certainly."

"Will you put yourselves in his place, and receive the proposals I should make to him?"

"With pleasure; but, holding him dead, we will consider your proposal in reference to his heirs," said Mr. Hunter.

"That is as you please. Sixty-three thousand pounds is a jeweller's appraisement of those stones. He would have found me the money. I ask ten thousand pounds for restoring them."

"Plainly, Mr. Shaw, your Portsmouth jeweller taught you no lesson," said Mr. Hunter; and the other partner arched his eyebrows.

"Be open with me, gentlemen."

"Why, sir, we consider your request a very modest one."

"Then what I will ask you to do is this: give me a letter stating that you hold these stones for me; get them appraised at your convenience. I will write to you in the meanwhile, giving you my address, and you will then send me bank-post-bills to cover the sum I ask."

The letter was written, the number of stones specified, and within the space of twenty minutes Cuthbert had left the office.

Both parties shook him cordially by the hand, and Mr. Hunter attended him, bareheaded, to the door.

It was a rich morning's work for them; for in those days "commission" was as keenly understood in the City of London as now.

CHAPTER XII

CUTHBERT

"Now I am comen home to reste."
SIR JOHN MANDEVILLE

BRONZED by the sun and thin in the face.

But emaciation was the only change in him.

And it was a change to mar nothing of his beauty, which, because of the ingrained expression of pensive thought, such as a man might wear in whose heart sorrow languishes but will not die, was of a noble and truer type than what it had been in the lighter months before.

When a man lives a bitter lifetime in a short while, his face will be a mirror to reflect the violent compression of experience.

By the earnest, plaintive gaze of the eye, by the habitual fixity of the mouth, by the unsevere resolution of feature, Cuthbert explained to the shallowest sight the harshness of his ordeal, though its nature remained his secret.

But to this distinctive expression which his face had taken—stamped there by lonely contemplation, by unutterable longings, by helpless chafing, by many fits of mental agony, by hope fallen sick and spiritless, by such things which do really and truly of this life make a hell without participation of conscience, as there are sufferers to swear—was super-added at this time, as he walked through busy thoroughfares, a painful anxiety so acute as to fix upon his heart the shadow of physical torment.

With quick steps he pressed forward, glancing on his passage at every clock, until he had crossed Blackfriars Bridge, and arrived at the famous hostelry which, in those days, was the starting-point for the coaches to that part of the coast where Greystone lay.

Here was the coach drawn up, and passengers clambering to their places, and another five minutes of fog had lost the returned hero a night.

There was room and to spare, happily; but no time for the hot drink, which the rest of the travellers had stowed under their small-clothes. Vapour was still in the sky to darken it, and a leaden dulness on the massive city; but when the horses' heads were down, and the wheels spinning, the sky grew light, and fold after fold of fog peeled off until the blue heaven floated clear, and then the tune of the wind grew merry.

This coach was the "Rattler," and famous for good runs. At every stage did it halt, as punctually as trains at stations do now; and for a careless heart the passage was a glorious journey to make. November's yellow light upon the land, upon the hill-tops a full-toned colouring that kept distant the blue of the sky, between the ridges masses of shadow, the brown of loam, and the dwelling of sunshine on green.

At eight of the evening the coach swung through the streets of a half-way city of the road, where some relinquished the roof for an inn-fire and a bed. But Cuthbert kept his place; so that faithfully at the hour of twelve, by the deep-voiced city clock, the coach arrived at that ancient place whence diverged the road to Greystone, and here Cuthbert quitted the vehicle.

The suggestion of a bed seemed like a landlord's mocking of a restless spirit; yet to a bed in the Old Bell Inn he betook himself, laying urgent commands upon the host that a post-chaise should be ready for him by six. Even an hour's sleep could do him no injury; and this he got, which relieved the veins of his head from the fulness of the blood poured into them by intense mental anxiety, and toned the heart into a softer beating; so that when he was aroused he was better prepared for the end of his journey.

The distance to Greystone was twenty-one miles, and this the post-horses could run, with one halt for a bait. At nine o'clock the chaise-wheels took the stones of the High Street.

He was in Greystone at last; amid the familiar scenes that had been present to him in vigils which had made his eyes a torture to his head for the heat of them, in the frightful loneliness of the deep, in the hour of battle, in the shrieking time of shipwreck, in the long and crushing pause of idleness forced upon him by the tardy movements of the little ship that had brought him home.

In Greystone at last! And as in the High Street he stood, the smooth sea stretching its grey lustre to the sky from under the fronting houses, and the keen wind whitening the roadways—unnoticed, for the cold, by the few persons abroad, who hurried past, hugging themselves in folds of frieze—a passionate fear came upon him and held him to the pavement.

For right in his sight, looking now through bare tendrils of creepers, was the shipwright's wooden house; and that it might be a desolate place for the want of his wife, and a tomb for the echoes of memory only to sound in, was a dread of the awful kind that repels the heart with horror from the determination of it.

He took courage presently and went forward slowly, with his eyes fixed upon the house, until he was at the gate of it, and then he walked quietly to the door. He knocked and fell back a pace, that every window might be visible to him; and whilst he stood, looking first here and then there, the door was opened, and a respectably dressed woman stood forth.

He could barely speak for the constriction in his throat, and in a quite faint voice asked if Mrs. Strangfield was within.

"Oh, dear no, sir. Mrs. Strangfield has been gone these three months," answered the woman, looking at him with surprise.

"Where?"

"Why, to a house in Winston. Do not you know her husband be dead, and the business sold to Mr. McAndrew?"

"They were friends of mine, and I am just returned from a long journey." And in a wild, quick way, like a cry over-leaping decision, he said, "And what of her daughter?"

"Mrs. Shaw? She lives along wi' her mother. Her husband be dead too, ye know."

"She lives with her mother, and is well, I hope?" he said, the flush brought to his face by the violence his question did him yielding to a deadly white.

"Quite well, I believe, sir. She's niver i' Greystone. They say she's known a deal o' sorrow, and there's some shame in it that keeps her i' hiding. Poor heart! A sweeter woman there is not; truly there is not."

She looked at him hard as she said this, the gaze growing keener and keener, the eyebrows lifting to it, and something like an expression of consternation coming into her face.

"I am Mr. Shaw," he said, anticipating the question that was already parting her lips.

"You!—an' she thinks ye dead!" the woman shrieked.

With a toss of the hands he turned his head to look up the High Street.

"Is it known," he said, confronting her, "that I was impressed in error by a gang of sailors? What did my father think? Do you know him?"

"Dr. Shaw, of the school-house? Well by name, sir. Ye know, of course, that he be well, and is giving up teachin'? A man hath come from some city i' the north to buy the school from him—so I heerd but a week since," said the woman, so fascinated, not alone by the romance of Cuthbert's return, but by the beauty of his face, that she could not lift her eyes from him.

"Is it known that I was impressed?" he asked again.

"I cannot tell ye for sure, sir. Some talk there was, I think; but them as it went among were but little known to me. And before my husband bought this business we lived at the white house, away down by Callow Bay, which kept me out o' gossip."

"Is Mr. Franklin alive? or, where can I hire a coach?"

"Oh, Mr. Franklin is nicely, sir. Will ye not come in and sit down? And my gel shall fetch you a coach as quick as iver it'll come for thee."

He thanked her for her civil offer and entered the little parlour, never before beheld by him, and even unfamiliar to us, now that the quaint furniture of the Strangfields was gone, and the simple old sea-pieces.

He breathed quickly as he stood alone, looking around him. This had been his darling's home. Through the window, into which Mr. McAndrew had let clarified glass, he saw the old bay tree, and the shrubbery and green stuff, amid which he used to slip his letters to his sweetheart after dark, appointing meetings for the morrow. The walls around him had echoed to her voice. Her feet had trodden the ground on which he stood. Yonder was the scene of street and market-place, which her timid eyes had swept again and again that night when she waited for him to come and tell her father that she was his wife.

Mrs. McAndrew returned with a tray of wine and biscuit, and pulled a chair to the table that he should sit.

"I'm all of a tremble with astonishment, sir, truly. 'Tis the wonderfullest thing that ye should be there looking at me, and your pretty wife thinking herself a widow, not five mile away. I've sent the gel for a carriage. Ye'll have patience for five minutes, sir; and if this wine's not to your relish, I can draw ye a proper head o' beer."

He seated himself, looking vacantly at the woman under his lowering brow.

"You cannot tell me that my wife *knew* that I was carried away to sea by a press-gang?" he said presently.

"I can't own as iver I heard say she knew it, sir. But I can tell you that some trouble came upon the sweetheart after ye were missing; her father was cruel, and that she were married he would not believe. That's what were said. Then afterwards it were proved by Dr. Shaw she was your wife, sir. And that broke her father's heart, they said. One thing I reckon sure, howiver wrong be all else I say: your wife ran away from Greystone for the shame that evil-thinking gossips put upon her; and her mother, as she now lives with, told me herself that her reason for sellin' the business was because Mistress Shaw had vowed niver to come to Greystone again, after she had kissed her father, lying dead on his bed for grief."

"May God forgive them all for wronging her! Poor little one! Could her father look at her and doubt her? Oh, madam, the carriage is a long while coming. This delay is a heavy trial to me!"

He went quickly from his chair to the window, where he stood a while, tapping the ground with his foot.

"How did my father treat her, do you know?" he asked.

"Why, sir, very honourably, I believe, from all reports. An old Mrs. Mead, whom some call 'mother,' was telling me a while back, that your father asked Mistress Shaw to go and live with him, promising to pack the boys home and give up the trade if she'd come. But your lady hath a proper spirit, and Mrs. Mead, who loves her, said, 'How should she stay with the old man as doubted her honour once?' Though I'll own I answered her, that, all things considering, seeing your lady could not prove her marriage, as 'twas said, and that you were not by, it was not what you might call onraisonable for Dr. Shaw to doubt her."

"Not prove her marriage!"

He dropped his head and swung himself to the window, exclaiming under his breath, "That was my fear, always."

"Well, sir," continued Mrs. McAndrew, "ye see, accordin' to Mrs. Mead, it were this: ye had charge o' the marriage paper, and the mistress could not remimber the name o' the church in London. As how should she, if it were ne'er told her? Once in all my life was I in London, and dazed was I by the noise, to be sure—in some streets 'twas like a bull roaring—and though my cousin, who is a London man, showed me a score o' churches, and named 'em, too, clear in my hearing, not if you was to say, here be a hundred pounds for thee, if ye'll gi' me the name o'——"

But before she could make an end the hackney-coach came rumbling to the gate, with the maid inside it. Thanking her for her civility and information, and learning from her that "onybody i' Winston'll tell ye where Mrs. Strangfield lives," Cuthbert shook Mrs. McAndrew's hand, jumped into the coach, and was driven off.

CHAPTER XIII

HUSBAND AND WIFE

"But seas between us braid hae roar'd
Sin' Auld Lang Syne."

IT was a bright day, but the wind very keen, and the country white-looking for it, though there was no frost. From side to side Cuthbert's eyes roamed as the coach rattled him up the High Street, but no familiar face did he encounter. Yes! one there was—an old boatman, who stood sucking a pipe at the door of an ale-house. Always, when Cuthbert went fishing, this was the man who had rowed him out to sea. He was past in a moment, and out of the High Street rolled the coach on to the level country road. And now, by changing his seat, might Cuthbert have caught a glimpse, on his right hand, of the roof and chimney-pots of Greystone School. But he did not change his seat, nor turn his head, nor give his father a thought. That his father was well was news to satisfy into silence the faint filial instinct that stirred in him. Why, it was his own foolish silence, and the trick of a secret marriage, that had brought the shame of scandal upon his wife; but, pricked by memory of the cold restraint that had kept him a boy when he was a man, he would have been an angel not to refer all his own and Jenny's sorrow to his father.

With his arms folded tightly upon his breast, and all his heart given to violent strife with dismaying emotion, and the terror of great love, wrought by expectation and hope to the extreme point where other passions begin, Cuthbert was carried at a sharp trot along the hard road, and over the ruts which the cold had congealed into iron; past the brown land of fields and leafless hedgerows, where balls of birds perched without flutter; and the steam from the horse's nostrils drove out from either side the coach like throbs of an escape-pipe under the hammering of a cylinder.

At last came up a grey stone front, with green ivy flourishing upon it, and the wheels rang out a multiplied echo.

Cuthbert called to the man to stop.

"This is Winston?"

"Ay, sir."

"I'll get out here."

He alighted with his travelling-bag, and put money into the driver's hand, which set the fellow groping for change, until he found the passenger walking away.

A man was standing at the door of the Greyhound Inn. He touched his cap to Cuthbert, thinking him a customer for Sally; for this was Mr. Walker.

"Will you please direct me to Mrs. Strangfield's house?" said Cuthbert.

"You can see him from here, sir. Come vheer I stand. There; him with the top window built out. I reckon the old lady's seein' company to-day," exclaimed Mr. Walker.

"Who is there?" inquired Cuthbert, quickly.

"Well, the little schoolmaster from Greystone's there; and then there's yerself, master. One an' one maketh two; that's company for Winston. An' if it warn't for my garden-stoof, the Lord help my landlord!"

"Is Mrs. Shaw there?"

"Ay, day an' night," answered Mr. Walker, taking a close look at the speaker at this.

Cuthbert noticed the glance, and went forward.

The house stood back from the lane, with a space of twenty feet or so of garden before it. A big and pretty country cottage, with the old equipment of porch and eaves, and bay-windows trenching upon the oval plot of grass.

When he was at the gate of it, the hammering of his heart confused his head, and for some moments he stood unable to advance, hidden by the railing and the impenetrable tangle of evergreen within.

Courage came to him then, and with a swing of the body he passed through the gate and struck the door.

It was opened by Mrs. Strangfield herself. He knew her instantly, and she him. But wonderful it was to behold in her face the stupefaction of surprise, yielding to incredulity and fear, then to prodigious doubt, then to a light of wild rapture.

In a breathless voice: "Cuthbert Shaw! Oh, Jenny! Oh, my darling! it is well with thee at last! it is well with thee at last!" and her hands fell upon his arm, and she drew him in.

"Where is she?" he exclaimed, lowering his voice to a whisper. "Break the news to her gently. She thinks me dead, I hear. Is that room empty? Hush! I think I hear her."

He drew a fierce, short breath, and on tiptoe stole into a room on the left of the hall, beckoning to Mrs. Strangfield to follow him.

The poor woman closed the door, and with her back against it stared at him as though the ideas his presence gave her were not to be mastered.

"Is she well—quite well?" he asked.

"Oh yes, Mr. Shaw, she is well. Dear heart! how wonderful to see thee! Ay, is she well. But, pretty dear one, God knows she has suffered for thee! Truly she thinks you dead! Were not you in a ship that was sunk? Alack! but a minute ago you were drowned, and now are you here! Oh, my head! my head! Why, who is with Jenny now, but thy very own father! Often doth he come to see his daughter—for that is she now to him, and so he terms her, and truly loves her. Oh, Mr. Shaw, what will she say to hear of you—to see you!"

Her excitement was past weeping. She was distracted by the sight of him, and could not yet believe her senses.

"Mrs. Strangfield, pray go to her at once, and tell her I am here. Go, I beseech you. I *cannot* endure delay."

And saying this he went to the door, from which she drew away, and held it open, and she passed out.

Now in the adjacent room, toasting his feet at the fire, and his frill showing frostily upon his breast, in contrast with the ruby light from the grate, sat Dr. Shaw, snuff-box in hand, cosily nursing his figure in a good armchair. Facing him sat Jenny, in deep mourning, her pale loveliness taking from dejection and the sombreness of her apparel a fine and unapproachable delicacy.

Her hands were upon her lap, and her head drooping, and in that pose she listened to Dr. Shaw, who was explaining to her the offer he had that morning received for the transfer of his school.

It was easy to see, from the manner in which he addressed her and the expression in the eyes that he bent on her, that she had made her way to his heart, and was, indeed, to his soul what he named her with his lips— daughter.

Otherwise it was not in nature that it should have been. He was a lonely old man now, for whom his calling held no more relish; quite friendless in Greystone, with an ever-present ache in his heart which his proud face might dissemble, but which ruled his conduct.

This had brought him to the tender girl whose honour he had once rudely doubted; and she, for the love she bore his son, had given him her love, and he had no happiness away from her.

Thus they sat, and he was telling her that he should accept the offer made him, when Mrs. Strangfield came in.

Jenny turned in her chair to look at her.

"Mother!" she cried, jumping up, what is it?—who has come? Is it bad news? You are ill!"

"Oh, Jenny! Oh, Dr. Shaw! be seated, dear heart!" exclaimed the poor woman, involuntarily wringing her hands in her desperation; for the news she had to deliver was like a load heaped upon her back, above her power to support, and she reeled and trembled under it. "Something most wonderful—oh, how shall I tell it you?—something God hath done to make us merry! Oh, my darling, come to me!"

She held out her hands; but Jenny, leaning on the back of her chair, stood motionlessly surveying her, and the blood came and went in her face like the shadow of clouds on moonlit land.

"Mother," she said in a deep whisper, "speak! What hath God done for us?"

The doctor had left his armchair, and was peering with a pale face at Mrs. Strangfield.

"Is it—is it Cuthbert?" he said.

"Ay, as the Lord is just, he is here! Jenny, he is here!" the mother shrieked.

The girl stared at her mother with eyes that looked beyond her. She moved, but fell back again with her hand upon the chair, and turned her eyes upon the doctor, and then gave a wild, hysterical cry.

"She hath a brave heart, and will meet him bravely!" wailed poor Mrs. Strangfield; and opening the door, she cried, "Mr. Shaw! come to your wife—she is waiting for thee."

Cuthbert crossed the hall, and stood at the open door. Eyes for his wife only had he. Their glances met, and with the gladdest, maddest cry that ever rung from a woman's lips, she fled to him.

Dr. Shaw fell, with his face in his hands upon the table, and wept.

Of all violent shocks sudden joy is the hardest to bear. Great grief, dreadful calamity, oppression tragical and crushing mercifully will make stone of the heart it falls upon; but joy finds the heart living, and sore and tender, and its blow may well kill.

The wonder of love was in Jenny's actions: the quick cries, the passionate clinging, the sudden release, the mad and laughing closing again, the crazy frown of bewilderment, the glorious illumination of conviction—these were hers.

Piteously sobbed Mrs. Strangfield behind, with restless strides making little pluckings at her daughter, as if to stay the excesses of this distemper of bliss; until a kind of silence fell, and the wife, with heavenly consciousness upon her, lay in her husband's arms—peaceful and beautiful and smiling.

"Cuthbert," cried Dr. Shaw, suddenly lifting his face from his hands, "is it not my turn?"

"Kiss him, my darling one—kiss him," Jenny said, and stood firm, to ease his support of her. "He loves me as thy wife, and—oh, mother! how good is Almighty God!"

Father and son met in close embrace; but there was sadness in the sight of the old man's trembling, the passionate play of feature which the pride of Satan could not have restrained under the inexorable dictation of natural emotion; and when their arms fell to their sides, the doctor turned to a chair, and dropped upon his knees before it and said—

"Master, as Thou didst teach, so now I say, giving thanks: For that my son is ever with me, and all that I have is his. It is meet that we should make merry and be glad: for my son was dead and is alive again; and was lost, and is found."

And so saying he arose, and there was tranquillity and joy in his face.

Such a meeting as this makes amends; and the story of sufferings endured and hopes delayed, and the fears and the bitter convictions arising, shall be told with kisses and smiles and sighs.

Cuthbert shall relate how by shipwreck he made his fortune, and wonder shall unfold all the deeper beauties of his darling's eyes.

The doctor shall tell his story. The mother hers.

And, over and over again, the wife her story, claiming for her one old friend, the ancient gossip Mead, the affection and the gratitude of her husband, and a more shining tribute of his respect withal—as who needs to be told?—

while the darkness of the November afternoon gathers around, and shadows swarm in the fire-play, and the spell of winter holds the world pale and still outside.

This must be. Yet is there not irony in all recurrence to emotion that has played its part in "Auld Lang Syne," and is now asleep in dust?

God be merciful to us sinners, and make us charitable one to another.

www.ingramcontent.com/pod-product-compliance
Lightning Source LLC
Chambersburg PA
CBHW051548250626
47157CB00001B/229